PACK REJECT
THE SPLINTERED BOND

MERRI BRIGHT

Editing by Aubergine Editing

Cover by Get Covers

 Formatted with Vellum

This one is for my Bearman Betas.
F*cking Holly!

CONTENTS

CONTENT ADVISORY

Pack Reject contains on-page, graphic violence/death, profanity, decapitation, physical assault, loss of a loved one, mention of past sexual assault, mentions of past domestic abuse, child abuse, and an incidence of non-consensual spying during a bathing scene. This is a medium-dark, slow-burn reverse harem romance, with scenes that may be disturbing to some readers. Please be kind to yourself when choosing to read.

I

THE NIGHTLY HUNT

FLOR

The nearly full moon hung over the rooftop of the dorms for unmated shifters and the nearby woods like a bulging threat. From my place high in the branches of a sweetgum tree, I held perfectly still. I knew I was well hidden, though my feet prickled with the urge to flee to a safer place. But any help the bright night sky loaned me when it came to spotting the males who hunted me would be lost if I moved, or made a sound.

The night was quiet, with not even a hint of a breeze, the only noises the trill of frogs in the creek and the hum of an air conditioner at the distant Pack House. But that didn't mean I was safe.

Or alone.

As if I'd summoned them with my thoughts, the hunting pack appeared over the ridge, soundless. Stalking. A hundred feet away, one shadow slid along the ground, then another. The sharp, musky tang of the ones searching for me floated on the air.

A trickle of sweat ran down my temple. I ignored it and held my breath, concentrating on staying silent. I didn't bother praying. Praying had never saved me from pain. My own feet, fists, and the ball of rage that filled my empty belly were all that had ever helped me survive.

One more shadow slunk after the first two, but I knew there were two more to come. These five pack Enforcers always hunted together.

Hunted, ate, slept, and fucked together. Their pack instincts did make them easier to avoid, sometimes. But not during the Hunting hours.

Every night, from dusk to midnight, I had to stay silent and motionless in the middle of a marshy community made up of wolves who tortured me for shits and giggles on a bad day, and pretended not to see me on a good one.

Of course, I hadn't had a good day in four years, since Van Blackside, our Head Enforcer, had announced I was the latest quarry in the pack's nightly Hunt.

Only a few more days. I lifted one hand to my metal ear tag and rubbed it for good luck. *A few short days until I can stop running for my life. Until the other North American packs start to arrive for the Conclave, and I can run away for good.*

The last two shadows raced past, and I finally let out my breath, loosening my rigid grip on the branch, preparing to slide down to the rooftop. Almost too late to stop, I heard noisy, running feet, and high-pitched male voices, whisper-shouting. It couldn't be more Enforcers. They sounded too young, and too loud.

"I told you, I think I smelled her!"

Two boys, no more than fourteen, stopped almost directly below my perch. The moonlight shone on their greasy hair and pale, skinny arms. "Leroy, what're we gonna do if we catch her?" The boy's voice cracked as he scratched his hair—at fleas or lice, most likely. Lots of the younger shifters had lice in the spring. "I mean, we ain't even shifted yet. And I ain't never... *you know*, with a girl."

Leroy sniggered. "Course not. Your balls ain't even dropped. Listen, Bo, if we catch her, we'll just... I don't know. Kiss her, that's what girls like. We ain't gotta mate her for real. It's a game, right?"

Bo swallowed so loud, I could hear the spit go down. "Naw, I heard the older guys talking. They said it's real."

Leroy shrugged and sniffed the air. "Well, we don't got a choice. It's mandibular."

Bo thumped his head. "*Mandatory,* stupid."

"Call me stupid when I bring her in and get promoted to Enforcer at thirteen," Leroy sneered.

Thirteen? I almost fell out of the tree. What in the hell was a thirteen-year-old kid doing trying to catch a mate?

Of course, I was only six years older than him. I tasted bile, picturing being tied for life to one of these little shits.

Leroy was still talking. "I think she's pretty, even if nobody else does."

Bo scoffed. "No tits. She's too skinny."

That little shit. Like being skinny was a choice? Honestly, both of these kids were almost as thin as I was.

Leroy kicked at a pinecone on the ground. "Yeah, but she's got those pretty gold-ish eyes, and that long red hair. Plus whoever gets her, gets their own house, Alpha Callaway said. And double food rations. I'd mate a gator for double rations."

The promise of double rations was probably the only reason they'd joined the Hunt. The older males were more interested in getting a promotion to the Enforcer ranks, or the house and bump in pay that went along with mated status. Supposedly, some of the older Enforcers had placed bets on who would catch me, and on what night, as well. But these little boys just wanted food.

"You don't even know how to mate, Leroy Johnson. It ain't just bitin' and shackin' up."

"I know about fuckin'. It ain't hard. All ya gotta do's stick your tallywhacker in between her legs and move it around for a bit."

"We better find her and mate her soon, is what I'm thinkin'. Mama'll be pissed if I'm out much longer."

Leroy grunted. "Once we get her, it won't take long. I watched Trevor screw Megan McReady last week behind her house, and he was done in like a minute. Maybe less."

Bo scratched his hair again. "I can spare a minute, I s'pose."

"Listen, we gotta move. It's ten minutes to midnight. Trevor said she smells like cinnamon toast, and I *swear* I smelled cinnamon right over there. Take a whiff."

I smashed my hand over my mouth to keep from laughing. The older unmated males had hunted me for years, and most knew better than to fall for the false scent trails I'd laid. Because I didn't rub my clothes on bushes and trees; I sprinkled a dry powder of cinnamon and ground-up ghost peppers wherever I needed to hide my tracks. And when they got their noses deep enough for a good whiff...

"Ahhhhhh!" Both boys got a snout full of ghost peppers at the same time, and went running, screaming unintelligibly. I didn't let myself laugh, though, or shift position. I hoped they were the last ones out on the Hunt, but hope had screwed me six ways to Sunday before. I didn't trust it.

I stayed where I was for a few more minutes, until I heard the air horn that indicated the change of the front gate guard's shift—midnight precisely. Then I slipped down the tree, careful to stay in the shadows on the way to my room. Hunting hours might have ended for the night, but that didn't mean I was safe in this pack.

I was never safe, but I should be okay until morning.

Three more days.

I WASN'T EVEN safe for three hours.

"Florida... Floridaaaaaaaaah. I can *smell* you." The oily, nasally voice slithered into my dorm room and woke me from a restless sleep. "Mmm, smells like my mate-to-be in there."

Trevor the Toadfucker Blackside.

Instantly alert, I stuck a hand through the slit in the side of my mattress, grabbing the contraband knife I'd fashioned out of a piece of broken pipe, some hemp rope for a grip, and a lot of duct tape. "You're disgusting, Trevor. Get away from my window," I hissed back, glancing at the glowing wall clock. It was just past two in the morning.

What was he doing here now? His dad Van had made new rules for the Hunt a few years back, and the most important one for my continued survival was that it ended at fucking midnight. Maybe Trevor didn't know what time it was.

"You know you're not allowed to hunt me this late. You're gonna catch hell."

"The Alpha won't know. Dad don't care." His dark laughter gave me chills. "By sunup, you'll be mine, bitch. My property. My mate. Mine to do whatever I like with, by pack law."

2
A HIDDEN KNIFE
FLOR

F*uck.* I hated that Trevor was right. The law of our pack was clear. Any female, once she was mated to a male, had to answer to him for the rest of her days. Any order he gave was like a command from the Moon Goddess Herself, and no one other than the Alpha was allowed to interfere when a male was disciplining his mate.

If Trevor Blackside got in here and got his teeth into me, my life was as good as over. He'd lock me in a room and shackle me to his bed for his use, and most likely for his friends' as well. If I cried foul, said he'd claimed me after Hunt hours? It would already be too late. No one would believe me, or even care if they did.

"Shit," I whispered, trying to make a plan. I couldn't yell at him or draw any attention from the other girls on the floor, or worse, the dorm warden, Holly Grier. As she reminded me on an almost daily basis, I was only one more incident away from being kicked out of unmated housing.

It didn't matter that every "incident" so far had been males harassing me, clawing me when I walked past—and that was during the hours they weren't chasing me down outside.

I tried not to think about the evenings I'd spent running, holed up underground in the storm sewers, or perched in the highest branches of trees, even in bad weather. After four exhausting years of it, I was almost tempted to give up and let one of them catch me. I'd be mated, and the Hunt would move on to the next unfortunate girl.

But the males hunting me all made my stomach churn with disgust and rage, and Trevor was the worst. He'd caught me once, and Mama had almost killed him defending me.

She'd been punished severely, banished to die outside our pack's border, for daring to try. Trevor had taken great pleasure in telling me that he'd heard her being torn apart outside the main pack gate by rogues. Smelled her blood.

"She cried like a pup when they went for her throat," he'd taunted me only days after she'd been sentenced. "She shit herself, and talked gibberish like the crazy ass she was. Our pack's well rid of her."

I'd been tempted more than once to follow her out the gate, and let the rogues take me as well. But I was just stupid enough to stay alive, even when I had no reason to. Mama was dead, and I was alone. If I wanted to survive, I had to fight as hard—and as dirty—as I could.

I was allowed to hurt the ones who hunted me, if I could. Van had announced that if a scrawny, five-foot-one, teenaged female who hadn't even shifted yet could hurt a ranked male, then he deserved it.

That's why I'd fashioned a knife and hidden it in my room, deep inside the old mattress that smelled enough like piss to keep anyone from touching it, and was lumpy enough that no one would feel it in there. And when I heard the metal bar latch on my window bending with a dull squeal, I knew I'd made the right call.

I had my plan.

"Not today, Satan." I stalked across the room, my makeshift shiv held low. Sure enough, Trevor's massive hand appeared through the gap as he clawed for the latch to open it the rest of the way. "Last chance, Trevor. Get away from my window."

"Not 'til I get what I came for, bitch. Don't worry none. Holly won't bust up the party until we're done."

Aw, snakeshit. Holly had a thing for Trevor's dad, even though he was mated. I'd bet my last dollar she'd given his waste-of-space son permission to creep into my room, breaking the Hunt rules, on the off chance his dad would appreciate her "help."

"Don't say I didn't warn you." I took a breath and lifted the knife, stabbing down with every ounce of strength I had. The rope burned my palm slightly as he yanked his hand around, screeching.

Double snakeshit.

I pulled out the knife, accidentally running my own hand along the exposed edge and adding my blood to the spatters on the floor. Loud footsteps thudded in the hall at the same moment that Trevor dropped to the ground outside, wailing like I'd cut his hand off entirely, not just stabbed him.

What a crybaby. He'd heal by sunrise.

It took two seconds to leap across the room to the tiny bathroom, where I chucked the knife into the toilet, tossing a wad of toilet paper on top of it. Then I hunkered down on the toilet seat, trying to look surprised when the door to my room slammed open. I wiped my bloody hand on the bottom of my t-shirt, and waited.

"What's goin' on in here?" Light flooded into the room and through the open bathroom door, blocked only by two long shadows. Holly barged through the open door, her house shoes squeaking on the tile. She wasn't alone; an Enforcer stood right behind her.

My heart raced when I saw it wasn't just any Enforcer. It was Luke.

Tall, muscular, raven-haired, Adonis-wolf Luke Callaway. Luke, who always smelled like melting caramel to me, and made my mouth water every bit as much.

My one and only crush. And so far out of my league, we might as well have been on different continents.

Luke was the Alpha's adopted heir, since Calvin Callaway hadn't been able to have any sons of his own. He had been adopted into the pack when he was a little boy, coming from some pack in France. So even his slight accent was sexy, not the pronounced Southern drawl like the rest.

Now the gorgeous, silver-blue-eyed shifter who had featured in almost every one of my PG-13 to X-rated fantasies over the past few years was staring at me... while I squatted on the toilet. With a bare ass.

I squeezed my eyes shut, wishing I could disappear. It didn't work. When I opened them, he was staring at the rust-stained tile floor, as I squatted over a bloody toilet bowl in a loose t-shirt, my cut hand now wrapped in the ragged underwear around my knees.

"What the hell's goin' on?" Holly demanded again, screeching as she crossed to the window and glared first at it, then at the blood all over my shirt.

Behind her, Luke arched one eyebrow, his face revealing nothing but slight interest.

"I, um, woke up in the night because..." I scrambled for an explanation for all the blood, and quickly pressed my other hand over my abdomen. "You know how periods can be, right?" It was tricky, talking around the truth to answer a direct question, and not be caught in a lie. Mature shifters could smell lies. Or most of them could.

"You're disgusting," Holly spat. "You mean to tell me you made this mess?"

"Well, heavy periods are the worst. Blood just gets all over, you know?" I made a motion to myself, my under-wear, and the floor around me. Luke's eyes widened, taking in the splatters. Probably wondering if my entire uterus had fallen out.

I had to be careful how I phrased things, staying just on this side of true. "I ran to the toilet, and I was just sitting here when I heard noises. I thought I heard a voice outside. Is somebody there?"

The dorm warden strode to the window, throwing the bent bar latch to one side and peering into the still night. "Not now. But there was!"

Luke's calm tenor voice interrupted her screeching. "A male was outside the unmated female dorms? Did you scent him, Ms. Grier?" he asked quietly. "I'll have him brought before the Alpha. There are consequences for attempting to enter this dorm after hours."

"N-no," Holly sputtered. "I didn't scent—it could be anyone. She draws that kind of male, like shit draws flies. She likes the attention."

"That's not true," I protested before I could stop myself.

She tightened her bony hands into fists, the cold gleam in her dark eyes promising violence as soon as we were alone. "You insolent little bitch. You don't get to take that tone with me. I'm all you've got, the only one who'd let you stink up this place for all these years. You give me lip again and I'll throw you out; you've been nothing but trouble—"

Luke cleared his throat. "Ms. Grier, it appears the young lady needs assistance. If I may?"

"You may not," she hissed. "I called you tonight to... search for contraband." Ugh, she was lying. I knew that, even if I couldn't smell it. And from Luke's stern expression, he knew it, too. She had called him to "catch" me and Trevor in the room together. But now she had to make some excuse.

"Really, Ms. Grier?" Luke asked coolly.

She sniffed. "Well, I had a report that she has something in here that isn't allowed. I insist you search her room, Enforcer."

"Yes, ma'am," he answered. He kept his eyes averted, which only made me more embarrassed. "Close the bathroom door, and I'll search out here."

"No," she sneered. "Leave it open. She'll try to get rid of something. She's sneaky, this one. Comes from trash, and lives like it. Look at this place."

I blushed as Luke scanned the room. It was true; I didn't have much. Just a few books I'd scavenged from the pack's garage sale when everyone else had done their shopping and the remainder had been put out with the garbage, the nubby ends of some pencils, and my drawing supplies. Luke actually thumbed through a couple of the pages of my sketches before I growled and he backed away, nodding an apology.

My clothes were the worst. Watching Holly paw through my drawers—holding up my saggy, bargain basement underwear for Luke to see, as if they might find drugs in the torn crotch—made my stomach churn.

I pushed down my rage, my humiliation. Holly picked

up my one good pair of jeans and tore at the pockets, ripping them down the side seams as she pretended to search.

Could I make it three more days? I had to.

It was only days until the Conclave, and then the Enforcer Games. A few short nights before I could fight my way out of this hellhole pack and win a spot in another one. I'd go anywhere. It couldn't be worse than where I was now.

"Get up," Holly growled. "Get off the toilet. I need to search in here."

"I don't have a pad. I'll bleed... more." I stared at the floor.

"I'd like to see you bleed more," she muttered.

Luke gave her an odd look, like he wanted to intervene, but he didn't. I wasn't mad about it; Enforcers had to be seen as impartial. And Luke had never been a friend. He was eight or nine years older than me, and we'd never spoken more than a few words.

Recently, though, he'd been the Enforcer on guard more than once when some random shifter had decided to hunt me during what were supposed to be my safe hours. I had the feeling that might be one reason I'd made it this close to the Conclave without getting forcibly mated. Luke was all about the rules.

"Stand up, girl," Holly demanded.

"Get her something for her period," he requested quietly. "I'll check this room."

She stomped away, grabbed some of my ruined under-wear, and thrust it at me. "Use this."

"I'll need space to move, ma'am," Luke insisted, gesturing for her to leave the tiny bathroom. She left, still snarling. "Can you stand now?" Luke carefully kept his eyes on the wall. Face flaming, I stuffed the underwear in between my legs to staunch the imaginary blood flow and stood. I hoped the wad of toilet paper I'd thrown on top of the knife had been enough to cover it.

He peeked down at the bowl, slid back the mildewed plastic shower curtain for a moment, then made a fuss of inspecting the cup that held my toothbrush while Holly watched. He opened the mirrored makeup cabinet and stepped back with a scowl. It was empty, except for a few mini tubes of toothpaste the pack dentist had handed out for free. Before he could stop himself, he shot me a questioning look.

"What?"

"No... girl things?" He let the question slip, then clearly regretted it.

"Tampons, pads, makeup?" I shrugged. "No job, no family, no money. Not all of us get to experience the protection of the pack." For emphasis, I flicked the small steel tag that hung from the top of my ear, denoting just how far down the pack hierarchy I sat. "Welcome to life at rock bottom, Your Heir-ness."

He frowned; the nickname bothered him. Good. There was nothing I could do to repay him for tonight's humiliation, but it was a tiny start.

His face twitched as he fought to respond. "The pack keeps us safe." It was the creed of every pack, the foundational reason packs existed.

I couldn't help it. I laughed so hard, I gasped for air. "This pack? This pack doesn't give a shi—"

"Shut up!" Holly's screech interrupted the grave mistake I was about to make. I was almost grateful.

"You're right," I replied, keeping my tone soft, feminine. Submissive. Fake as fuck. "I should be grateful to have the strength of the pack behind me. I'm sure the pack will keep me... as safe as it always has."

Luke's eyes had gone hard, his scent slightly bitter, and he dropped the lid down on the toilet before he left. Taking my first deep breath of the evening, I sat back down on the lid, listening as Luke and Holly exited my room, then the hall.

I sat there for a few minutes, shaking for many reasons. Trevor's attempted attack. The blood all over that stung my nose, all iron and salt. The knowledge that now I didn't even have a window that would lock, and three days left to survive. The effect of Luke's presence on my nerves.

Ugh. Crushes were dumb.

I wrapped a washcloth around my hand, wiped a few drops of blood off the floor of the bathroom with a handful of toilet paper and, without thinking, opened the lid to drop it in.

The knife I had thrown in the toilet was not covered at all. In fact, the wad of paper I'd thought had covered it hadn't even landed in the water, but gotten caught on the side. The blade shone, blood on the rope handle, pink-tinged water making the metal glint in the flickering fluorescent light. I pulled it out, wiped it clean, and carried it back to my bed, stuffing it back into the mattress.

Why hadn't Luke said anything? As Enforcer, it was his job—no, his pack duty—to turn me in for breaking his precious rules.

It wasn't like I'd get the chance to ask. But for the first time in a long while, I wondered if the pack leadership wasn't entirely rotten.

3

LITTLE SPILL, BIG CONSEQUENCES

FLOR

T he thought that Luke might not be the Boy Scout I'd figured he was stayed with me the next day as I worked. I didn't mind work. I even liked parts of my job in the kitchen, though I wasn't much more than a maid and waitress.

Mopping the pack dining hall in the evenings was about the best my life got. I was alone with my thoughts and dreams of leaving the Southern pack for good. If I worked fast and made sure the dining hall doors were locked up tight, I could sometimes get some bo staff practice in, using my mop handle as my weapon.

But cleaning up in the mornings, while the ranked shifters got to sit and eat what I served them? Acting like I respected them, taking their shit? That sucked harder than a starving mosquito, and after only two hours of sleep, this breakfast shift was worse than ever. At least the other packs would start to arrive later today. Even if it meant more work in the short term, there was some light at the end of the damned tunnel.

"Flor, can you come take care of this? A little... spill here." Grant, one of the unmated males who was planning to fight in the Enforcer Games and talked about it constantly, pointed at the floor beneath him. Grant was strong, but shorter than the other Enforcers, with a weak chin and habit of picking his stubby nose when he thought no one was watching. He liked to show off, and had a mean streak a mile wide.

I stepped closer, holding the mop in front of me just in case any of his friends decided to pay attention to me instead of their food. "Where?" I asked, peering at the floor until I realized he was pointing at something else.

His crotch. Of course.

"Nice, Grant. Enjoy your breakfast."

"Whoa there, Flor. I said there was a little spill." He thrust his pelvis forward, then licked his narrow lips. "Clean it good."

His friends looked up, their conversations stopping. *Shit.* It was almost the end of breakfast, and the shifters were less hungry for food than they were for drama. This wasn't going to end well.

I shot a glance at the window to the kitchen where the pack cook and my only friend at Southern, Del, shook his gray head at me. "Don't do it, girlie." He spoke softly, but I heard him. One of the curses of shifters—we heard everything. Which meant I was busted every time I muttered something sassy at one of my "betters."

"Florida!" Grant stood, the bulge in his sweatpants tenting out the fabric a little. But just a little. I bit my lip and prayed I could hold back the comments that ran through my brain. "I said I need you to take care of this. Why aren't you rubbing it clean? It's your job, ain't it?"

"Well, Grant," I said, loud enough for everyone to hear.

"You said you had a little spill. I can't see any 'spill' at all. Must be pretty small. I bet you can take care of it on your own." I tore off a tiny piece of the paper towel roll that I had on my mop bucket and gestured at his groin. "This much oughta do it."

The room erupted in laughter, howls, growls, and curses. In the kitchen, Del shouted, "Damnit, Flor!"

I knew better than to mouth off. But the thing with Trevor had sort of wrecked me, and I was so done with this whole place. Before I could duck, Grant's plate of food sailed across the table and glanced off my cheek, cutting the skin by the side of my eyebrow. I wiped my eyes clear as fast as I could; I had to be able to see who was coming next.

And they would come. His friends, the other Enforcers, they would all want to take their pound of flesh.

But someone unexpected was coming, someone worse, right behind Grant. My heart fell, my stomach churning. I needed to look busy, and fast. My gaze was plastered to the floor as I moved my mop around to start cleaning the food splattered across the white tiles.

"You bitch," Grant roared, red-faced as he vaulted over the table, ignoring the wave of harsh power that was forcing all the other diners to bow their heads. "Who do you think you ar—"

His rant was cut off as one huge hand closed around his arm, another on his neck, threatening to crush his windpipe. The hand on his throat was attached to an arm that was tanned and burly. An arm that led to a barrel chest that had to be muscle underneath the denim shirt—male wolves usually didn't store fat, even ones in their mid-fifties like this one—and a six-foot-four frame that cast a long shadow across the table.

"What?" Grant croaked, confusion whirling in his dull

eyes. Our Alpha never ate in the dining hall with the rest of the Enforcers. He had his own private dining room, not that I'd ever seen it. Well, not *officially*.

"What have you done here, Grant?" The Alpha's words fell like dangerous grenades into the suddenly silent dining hall. Del had stopped the dishwasher so there wasn't even the sound of water running, only Grant's wheezing breath as the Alpha lifted him by the neck until he was standing on tiptoe.

"Sir?" The stench of fear filled the area, and for once, it wasn't just mine. Grant's bulging eyes darted to his friends. None of them offered any help.

Alpha Callaway shook him by the neck, like a dog killing a rabbit. "What did you call me, boy?"

Grant's reply was quick and apologetic. "Alpha. Sorry, Alpha."

I felt his eyes on me. "Should have known it was you."

I didn't answer. Didn't move.

Alpha energy had a weight to it. Every other shifter in a pack had to answer to it, when and if the Alpha decided to let loose. Some of the shifters in Southern couldn't even stand when our Alpha was in the same room. They'd drop to their bellies, in human form or wolf, and whimper until the beating drum of his power was far enough away to stand, and breathe. Or run.

Running from him now wasn't an option. He was close enough to touch, not that I would dare.

The Alpha's gaze raked across me, and I tried to hunch down even lower on the floor. I knew better than to even glance above his knees. Forgetting that important rule was how unranked shifters like me went blind, one plucked eyeball at a time.

"I asked what you've done here?"

"She disrespected me, sir." Grant's voice wavered, but his muddy brown eyes met mine with clear intention. He blamed me for this, and was going to make me pay.

I had disrespected him, and I knew what I'd pay, too. I'd had enough beatings in the courtyard, with the whole pack watching. I'd been left out in the sun to bake, tied down on a cut log, with blood still running down from the gashes left by the leather whip.

I couldn't afford for any of that to happen now, so close to the Games. To my one chance to get free. If I was stronger —if I hadn't been starved my whole life, and gone without a decent night's sleep for years—it might not have been that big a deal.

I held my breath, waiting for my sentence.

The Alpha only tsked, shaking his heavy head of chestnut hair. "So, you threw away good food?" He dropped Grant back on the table, the Enforcer's ass smashing the remaining "good food" that had been uneaten. I wanted to groan; that would have been a decent breakfast for me and Del. But I stayed silent, hoping against hope to live through this encounter. "I don't think you appreciate the work it takes to prepare our pack's meals. Gotta remedy that."

"Alpha?" Grant had never been the brightest bulb in the pack. But I think he was starting to get the idea that I wasn't the one in trouble here.

Or at least, not the only one.

"You'll spend your next three days' duty shifts here in the dining hall, serving and cleaning for the other unmated shifters until the Games."

"But Alpha, the other packs are supposed to start arriving today. I'm an Enforcer." Grant's voice trembled with suppressed anger. "You're making me work under an unranked shifter?"

That was unheard of. Males in our pack were either ranked or unranked. Ranked males had the chance to work as Enforcers, protecting the pack. The unranked males were the weaker wolves, and their lives were shitty, since they were seen as close to useless. Female shifters weren't ranked unless they mated to a ranked male, so pretty much every girl was angling for guys like Grant, even if they weren't "true mates," the one soul in the world who the moon had made for you.

Whatever. A girl couldn't eat true love, or survive for long in this pack without a ranked mate.

Alpha Callaway laughed. "Don't be ridiculous." I felt his eyes on me like a laser, burning into the back of my neck. Then I felt something worse.

His hand.

He'd gripped the metal tag that hung from the top of my ear, and he yanked it now, shaking it roughly and moving my head back and forth. I bit my lip, hoping he wasn't going to rip it out and force me to get it re-pierced.

The shifter in charge of piercing always strapped the unranked females down while he attached our tags, and he had wandering hands. I'd been eleven when I'd gotten this tag, and I still remembered the way the bastard had run his thick fingers over my neck and shoulders, his whispered promise of, "Someday soon." I'd been lucky; I knew he'd done a lot worse in that chair to other unranked women and girls.

The Alpha gripped the tag even harder, and I felt a burning pain. *Shit.* I tried to lever myself upward slightly to stop the tearing as he went on. "Work under *this* female? Rank is everything. No, you'll be in charge of this one for those three days. Make sure the little bitch learns to respect her betters. She'll work under you, in whatever way you tell her to." He let me go. "Don't disrespect him again, do you hear? He's your boss now."

Oh, hell. I'd rather be whipped. I could almost taste Grant's combined rage and lust on the air.

The Alpha had just pushed his way through the door when I was saved by the bell—literally. The bell that announced the start of classes for younger shifters and work shifts for adults rang out loud enough in the dining hall that every shifter winced and shook their heads to clear the ringing in their ears.

Except me. I had already run for the kitchen, taking advantage of their moment of disorientation. "Del, hide me," I whispered. He shook his head disapprovingly, but gestured with one thumb to the walk-in freezer. It was right next to the door to the outside, and I almost decided to take my chances and run, when I thought better of it.

Del never steered me wrong. He was the only one who didn't.

I slipped inside the freezer and ran to the back, squeezing behind the cases of raw meat. I sniffed at my arm. The food Grant had dumped on me would do double duty now. I could eat what had landed and stuck to my clothes and skin, and the rest would hide my scent as long as anyone hunting me gave a cursory sniff and no more.

Outside, I heard Grant's demand. "Where'd the bitch go?"

And then a mumbled, "That way," from Del.

I crouched down even lower, waiting for the light from outside to shine on me, revealing my hiding place. The freezer didn't open, but I heard the door that led to the training yard close with a resounding slam. For a moment, I relaxed.

Then I heard my name. "Florida, get your stupid ass out

here." Del stood in the open freezer doorway, arms crossed over his chest, a look of utter frustration on his scarred face. It was his usual look when he was dealing with the repercussions of my attitude.

I slipped out quietly, picking a tiny piece of bacon off my shoulder and popping it into my mouth. "Sorry about the mess."

"You've made a bigger mess for yourself than some food, girlie," he replied, running a hand over his buzz-cut salt-and-pepper hair. "You know you can't stay here."

"The freezer? You're right. I'd freeze to death." I grinned. Del was the only shifter I could sass with impunity. I think he kind of liked it.

He leveled a dark look at me. "I mean the compound. You've got to get out."

Did he mean I needed to leave the pack? "I can't. It's three days until I can get away for real. Officially."

"Grant will find a way to kill ya before then. He's not right in the head."

We both spoke so softly, our voices were less than whispers. We knew better than to draw attention to this conversation. With a nod, Del directed me to the leftovers he'd salvaged from the breakfast plates. Not much, but it was all the food he and I would get until dinner, so we ate fast, stuffing burnt ends of toast and scraps of eggs in our mouths.

I swallowed hard. "Best breakfast in the whole state of Alabama," I whispered, forcing a smile. "Tastes better than ever."

He huffed, and replied with his mouth full, "You'd eat a rat sandwich, Flor."

"I have eaten one, Del," I teased back. It was true, and I wasn't ashamed. I'd caught that rat myself, cooked it, and seasoned it with discarded salt packets, back when I was eight. It hadn't been the worst meal of my life by far.

"Shut up and eat." Shaking his head, Del sat on a stack of red-printed rice bags. He stuck his legs out in front of him, and we both stared at the prosthetic one, pondering the shit pile the morning had become.

"Want me to rub it?" I usually gave him a massage on the muscles near the end of his stump, above the knee. He said I had magic hands. The truth was, contact with other pack members helped with pain, whether it was physical or emotional. Since Del had lost his leg—I'd heard it was some sort of accident that had happened when I was still a baby, but had never been stupid enough to ask him outright about it—he'd lost his rank. That meant he'd lost the right to stay with the other Enforcers. He'd never been mated, as far as I knew, so he didn't even have family to help out. If he'd had other relatives, they'd all bailed when he was hurt.

Most wounds, even severe ones, healed within days on mature wolves. Shifters who hadn't shifted, or really low-ranked ones who were either born weak or starved that way, healed a lot slower. It could take weeks for a deep cut to close up on one who hadn't ever shifted before; I'd had wounds that had taken a year for the scars to disappear. So shifters with the kind of injuries that would never heal, like missing eyes or limbs, were treated as if they had no value at all.

If you asked me, even without one leg, Del was one of the strongest and best wolves we had.

Before his injury, he might have stood a chance of taking our Alpha's spot in an official challenge. Now he was only slightly more valuable to the pack than I was. He was everything to me, though. Del was the only shifter who hugged me, who talked to me like I wasn't trash. He was definitely the only one who knew my secret plan for the Conclave.

He was all the family I had.

"Come on. Rub time."

"All right, girlie," he sighed, rising to lock the doors. When he sat back down, I pulled off his prosthetic and started rubbing. "Probably the last time I'll get to feel those magic hands of yours." He grunted slightly as I worked on a bad knot of muscle at the bottom of his torn quadricep.

"You're right. Grant's gonna kill me." I let out a groan. "*Actually* kill me. Three days until the Games start, and I couldn't keep my mouth shut."

Del nodded. "Gonna have to move to Plan B," he muttered, shocking me.

"There's a Plan B?" I perked up. If Del had a plan, all wasn't lost.

"There is," he said slowly. "But you're not gonna like it."

"I'll like it better than being force mated to Trevor, or killed by Grant, I bet," I snapped back.

Del shushed me and strapped his prosthetic back on. He moved efficiently around the kitchen, grabbing handfuls of things and stuffing them into an old camping backpack. I narrowed my eyes as I took note of the odd assortment. A few of the airlocked packets of dried meat that the Enforcers usually took on training runs, his favorite butcher knife, an old canteen that looked like it had been through a war—the Civil War, maybe—and lots of other things.

He thrust a baggie into my hands. "Get up. Fill this while I talk."

I stood and pulled back the drawstring on the open oatmeal bag by my side. "Who are we feeding today?" The pack bought rice and other staples by the hundreds of pounds, though only ranked shifters had access to the dining hall. These days, our unranked shifter families were literally starving, so Del and I had started sneaking rice and grains out, delivering it anonymously to their back doors with whatever meat I could hunt with a slingshot—squirrels and rabbits, mostly.

"It's for you," Del answered. "You can get to my house?"

I nodded. The hole we'd made in the fence between the compound and the pack's hunting grounds wasn't that far from his house. Well, his shack.

"Take this." He lifted up the backpack he'd filled with the food and added a few other things to it. "Get to the hunting grounds. Go by my place first; pick up anything you need. We can't get you back to the dorm for your own stuff."

"I don't have anything there except a toothbrush anyways."

Del shook his head, like my words had hurt him. "It's not like this in the other packs, you know. This ain't how shifters are supposed to live."

"What do you mean?"

"Our pack, the Southern pack, is backward. Worse than the other North American packs by a long shot. The way we treat the unranked, the females—hell, even the elderly—is not normal, not lawful."

"Alpha reads out pack law every full moon, Del."

"He does no such thing." Del barely breathed his words. "He reads the parts that make what he's doing sound acceptable. There used to be more read aloud before the war, before *this* Alpha."

Before Callaway? He'd been Southern's Alpha for over twenty years, longer than I'd been alive. I knew he'd taken over for his uncle, who must not have had kids of his own. The war with the Russians had wiped out most of the older shifters, not only in our pack, but in all of North America. At least, that's what I'd learned in school.

The packs had established firm borders, and everybody more or less kept to themselves. Though only Callaway had decided to build an actual fence and make everyone live inside. Since Southern only had a few hundred adult shifters anyway, and a handful of kids, he said it was necessary to keep us safe.

Keep us prisoners, more like. I wondered exactly what parts of pack law he'd been skipping on the full moons.

I was about to ask Del for details, when he stopped me with a finger to his lips. Someone was outside, in the dining hall. We both waited, barely breathing. Finally, Del decided they were gone.

"There's some clothes in a drawer," he murmured. "Boy clothes. Change. Cut your hair with the knife, short. If anyone sees you walking to the fence, they'll think you're a boy."

I nodded. Maybe some girls would give a shit about their hair—and to be honest, I would miss it, as it was the only attractive feature I had. Long, thick, stick-straight, and a deep red that I covered with soot on full-moon nights in the Hunt, in case it gave me away, my hair was objectively pretty. Other girls had said so, though they'd never complimented me to my face.

My hair was about the only way you could tell I was female at all. I mean, if I'd had more to eat growing up, I might have curves like the other girls. But I was skinny, pale, often weak from lack of protein, and my eyes were constantly bloodshot from lack of sleep. It wasn't like I'd lose my shot at Miss Shifter America if I cut off my hair.

"Got it."

"Go as far as you can. Don't start a fire for cooking

unless it's night, and the wind is blowing away from the compound. If you can, eat raw. Stay there until the Conclave. You'll see the other packs arrive. Some of them might camp on the hunting grounds, so stay back. But still on packlands."

I nodded. Leaving the packlands was death, if you ran into the rogue shifters that haunted our borders. But there was an obvious flaw in his plan. "Del, you know they'll notice I'm gone. They'll track me, smell me."

"This is the part you're not gonna like. You've got to get rid of your scent for the first few miles at least. I want you to roll in the pit latrines on the way out, then walk above the sewage lines as far as you can."

"The leaking ones?" The infrastructure of our pack was as rotten as the shifters who ran it. Our lines had plenty of leaks, so the soil above them was often rank. I'd used the sewage lines to cover my tracks before, during the Hunt hours. Most shifters kept clear of them.

Del nodded. "You know how it works. The marsh out in the woods has pockets of gas. Stay near those once you're outside the fence, in the hunting grounds. No one should notice a little more stink."

"Fine." I knew better than to argue about something as insignificant as smelling bad. I'd roll in a rotting skunk carcass if it meant staying away from the Enforcers. I'd need to bathe in one of the creeks in the forest once I was loose, that was all.

Del's eyes sparked with what I hoped was pride. "You still want to fight in the Enforcer Games?"

"Hell yes."

"I'll get you signed up for the first night then. Keep practicing your bojutsu until then. Use a branch or something."

"You trained me, Del." I leaned over and gave him a tight hug. "I'm sure I'll beat at least one guy and get picked up by another pack."

He let out a heavy sigh. "Sometimes I wish you were more like the other girls. You could find your true mate at the Conclave, you know. Sneak back into the compound for one of the social events, meet as many of the outsiders as you can. That's a way out, too."

"Are you kidding me? You know I promised Mama I'd never mate." He grumbled for a second, until I whisper-yelled, "Mama's true mate tortured her, left her covered with scars, then screwed every female he wanted for fifteen years and drove her insane. He broke her!"

Del had told me once that her mate must have been trying to sever the mating bond, but it hadn't worked. I remembered the countless nights she'd screamed and torn at her own throat, trying to end the pain. Every time he'd fucked another woman, she'd acted as if her blood had turned to acid. It would have made anyone crazy.

"I know all that," Del growled. "Only good thing he's ever done was—"

"—make a sperm donation," I finished. Mama had gotten pregnant the same night she met my asshole father, and Del had delivered me nine months later, taking over the parenting duties that my mama tried so hard to do. But she never could; she was too broken.

In every way that mattered, Del was my real dad. The only person I loved, who loved me back.

His dark eyes went soft as he gazed into my face, staring like he was trying to memorize my features. "True mates aren't all evil, Flor. You might end up with a good one, and he'd take you away from all this hillbilly shit. You could finish high school, get a job. Not make yourself into some sort of warrior."

I wasn't going to argue this with him again. He knew how I felt. "If I get to be a warrior someday, I'll come back and take you out of this shitty pack, Del. You got a lot of fight left in you."

"I hope so," he said in a way that made my ears prick up. What did he mean?

A sound came from the dining hall again. Footsteps, getting closer.

Del's nostrils flared. "Go, *now*."

4

DESPERATION AND DISGUISE
FLOR

I padded across the kitchen floor silently, opening the door to bright sunlight and a blast of damp heat. June in Alabama was always hot and humid, but it could be worse. At least the Conclave wasn't held in August.

I blew a kiss over my shoulder to Del, who was growling quietly, staring at the door to the dining hall like he knew who was there, then slipped out into the deserted courtyard. Once I was away from the kitchen door, I walked as close to the buried sewer lines as I could at a normal pace, knowing the worst thing a person could do around a pack of predators was run.

At the latrines, I stopped and took one last deep breath before I stepped into an empty stall. My lungs aching, I scraped shit off the side wall of the pit toilet with a piece of paper towel and rubbed it onto the bottoms of my shoes, my legs, splattering it over my arms. Finally, I tucked my hair into my collar, wishing I had a hat.

Trying not to breathe through my nose, I stepped out of the latrine and set a quick walking pace for Del's shack. For the first time in forever, luck was with me. The few pack members I saw were far enough away that they stared for a bit or nodded, but didn't come close. That was normal, since none of the other shifters even spoke to me regularly. Who wanted to be friends with the "hunted girl", the Alpha's least favorite pack member? Or even talk to her.

I wasn't going to miss one damned thing about this pack. Except Del.

I slipped in the back door at his tiny house, feeling guilty that I was about to track literal shit though his rooms. That smell wasn't coming out soon. "It was his idea," I whispered, trying to ignore my own horrific funk as I worked.

I grabbed a toothbrush—he had a new one on the counter—and ran to his dresser. Inside the top drawer was a set of boy's clothes, just like he'd promised. Did he have another pack kid he took care of? But then under the clothes, I saw a bunch of muslin: long strips to wind around my body and hold my small breasts flat.

He'd been planning this for a while, then. Taking care of me in ways I hadn't even known about. I'd find some way to thank him. Somehow.

In five minutes, I'd wrapped myself up, thrown on the clothes, and had hacked off my braid and most of my hair, flushing it all down the toilet. I was ready to leave when I spied something near the back door.

A package, no larger than a few slices of bread, wrapped in brown paper with my name on it. I picked it up, feeling fabric inside. For a moment, I was almost overcome by tears. It was the first real gift I'd ever received from someone besides my mom.

Outside, far enough away that I couldn't make out the words, an alert sounded on the compound's PA system. I slipped the present into my backpack and walked calmly out the door, turning back at the last minute to grab one more thing from Del's kitchen.

It was hard to stay calm. I moved as normally as I could, but in the distance, I could hear shouting, even make out some of the words.

"Del, where the *hell* is she?" It was Grant. Even though he was much younger than Del, he was still a ranked Enforcer and could cause serious trouble.

"Sir, I don't know exactly," Del answered. "Could she have run back to her room? She was pretty scared."

A low voice let out a short laugh. The Alpha. "That girl doesn't have the sense to be scared."

I had minutes, or less, to make my escape.

I kept my head down as I crossed gravel-paved street after street, hoping no one would notice me, stop me. Of course, when I reached the first row of houses, where the trees began to grow thicker, someone did.

"Boy, what is that *smell?*"

I stopped, daring a glance at the woman who'd shouted from her yard. She stood in front of one of the houses that bordered the second ward of the packlands, where the higher ranked, wealthier families lived. She looked like a maid, though, not one of the wives of the Enforcers.

"Sorry, ma'am," I grumbled, hoping I sounded like a boy. I coughed and thumped my hand against the backpack I'd wrapped inside a black kitchen trash bag at the last minute. "It's dirty diapers and, um, some sickbed things from one of the elders. I've got to get it to the burn pile."

"Yes, you do. It smells awful. Go back behind in the alley—I don't want that upwind from my clothesline, ya hear?"

Now that was a stroke of luck. You couldn't get into the alley unless you lived in one of those houses.

"Thank you," I muttered, and slipped past her across the lawn. The smell was bad enough that she didn't peer at my face. In fact, she ducked back inside the house as soon as I'd shut the gate.

The long gravel alley was choked with weeds and littered with broken glass and pieces of wood. You'd think people who spent time as wolves would care more for their environment, but this pack at least didn't seem to be bothered by living in filth.

I picked up my pace since no one was back there, jogging to the side of the compound where Del and I had widened a rabbit hole into one big enough to fit two full-sized squirrel hunters. This part of the fence was pretty far from the back gate to the hunting grounds, and surrounded by brush and trees. I knew the guard on duty at the gate couldn't see me. Still, as I slipped through, I felt the strange itch of eyes on me.

I paused just long enough to check for any nearby shifters. I wouldn't have been able to smell anyone coming; I stunk to high heaven. Nothing moved that I could tell, but the sensation of being watched didn't fade.

Finally, I let it go. If I was going to be caught, it was safer away from the compound. I unwrapped the black trash bag and stuffed it inside the backpack, not dumb enough to leave a clue as to where I'd vanished.

"*Aooooooh!*" A distant, angry howl that ended in a scream had me almost turning back. But Del had given me my orders, and he'd always kept me safe. So I ignored the uneasy feeling in my gut and the crawling sensation of being watched, and started running toward the hunting grounds.

THE COMMERCIALS I'd seen for camping had always struck me as hilarious. They made it look like it was a welcome break from real life. I wasn't certain what was so amazing about no toilet paper, air conditioning, or running water. For the thousandth time since I'd woken up that morning, I slapped at a mosquito and wished for a tent, or at least some netting. It wasn't that being eaten by bugs was new; it's just that there were so many more of them down here by the marshy part of the forest.

Our pack's compound was set near a gravel road that led into the closest small town. Well, ghost town. It was deserted, just some boarded-up trailers and a gas station that pack members who were allowed to leave ran to occasionally for magazines or junk food. Since humans supposedly didn't know about wolf shifters—though I wasn't sure how that could be, since there were thousands of us in the world, according to Del—it was usually only ranked shifters who got to leave and have jobs in the outside world. Unranked shifters were weaker, and didn't always have great control over their shifts.

I knew that was a sack of horse shit. For one thing, Del was unranked, and had more control and strength than ten regular ranked members. According to the Alpha, our pack had cultivated a reputation for being a religious cult of some kind, to keep people away. If that didn't work, the shitty, razor-wire-topped fence that stretched for miles on the edge closest to the pack's housing made it clear no one was welcome inside.

The tall fence circled the entire compound, with one

main gate at the front, and one at the back that led out to the hunting grounds, the unfenced part of Southern's territory that was still patrolled by our Enforcers. The hunting grounds stretched into a dense forest with hills that turned to mountains the farther north you ran. We all knew that the rogues who lurked at Southern's borders could be out there, and hunting alone was Russian roulette. Only Enforcers or ranked shifters who were accompanied by one were allowed to hunt game.

But I'd been hunting illegally on this land for years, and had never once come across any rogues. Of course, I'd figured they couldn't be much worse than Trevor Blackside and his asshole friends. I'd only seen signs of rogues when I'd wandered too deep into the hunting grounds: footprints that became pawprints, gnawed bones, and tracks that vanished into nowhere.

The area of the hunting grounds where I'd finally stopped smelling other Southern wolves—but was still close enough to be certain I wasn't in rogue territory—felt more like a swamp than a forest. In the past day and a half, I hadn't seen much wildlife other than a couple of water snakes, birds, and a few squirrels, but the mosquitoes were approaching the size of apex predators.

I dipped my canteen into the less-stagnant water at my feet and dropped another sanitizing tablet in before shaking it up. I would definitely have to thank Del for those little marvels later. Once I was able to shift to my wolf form, I'd be able to drink almost any kind of water, but until then, I was vulnerable to all the creepy-crawlies.

Some of the girls I'd known in school, back when I was allowed to go to school, had already shifted. It happened naturally after someone found their true mate. But if a female got too old without shifting, the Alpha would guide her through the change. Which sounded like a favor, but I'd watched more than one twenty-one-year-old go through the process, and it apparently hurt worse than childbirth.

That said, the males in our pack were all forced into their first shift before they turned sixteen, and it didn't seem as painful for them. Maybe the Alpha made it worse for the females. He was a sadistic prick, so I could see that being something he would enjoy.

Leaves rustled just beyond my campsite, and I hopped up, stowing the canteen. At the base of a nearby sycamore tree, I'd made a squirrel snare the way Del had taught me years before. As usual, I'd caught one. I twisted its neck and tucked it into the makeshift belt I'd made out of some rope Del had packed.

The guy had thought of everything. When I went back for the Games, I would find him, and after I'd fought and found another pack, I would ask their Alpha to take him, too.

I still remembered the night our Alpha had announced that the Conclave was coming to our packlands. Since it was a gathering of all the packs, the Conclave was supposed to switch between the four main packs every four years. But the Northern, Eastern, and Mountain packs had so much more money than ours, and so many more members, they hadn't come to our packlands for something like forty years.

The older females in our pack had been buzzing with stories about Conclaves ever since the announcement. I'd listened at more doorways and half-opened windows than usual, trying to figure out what exactly to expect. Especially if it would make my life harder, to be hunted at night with so many other packs here. It would be a real bitch to hide, with every room filled, and shifters everywhere.

Supposedly, Conclaves lasted for a week and were the main way that true mates who weren't in each other's home packs could meet. That was mostly what the pack women seemed fired up about.

The whole first two days, and every day for the entire week, there would be parties and even regional "cultural classes," with dances late into the night. Those were the events everyone around my age wanted to go to, since they gave unmated wolves more chances to interact. If you found "the one," and touched him or her, it was supposed to be super apparent to everyone around that you were fated. The packs would hold celebrations every night for the lucky wolves.

I had always been more curious about the other elements of the Conclave. There were pack political meetings, where any shifter could speak privately with the Council, the elite ruling group made up of the Alphas of the four main packs, their mates, and Head Enforcers. Any shifter, no matter what their rank, could report on issues within their own pack, with the understanding that there would be no retribution after the Conclave was over. Boy, would I have some "issues" to share with the big shots, if I could get close enough.

But the most exciting parts of the week were the Enforcer Games that took place on five of the evenings. They were really fights, not games, exactly. Del had said there used to be different types of competitions, so shifters who were great at tracking or hunting, or even stuff like memorizing pack history, could win. But for decades now, the only Games had been the evening fights.

Our Alpha had announced that any shifter could participate. When I'd pressed Del for details, he'd admitted that no, it didn't say in the Conclave bylaws that only male shifters were eligible. He said there was even one pack that had a few female Enforcers. Maybe that one would bid for me.

I ran a hand through my butchered short hair. Would I even be recognized as a female now? I sure didn't look like one anymore.

Grabbing the stout branches I'd found to serve as my practice staff and sword, I ran through the fighting forms Del had been teaching me for the past ten years. When he'd discovered me trying to teach myself how to use a broken wooden sword in the hurricane-damaged gym by the dining hall when I was almost ten, I'd thought he'd make me quit. But instead, he'd taught me.

Well, not taught, exactly. It was illegal to teach an unranked wolf to fight. But we were allowed to do forms without weapons. So, he'd handed me a mop instead of a staff, and a kitchen knife in place of a sword. I'd gotten pretty good, or at least, I thought so. Del had told me I was better than I realized.

I swung my branches, thinking about how the Games would play out. Supposedly, there were five evenings of scheduled fights after the Conclave began, where shifters would show off their strength, cunning, and fighting skills in human form, and wolf form if they could shift. Enforcers and even unranked shifters could participate. Mostly, participants were in it to gain glory for their own pack, but a shifter could announce after they had won a round that they were seeking a new pack.

And then, if another pack accepted them, they were taken on as an Enforcer in training.

My heart raced at the thought. No, the *certainty*.

I was going to be an Enforcer. All I had to do was win one round against another shifter and impress another pack. According to Del, most of the shifters tried to pick strong opponents, so when they won or lost, they were celebrated. No one cheered for the weaker wolves.

Del was probably going to sign me up for the scrawniest boy he could find. I didn't care. I'd kick his ass with style and get my ticket out of Southern. I swung my staff around one last time with flair... and hit a tree.

That *growled*.

"Oh, fucknuggets."

5

DEFINITELY NOT A TREE
FLOR

It wasn't a tree I'd hit. It was a guy. A really, really tall, angry-looking shifter.

All I could see at first was short red hair and green eyes that were so bright they almost sparkled, like gemstones. His lips were full and looked soft, but his clean-shaven jawline was hard. I'd never even imagined a face as sharp and perfect as his. He was a stranger, not one of my pack, which was a blessing.

I weighed my options. Should I run? Maybe not yet. It wasn't the hours for the Hunt. And something in my gut said I didn't need to be afraid of him, even if he was a stranger, and a male. Maybe he wasn't hunting me. Heck, he might not be able to tell I was a girl.

I backed up a step anyway, taking in the rest of him. "Um, sorry," I mumbled, trying to lower my voice like a boy's. "I thought you were a tree."

I tensed my muscles to flee, in case he didn't buy it. I wasn't sure I could run faster than him, though. He looked fit and fast, and his legs were long—he must have been six foot four. He also had on expensive-looking black running shorts, black tennis shoes, and nothing else. I tried not to stare at the defined abs that were flexing right in front of my face.

"You're tall as hell," I muttered at his abs. "It was an honest mistake." I peeked up at his face again. A muscle in his jaw twitched as he stared down at me. He seemed disappointed for some reason. No, *disgusted*.

The idea of that made my heart pang. Why should I care if some stranger thought I was trash? I was used to that.

"So, you gonna kill me or stare me to death or what?" I asked gruffly, annoyed at his silence and my own strange reaction to him.

"You're from Southern." He didn't ask, just stated it. His eyes flicked to the metal tag on my ear.

"Yeeahh," I drawled. I guess you couldn't expect that much hotness to also have brains. "You're not. What are you doing on our hunting grounds?"

"Running." He paused, like there was something he wanted to say but decided not to. "Your Alpha gave us free rein to exercise. We're staying at the Pack House."

"Dang, you came a long way." I glanced around the trees behind him. "You alone?"

"For now," he answered after a moment. "Lots of others are planning to take some pack runs, though. You might want to get back to the compound. A kid on their own? Bad idea with so many strangers coming into the area."

I noticed he hadn't said a girl on her own. Maybe my disguise was better than I thought. I stuck out my flattened chest. "I can handle myself. And I ain't a kid."

"Sure, kid." He strode casually across the clearing, glancing at my campsite, such as it was. He picked up another branch I'd found to practice with. "I see you know some bo staff forms."

43

"Yep," I agreed, trying for casual. "I'm gonna join the Games."

For a split second, his eyes glimmered with something. Curiosity? Concern? I wasn't sure. He was probably just like the guys in my pack, considering anyone as small as I was to be weak. I hated that condescending shit.

He twirled the branch a few times, testing its weight and balance. "Want to spar?"

I held my breath for a second, then let it out. I'd never sparred with anyone other than Del, and we'd only used mops. This could be great practice. "I'd love to." I gestured to the clearing. "This work for you?"

"Stay between those three pines?" He sketched a triangle out with his eyes.

I nodded eagerly. "Ready?" My voice squeaked, too high in my excitement, and I repeated myself, trying for a casual growl. "Ready?"

The corners of his lips turned down, but he nodded once. "Fight," he agreed.

He came at me fast. The force of his hits jarred just a bit, and I winced, wondering how powerful this guy really was. Del always held back, no matter how much I tried to get him to use his full strength. He said until I could shift, he wouldn't fight me for real, since my healing would take too long, and I was constantly being hunted by the unmated assholes. A shifted wolf could heal almost anything in a few days; human forms took weeks longer, and sometimes couldn't heal really bad stuff. Human form was what got Enforcers killed, according to Del.

The guy in front of me whirled his staff around for another hit. I returned his blow just as fast and danced away. We circled for a moment, and then I drew my branch out in a swift arc away from my hip, switching to an elegant sword-fighting style Del had begun teaching me a few months before.

The guy's eyes widened. "*Iaido*? With branches for swords?"

"*Hai*," I agreed, trying not to flinch when he switched his style to meet my branch with equally smooth parries.

Crap. He knew that, too.

He said something in what I assumed was Japanese, but I shook my head. "I don't speak it."

He frowned, like I'd let him down again. I wondered how upset he'd look if he knew I'd only finished ninth grade.

His strokes were coming faster now, and *Iaido* wasn't cutting it. I dropped low, rolling toward him and swinging my staff at an angle toward his knees. The staff connected, barely above the knee, and he leaped back, cursing.

"Dirty," he gritted out.

"Effective," I returned with a grin.

He was right, though. This was not a traditional style, more street fighting. But Del had said shorter and weaker fighters couldn't afford to fight clean. There was no way I could match this guy without getting a little dirty.

"I should have expected dirty from Southern," he sneered.

I laughed. He wanted to insult my pack? Be my guest. "You have no idea." I did a backflip, taking a chance that he wouldn't strike while I was showing off. For some reason, I wanted to impress him.

That was my first mistake.

He took the moment I was regaining my balance to aim a quick flurry of strokes at my head and shoulders, then managed to twist his staff under mine and pull. My branch landed across the clearing.

45

He bowed. "Well fought."

"Not done." I darted forward to grab his branch, tossing it away in a slick move with both hands.

He let out a laugh. "Got no quit?" He dropped into a jiu-jitsu stance, and I realized I was in for it now. He was huge, and his balance was so perfect. The only way I was getting out of a wrestling match was with luck.

Or more dirty fighting.

"Never got the chance to quit," I panted. I dropped low and set my fingers into the leaf mulch, grabbing for the dirt underneath. He leaned forward, arms ready to grapple. I pulled my hand up and out, spraying the dirt into his open eyes.

"What the hell?" He coughed, scrabbling back, scraping one hand at his face.

I shouldn't have done it, but I couldn't resist. While he was blinking away the dirt, I grabbed his arm, twisted my leg behind his knee, and pulled him into a classic takedown.

It worked, for a minute. I slid off with a muttered, "Good fight," thinking to get some distance in case he was pissed. I got about six inches away before I felt his hands on me.

"You little punk," he grunted and reached around my waist, grabbing hold of my sleeve and pulling behind me as he slammed me up and over his shoulder, then into the ground.

Pain exploded in my gut as all the air rushed out of my lungs.

He leaned close and growled while I fought to breathe. "You fight dirty, and you smell like shit." And then he sniffed me. Twice. "What the... What is that *smell?*" He leaned even closer, sniffing again, and the hand on my arm loosened slightly. "It's not possible."

I didn't know what he meant. I was dealing with my own impossibility. Something weird was happening as I gasped.

His touch was doing something. Freezing me in place, and warming me up at the same time.

It felt like a swarm of ants was rushing from where he touched me on my arm to the rest of my body. Maybe he'd broken something inside me. My chest suddenly ached, and then other parts, lower, started to echo the pulse. The shock of getting my breath knocked out of me was accompanied by a more stunning realization.

The man's weight on me should have been terrifying, but instead, I felt like I wanted him to press harder against me.

It felt *good*.

"Spicy and sweet," he growled, inhaling deeply.

What the hell was going on? "You like... the smell... of shit?" I managed to taunt, although it still hurt to breathe. I felt a hand on my ribs, then heard a curse.

"Can you stand?"

"Why?" I pursed my lips, drawing in tiny sips of air like Del had taught me. "You want me to hand you... your ass... again?"

It sounded like he stifled a laugh. "Whatever, kid."

And then I heard another voice, a low grumble. "Finnick? You done beating the crap out of baby rogues?"

These shifters thought I was a rogue? I wanted to laugh. Everyone knew rogues were feral. They'd lost their connection to their packs, and from what Del had told me, most of them couldn't even speak. They were less than human, and less than wolf.

Crazed.

Idiots. I might have a bad haircut and smell like I'd rolled in shit, but I... Well, okay. I might look a little feral.

The guy I'd fought—Finnick—let out another curse. "This one's not a rogue. Southern."

Another voice joined in, with an accent I'd never heard before. "Should have known from the smell. Worse than a New York sewer."

I managed to push up onto my elbows, blinking through the pain. "Say it... to my... face, asshole," I spat.

The clearing filled with laughter. I scrambled to my feet, trying to focus, but my head was still spinning. Or I was seeing things. The guy with the accent looked like an angel, or at least like an actor I'd seen playing one in a TV show. As tall as Finnick, but with blond hair that curled around his face, deep blue eyes, and golden skin, his jawline dusted by stubble. He wasn't as muscular as Finnick, but lean, like he ran miles every day.

"I didn't think anyone at Southern had this much fight in them."

I raised one eyebrow in a *come at me, bro* way. The angel laughed, and I swear, something in my stomach clenched in a way I'd never felt.

What the hell *was* that?

"Fights dirty," Finnick growled. His eyes were still red, his face blotchy.

I bared my teeth in my worst smile ever. "My teacher said to use every weapon you got in a battle."

His impossibly rugged jaw dropped. "We were sparring, not cage fighting." I shrugged.

The grumbly voice came from behind me. "He's just pissed he lost." I whirled around and blinked.

There was a mountain in front of me. A mountain that

moved, and breathed, and had ridiculous, boulder-sized muscles all over his body. And a lot of muscles were showing since he was only wearing shorts and a tight, navy-blue t-shirt.

He was the largest man I'd ever seen, seven feet tall or more. Massive, with long dark hair that fell on the sides of a close-cut bearded face. His eyes were a deep chocolate brown, almost black, and snapped with a strange fire as he examined me. He was so huge, I was mesmerized. My fingers itched to feel how soft his beard might be, though it would be a stretch to reach that high. He wasn't a mountain, though. Maybe he was a bear.

His eyes gleamed with something I'd never seen directed at me before. Something warm, and possessive.

I swallowed hard, saying the first thought that floated into my mind. "Are you... Are you a bear?" The other guys burst out laughing. My mouth kept moving, saying exactly what I was thinking. "You're enormous. Like a mountain of shifter. Are bear shifters a thing?"

The other two laughed harder. The grumbly shifter frowned. "You don't recognize me?"

"Um, no," I said, taking a step back. His gaze was glittering with something else now. Was he staring at my ear tag? I had to fight to keep from covering it up. "I've never met you."

"You should have," he growled, stepping closer. "If you really are part of Southern."

"W-what do you mean?" I stammered. "I really am."

"Then why weren't you there to greet the visiting Alpha Heirs yesterday afternoon? Your Alpha said all his males were there for the official start of the Conclave." Was it my imagination, or had he put extra emphasis on the word *male*?

49

Finnick coughed behind him. "Leave the kid alone," he muttered. "There aren't any rogues on packlands."

The blond angel wandered closer, pushing the supplies next to my backpack around with the toe of one sneaker. "I think there's one. Let's take him back to camp. Come on, kid. The Southern Alpha might let you join up."

I let out a laugh. "Join up? Listen, Blondie. If you think the Southern Alpha would let a rogue join his pack, or even let one live for more than a breath, you're bugnuts. You take me back, he'll kill me. Or worse."

The huge guy glared. "No decent Alpha would kill a child."

If he only knew. "Trust me, he might do a lot worse. I was born in this piece-of-shit pack. I should know." I shot him what I hoped was a scathing look. "And I'm not a child, Bearman. I'm almost twenty."

For some reason, Finnick let out a strangled sound. "Too young to be on your own in the woods." A clanking sound came from behind me, and I spun around.

"What the hell are you doing? Get out of my stuff!"

Blondie had stopped poking at my bag with his tennis shoes and was now pawing through the contents of my backpack with both hands. He held up the butcher knife Del had sent. "What's this for? Doesn't look like camping supplies."

"Give that back, asshole!" I shouted, and almost killed myself tripping to get to him. At the bottom of the bag, there was something I really didn't want him to find. Del had slipped in a few tampons, which I wouldn't need unless I was out here for another week. It had been thoughtful.

But these guys thought I was a boy, and I needed to keep that up. Who knew what they would do if they figured out I was a female? They might make me return with them to the compound.

Time to get aggressive. I pulled back my fist, pulling strength from my hip. I was close enough to Blondie to punch him in the face, or I thought so. But before I could connect, I felt a giant hand on my shirt, whirling me around. It was the bear shifter. I still thought he might be a bear; he couldn't be a wolf and be that big.

His chocolate eyes were gleaming with amusement now. "Please don't punch my friend Glenda right before the mating events. He'll need his good looks to get any girl to look at him twice, true mate or not. He doesn't have anything else going for him."

I stopped, my mind whirring. There was so much to unpack in all that. For some reason, the only thing I asked was, "His name's Glenda?"

Finnick let out a sharp laugh. "Glenda, the good witch of the North. See, you didn't need to be offended, 'Bearman.' This kid hasn't heard of him either."

"It's Brand, not Bearman." He rubbed one hand over his beard, and I fought the urge again to run my fingers through that beard. It was short, so it might be wiry, but it gleamed, and I had a feeling it would feel soft like a pelt. He was still holding my shirt, so he was close enough... I shook the thought away.

"Call me Glenda again, Finnick," the blond angel snapped, looking up from my backpack, "and I'll kick your ass, too. I'm more your size, so I won't even have to fight dirty."

"Still say we should take him back, Glen," Brand growled.

I tensed, ready to fight my way free if I had to. "Don't even try it." I tried to hide the panic I felt at the thought, but his grip loosened slightly, and his head tilted to one side, like he was trying to solve a riddle.

"Let the kid go, Brand," Finnick said. His voice sounded weird, and clearly I wasn't the only one who thought so. Brand and Glen gave him a couple of raised eyebrows. Finnick just shrugged. "Southern here has to be at the Conclave, right?"

"Yeah," I muttered. "I wouldn't miss it for anything." That much was true.

Glen perked up. "You plan to fight in the Enforcer Games, kid? What's your name?"

I was instantly suspicious. "Why?"

Glen's blue eyes twinkled. "Just thought I might sign up for a round."

"No!" Finnick shouted. "You can't fight a kid."

Glen rolled his eyes. "I can fight anyone. You'll be fighting on the first night. Unranked, right? I'll go easy on... What was your name?"

I sure as hell wasn't telling them my real name. But I couldn't think of a decent lie. "It's, uh, Wills."

Glen froze. What had I said? Then the world started again, and I wondered if I had imagined it.

"All right, Wills," Finnick choked out. Maybe he still had some dirt in his windpipe. "We'll see you back inside the compound."

"At the Games, sure," I said, hoping I could sneak in when none of these giants were around. I didn't just want to fight in the Games. I needed to win one round if I wanted a chance to get away from my pack.

If I wanted a chance to survive.

6

TRUE MATE, FAKE NAME
GLEN

"I 've never met a wolf who smelled that bad," I said casually, glancing at Finn and Brand as we jogged away from the strange little campsite. If any shifter screamed runaway, it was that one.

"Can't be nearly twenty. Too fucking small," Brand grumbled, sounding pissed, as usual.

I liked to tease him about waking up on the wrong side of the bed every morning. I'd change that to the wrong side of the cave now, though. *Bearman, ha!* It wasn't as bad as Glenda, but the look on his face when the stranger had said it was priceless.

Finnick mumbled something like, "Could have rolled in a latrine."

"Mhmm." I agreed with them both, wondering if that's exactly what the little shifter had done.

It was possible. None of us had ever been to Southern before. For all we knew, they didn't have bathrooms for most of the pack. They sure as hell didn't have clean, clear lakes to swim in like my pack in Canada, or Brand's. Their hunting grounds so far had been bogs, spindly forests, and streams drying up, though it was only late June.

But I'd never thought a bad smell would trick the noses of my best friends. I was going to have so much fun teasing them about this. "Brand, you're always going on about how observant you are, living in the mountains."

He shot me a dirty look. I winked back, knowing insults were his love language. According to him, I was practically a city wolf like Finnick. He'd teased me about my poor nose and minimal tracking abilities for years, even though he knew my parents had made sure I could handle myself in a forest. Hell, his own grandfather had taught me tracking and hunting one summer when I'd fostered at Mountain. I could hold my own.

Brand growled again. "I do live in the fucking mountains, Glenda. I have to be observant to survive. I hunt my food; I don't call a damned Uber to bring it to me."

By the moon, this was priceless. I couldn't help prolonging the moment. "So, you didn't notice anything particularly significant about our little runaway friend there?"

"What?" His glare turned suspicious. "What do you mean? Is he a rogue after all? Damnit, I could *tell* there was something about him. Let's go back there and—"

I reached into my pocket and pulled out the tampon I'd found in the backpack. "You didn't notice that 'Wills' back there was a female shifter, did you?"

Brand tripped over a fallen branch. "F-female?"

I let loose a laugh. "Some tracker. I don't know about you, but male wolves at Northern don't get periods. Is that a Mountain pack thing?"

He picked himself up. "What the hell is a little girl doing out here alone?"

Finn had kept quiet until now, which was strange. He was more or less the most talkative of us there. "Wills, she said. Her name is Wills."

"A fake name?" Brand mused, rubbing a hand over his beard in thought.

"Wait, no. Wills. Isn't that the last name of the girl they said killed the old Enforcer Del? The girl that went rogue?" It was the first thing Alpha Callaway had greeted us with when we arrived the afternoon before. One of his pack, an unranked girl, had killed an ex-Enforcer in cold blood only yesterday morning, and he'd asked us to be on the lookout for her.

I turned on my heel. "Shit, we have to go back and bring her in."

Finn stopped me with a hand on my arm. "No. Leave her."

Brand looked as disturbed as I did. "What the hell, Finn? She's a wanted criminal, worse than a rogue. A murderer. She has to be brought in, brought to justice." I wasn't surprised at the anger in his tone; Brand's mother had been killed by rogues, years before.

Finn scowled. "Justice in this moon-forsaken pack? You know Callaway will just execute her."

"If she's a murderer, then..." Brand went silent. "Maybe we won't turn her over to Callaway. We can wait until your parents arrive—"

Finn cut him off. "Listen, there's something I have to tell you."

Brand was already up off the ground and heading back to the campsite. "Tell me after I catch the rogue."

"She might be my mate," Finn blurted out.

"Oh *shit*," I muttered, wondering why my stomach had turned over at his announcement. Finding a true mate was a positive thing, right? I should be pleased for my friend. I shouldn't want to rip his throat out. *What the hell?*

I tried to smile, but had a feeling I was baring my teeth.

Finn didn't seem happy either. "I could be wrong," he muttered. "I hope I'm wrong."

Brand let out a deep growl. "I guess you're not thrilled about her smell? Or is it the murdering thing? She'd fit right in with your pack."

I held up a hand before the fight could start. "Tell me something, Brand. When the Southern Alpha announced this girl's crime, did you get the feeling there was something... odd about the whole thing?"

"This whole pack is odd. Too much inbreeding." Brand scratched his beard. "But sure, it was short on details. Long on how amazing the guy, Del, was. You know, I met him, a long time ago. At a Conclave."

"He was a big guy, Del," Finn said softly. "A great fighter, an Enforcer for the Alpha before Callaway."

I let out a low whistle. Callaway had been the Alpha for two decades, taking over for his uncle after he died in a fight with a pack of rogue wolves.

Finn went on. "I remember watching him at one Conclave when I was a little kid, before his accident. He was trying to teach my pack about street fighting, how important it was to use any advantage, even if it meant going low."

A memory surfaced from my own childhood. "Wait, my dad told stories about him, too. He said back in the day, Del was the best Enforcer Southern ever had."

Brand hesitated, something crossing his face. "He hasn't been an Enforcer for a long time. That's why he wasn't at the last four Conclaves. He lost a leg. Lost his rank along with it, Dad said."

"They stripped his rank?" Finn was shocked. "What the hell—they thought a fucking legend like him couldn't fight on three legs?"

I thought for a second, then added, "I didn't see a single member of Southern with any defect today. Not in the ranked wolves anyway."

"There were some skinny kids with injuries, though," Brand growled. "Skinny adults, too. Kept way back."

"Unranked, like this girl Wills?" I wondered aloud, while Brand muttered about the fucking ear tags all Southern's unranked shifters, male or female, had to wear. "I'm not sure it matters. If she killed Del, she has to be brought to justice."

"So, you really think a girl that size—a nineteen-year-old who obviously hasn't eaten a decent meal in a long time—would be able to kill one of the best Enforcers who ever lived?" Finn's voice was as quiet as ever, but filled with rage. "She even mentioned her instructor to me—had to be Del. She didn't flinch. Does she even know he's dead?"

I wondered how long she'd been living out here. I thought probably only a few days, but who knew? Finn's eyes met mine, and I let out a slow breath. "She was set up."

He nodded. "I think so. I've heard rumors of how Callaway gets away with things. Del didn't lose that leg in battle, you know. It was an accident of some kind. Logs rolling off a truck. He was passed out drunk on the ground."

"Drunk?" I shook my head in disbelief. "A wolf his size and age would have to chug five gallons of Everclear to get passed-out drunk."

Brand let out a string of curses. "Fucking Calvin Callaway, useless lump of Alpha shit. Can we go ahead and kill his ass?"

57

"Not yet," Finn said. "You know what our parents have said. Luke isn't ready to take the reins. Give him time."

"Luke is too naïve and weak to ever beat Calvin in combat," I reminded him. "And if Luke knew about this set up…"

"She's planning to show up at the Conclave." Finn spat out the words like they were poison.

"To the mate match?" I couldn't help smiling. "Why don't you go tell her she doesn't need to bother?"

"No, to the *Games*. She's planning to fight. She fucking told you that."

"Shit, I thought that was just talk. It had to be, right?" The idea of a young girl fighting male shifters in the ring sickened me. And *that* girl in particular. She could be killed. For some reason, the thought that I could lose her before getting to know her gutted me.

What the hell was going on with me? She was Finn's mate, possibly. I had no reason—no right—to feel possessive.

"I'll go back," I suggested. "I'll let her know about Del. Let her know she needs to bail on the Games, and we'll figure out some way to get her back to your pack."

Finn's teeth were going to crack if he clenched them any harder. "She's almost the same age as my sister. And she's… Southern."

For some reason, I imagined grinding his face into the dirt. And when I peeked at Brand, he looked similarly inclined.

"If she's your mate," Brand said, his voice too quiet, "you'll protect her. You can have one of our fathers call an emergency Council meeting, and beg for amnesty. True mate bonds trump everything."

Finn let out a breath that was half howl, half sigh. "What do you think will happen to her at my pack? You both saw how small she is, how weak. I can't bring a dirty hillbilly runaway to Eastern."

Brand took a step forward, like he was going to punch Finn in the jaw. I'd never seen him so unhinged. "You don't talk about your mate that way, asshole."

Finn stepped into range of Brand's fists. *Shit.* I had to stop this before it started. "Why did you think she was your mate, anyway? What was it that tipped you off?"

He tilted his head, thinking. "When I smelled her, it was like... by the moon, this is disgusting. But that shit didn't smell as bad as it should, like I wanted to claw my way to the bottom of that stench and scent *her*. Touch her."

"And what else?" I asked. "I mean, I've been attracted to some not-so-nice smelling females."

"Her punches and strikes. They hurt." He stood there, looking at us.

Brand was the first to react. "That's it? You think she's your mate because you like the smell of shit, and you're weak?" He let out a huge bellow of laughter. "I could have told you that already, brother!"

"Fuck off." Finn ran his hands through his short hair, his eyes flashing. "Why do you have to be such an asshole?"

"Listen, Finn. Whether or not she's your mate, she's in danger. Maybe she doesn't know Del's dead; maybe she does. That part's not important. She said she's planning to sneak back in for the Games. To try for a place in another pack, probably."

"But she knows Callaway wouldn't let her fight." Brand ran a hand over his beard, thinking. "Not as a girl."

"Yeah." I admired her commitment to the camouflage,

actually. "It's not a bad tactic. Dress like a boy, cut off your hair, cover your scent with shit—literally. It worked, and she's hoping it keeps working right up until she's in the ring, I bet."

Brand let out a shaky breath. "She's going to be killed. They'll be looking for her—all the packs will. Finn, you have to go tell her."

But Finn blurted out, "I can't deal with this, with her," and jetted away, leaves crunching underfoot as he fled. I stared at his back in shock as he ran.

"That *asshole*," Brand growled. "Fucking city wolf. Willing to throw away what could be his true mate. She'll be killed because he's a coward."

"Maybe not," I muttered, already planning how to sneak her out to my pack. "I'll go back and talk to her, make certain she didn't kill Del. Then I'll make sure she knows what she's walking into." I nodded at the path where Finn had vanished. "You follow Finnick and see if you can talk sense into him. Or keep him from doing something stupid anyway."

"Too late, brother," he grumbled, but took off after Finn.

I turned back toward Wills—whatever her real name was—and wondered why my heart pounded faster with every step I took. Probably because I was getting out of shape. I'd add a few more miles to my runs this week.

As I got closer to the campsite, I realized she'd left. I tracked her easily, following the scent of latrine for about a half mile, noticing a little too late that she had gone to the creek that ran along the far edge of the Southern packlands.

Before I knew it, I was standing in the shade of the forest, watching like a fucking creeper as the shifter I'd thought at first was a young male lay in the sunlight.

Her wet hair gleamed, her clothing drying on nearby rocks. She looked like some sort of forest nymph, small breasts with tight pink nipples bare to the sky, and a narrow strip of dark red hair between her legs.

She was a vision. A goddess. And I couldn't look away.

7
DISHONORED
FLOR

"Tell me I smell like shit?" I muttered out loud as I stalked to the creek. "Tell me I can't fight? I'll fight them all."

Flor, forget those guys, I told myself. *Their opinions don't matter.*

But inner, bloodthirsty Flor was not so forgiving. She kept imagining a battle royale where she handed all three of them their asses. Their very nice, very firm asses.

Asses I might fondle for a while before I kicked them from here to the Mississippi border.

Ugh. Maybe the sewage had gotten in my ear and infected my brain. I'd lost all my sense.

I grabbed the bar of hotel soap Del had stuck in the bottom of my bag, reminding myself again to thank him for thinking of everything. Well, not everything. I could have used some real shampoo instead of the hotel-sized bar of soap. But I'd made do with less.

I stripped down, unrolling the muslin strips that bound my breasts. The cloth wasn't that uncomfortable, but it left marks. I rubbed at my skin to erase them, running my hands over my breasts. They weren't big, but they definitely didn't look like a boy's. I let my fingers slide over the abused skin and circled my nipples with my fingertips, wondering why the faces of the men I'd just met swam through my mind as I did so.

"Turning into a pervert," I muttered, soap in hand as I stepped carefully into the water, aware of the slick moss on the stones near the edge of the creek.

I washed as quickly as possible, leaning over to let my short hair rinse clean in the tumble of water that fell over the rocks. I felt a little bad about using soap in the stream I fished out of, but it was sort of an emergency. Smelling horrible had kept me from being found by my pack's trackers, but I had to be halfway decent to sneak back in among the other Games competitors.

There should be enough strangers there to hide my scent. Enough scent and noise and commotion. There had to be. I wasn't certain even Del had a Plan C dreamed up.

The soap had left my skin squeaky clean. I sluiced off the excess water with my hands, then picked my way carefully across the mossy stones and grabbed my shirt and pants. I'd need to wear them again tomorrow, and they were the only set of boy's clothes I had. I used the rest of the tiny bar of soap to get them clean—they passed the sniff test, but just barely—then laid them out on a boulder to dry. I let myself lie next to them for a while, relishing the feel of the sunlight on my skin.

I allowed my mind to drift back to the moment in the clearing when Brand had grabbed my shirt. He'd almost touched me, and it had felt like a warm, syrupy ray of sunlight was running over my skin near his hand.

What would it have felt like if my shirt had shifted, if

his massive hand had closed around my bare arm, or my shoulder...

My stomach clenched again, the way it had when Finnick and I had been fighting. What was happening to me? I'd lived almost twenty years without feeling that... *whatever* the other girls talked about. I'd tried touching myself plenty of times to see if I could have an orgasm—hell, I'd read an article about it in some weird human magazine someone had left in the dining hall that practically gave step-by-step instructions. But I'd never felt anything amazing.

For some reason, the thought of Finnick, and Brand, and even that angel-guy Glen, made it seem like a good idea to give it another try.

Fuck it. Why not?

I reached down, my hands skating across my thighs, moving soft and slow over the hair at the junction of my legs. Opening them the tiniest bit, I let a finger explore for a moment. At first, it wasn't any different than before, but then for some reason, Brand's massive form popped into my mind.

Brand, with those big hands holding me, wrapping around my thighs, keeping me still. His finger, much bigger than mine, reaching down and spreading me open, finding my slit. Those dark eyes going liquid and sweet as he murmured for me to relax, to open to him, to give him my pleasure. Whispering words of praise, telling me what a beautiful, sweet, perfect woman I was. How he'd devour me, if I just let him in.

I widened my legs and used my own hands to play the part of Brand in the fantasy, at last feeling the sensation the magazine had described. The pulsing intensity, the waves that crashed and receded, and grew again... until after how long, ten minutes? I didn't know; it became almost unbearable. My heart raced, my breath stuttering.

But I didn't stop circling my clit, moving my fingers as the pleasure spiraled higher.

In my mind, Brand was naked, his chest covered with dark hair, his scent musk and salt, holding me down, sliding his fingers over my flesh, touching me lightly, and then deeper. Almost... almost...

Then my mind skipped like a stone over a still pond, and it was Finnick instead of Brand. Those soft, full lips moving on my clit, his cheeks smooth on my thighs, his tongue delving closer, deeper, sending me higher...

Until at last, Glen joined in, pinching my breasts, one hand reaching around my throat, grasping gently but firmly as his friends plundered my body...

I shouted his name as the sensations overtook me. "Glen!"

My pulse was still pounding in my ears as I heard his voice answer me. "Fuck, yes."

That voice wasn't in my mind. My eyes flew open, and I stood so fast that I felt dizzy, disoriented. "What the hell? What the hell are you *doing* here?" I scrambled for my clothes, but they were still wet, and I struggled to get them on, the sleeves sticking to my wet skin.

"I'm not looking," Glen insisted from the shadow of the woods.

"How do I know that, you creep?!" I screamed, my voice high. Like a girl's.

Well, it was too late to keep up the boy pretense. He'd seen the show. My first show. *That douchenozzle.* My fists balled up as I thought about pounding his perfect face into a bloody pulp.

"I swear on my pack's honor, I'm not looking. Not now," he added.

"What kind of an asswipe watches a girl *masturbate?*" I almost choked on the final word. "For the first time in her life," I whispered.

I was so humiliated. Ashamed.

"Oh shit," he said softly, but not so softly I didn't hear. Fucking shifter hearing.

I tried not to let out a sob. Males had taken so much from me. My mother, my childhood, any sense of safety or belonging in my own pack, and now this... My first time feeling like maybe I wasn't abnormal. Maybe I could feel normal girl things, and no one would hurt me.

And now this stranger had taken that as well.

I felt a sob burst out before I could stop it. And another. Fucking weakness. I knew better than to cry, to be vulnerable, in front of a predator. A male.

"By the moon, Wills." Glen's voice sounded as raw as I felt. "Please forgive me. I didn't mean to see you. I couldn't... I should have looked away. Gone back."

Suddenly, he was in front of me, next to me. I crab walked back, but he wasn't looking at me. His face was averted, his gaze on the ground, oddly... submissive? Submitting to me, an unranked girl? It had to be some kind of trick.

His voice was raw when he spoke, still not meeting my gaze. "I have dishonored myself, and the Northern pack. I now owe you a debt of honor. As Heir to Northern, and in the name of Alpha Bradley Hillier, I swear that you will never receive harm from me or mine until the debt is paid, and I will do anything in my power to make restitution for the crime I have done you."

"What?" *Crime? What is he talking about?* I pulled my pants up and buttoned them, but he didn't budge.

Finally, I reached out to get his attention, my hand hovering above his arm. His *trembling* arm. He was shaking with... shame. I recognized the scent of it, sour and dark, although his eyes were still firmly fixed on the ground.

"I-it's okay," I managed to say, even though it was very much not. "It wasn't that big a deal..." I trailed off, remembering what he had said. "Wait, who are you again?" I stepped a few feet away, suddenly nervous. "You're the Alpha Heir? You're from Northern?" Northern was Del's second favorite pack, after Mountain. He'd told me a ton of stories about his trips to those two packs before he lost his leg.

Glen stood, keeping his head lower than mine and his eyes on the ground. *Wow.* He had this submissive apology thing down.

"I am. And I'm so sorry. I took something from you I cannot return. You have my sincere regrets."

I was surprised to hear myself laugh. He was surprised, too, and glanced at my face. I tugged at the short ends of my hair, wishing I had enough to pull over my face to hide my embarrassment. "It's not like I haven't had worse done to me. Lots worse." He cringed, and I reached out and touched his arm, hoping to get him to stop staring at the ground.

It worked. He looked up, his eyes as blue as the ocean must be, and deep—and captured me, drawing me in, drowning me.

Remaking me.

Something spiraled up my hand to my arm to my chest, stopping to spin around like a tornado of emotion in my stomach and then out through my limbs. I let out a shaky breath.

Glen let out a matching exhalation, his hand meeting mine. His face transformed into a look that perfectly matched the picture I'd seen of an angel in a children's book years ago. Adoration and joy and... something else, something significant.

And then his hand was on mine as he spoke into the shining, shimmering moment. "It's you."

8

NOT READY
FLOR

"Yes, it's me," I agreed, wondering what was going on. I shook away the strange spiraling sensations that had moved through me and focused on the slack-jawed male at my feet. "It's me. Flor—I mean, Wills."

He nodded, his smile dimming. "Oh shit," he murmured.

I gave my arm a sniff, pulling it away from his strangely magnetic grasp. "Not anymore, I don't think. Should I take another bath?"

He shook his head, and I watched as the strangest series of emotions played over his face. Sheer happiness, then consternation, then anger, then excitement. What was he thinking?

"Tell me what you're thinking," I demanded. "I'm super confused right now."

"Um," he said. "Um."

I waited a long moment. "So. You're not a public speaker then." What was it with all these excessively pretty, unbelievably stupid men?

He gulped. "I'm actually very good with words. Usually. But you... I wasn't ready for you. For this."

What did he mean? Not ready to creep on some girl in the woods? Well, that made him different from the guys in my pack at least. Maybe he wasn't that bad.

Even if his grip did make me feel like I was riding a merry-go-round.

"Yeah, welcome to my life. Never ready, no matter how many plans I make." I shrugged. "I always thought if I could get away from my piece-of-shit pack, I could do more than just react, you know?"

"Yes." Glen's voice was once again confident, but his expression severe. "Let's talk about your pack, shall we?"

I wasn't sure how I was even able to speak after the embarrassment of him catching me, but this guy had the weirdest way of making me feel at ease. Comfortable, even. I'd never felt that before, especially not around a guy close to my age. I thought he was anyway; he looked to be around twenty-five, though it was hard to tell with most shifters. I almost asked, though I knew better. He felt safe, but that didn't mean he was.

The feeling might have been because he kept his eyes down, even as he more or less interrogated me. I wasn't used to anyone showing me that level of respect. Maybe it was his manners. He was more polite than anyone I'd ever met.

The questions he asked were odd, though.

"Can you tell me about your childhood?" he began.

"I'd rather not." My wet clothes were plastered to my skin, and since I didn't have my muslin cloth binding my breasts, I was more than a little self-conscious about the way I looked. My nipples were sticking out like they were trying to get this guy's attention. *Stupid nipples.*

"About your parents, then."

"Mama was around," I said slowly. I swear, if a shifter's human form could swivel their ears, his would have.

"Was? She's dead?"

"Well, it's a good bet," I replied. "Killed by rogues is what they told me. She got thrown out of the packlands four years ago."

He made a sympathetic sound. "Why?"

"She, um..." I'd never had to tell this story; everyone in my pack already knew it. "She was protecting me from this toadfu—um, this guy, Trevor. I'd started looking more like a girl." I laughed self-consciously, tugging at the ends of my hair. "You'd never know it, but I was slightly cute at one point."

"I'd believe it." His voice was like chocolate, dark and sweet.

"Well, anyway..." I went on, flustered. "I didn't want him, but I was unranked. He caught me the first week I was the prey in the Hunt."

"Hunt?" A slight growl had entered his tone, and I shrank back slightly, until he relaxed.

"It's a pack game the unmated guys play," I said, not wanting to explain. It was so humiliating, and I didn't want this guy to see me as weak. As prey. "Anyway, he caught me and said I had to mate him."

He sucked in a sharp breath. "Wait, mate him for real? You said it was a game."

I snorted. "Yeah, well, a game with consequences."

His eyes flashed with blue lightning. "You would have been sixteen?"

"Yeah, actually fifteen, I think," I mused, remembering how upset I'd been that my boobs had started to appear near the end of ninth grade. That was late for shifter girls, and the pack boys had started to notice. "I was a late bloomer. But he's the oldest son of our Head Enforcer, a real bastard named Van."

It was actually Van who had helped Trevor catch me. Del had been ordered to help cook for and serve in the Alpha's private dining room. I'd had to handle the whole pack dining hall and the cleanup, and hadn't been able to get away before the Hunt began that evening. Van had chained the doors to the dining hall from the outside so I had no way to get out, and then he'd given his asshole son the key.

The Hunt would have been over for me that night. Except Mama had shown up, sent home early from work.

His eyes narrowed. "The Head Enforcer. I thought that was supposed to be... what was his name, a fighter named Del?"

For the first time, my instincts were triggered. He knew something about Del. The faint, familiar scent of deception —like old metal rusting, stagnant water pooling—teased my senses. He wasn't lying outright, but he wasn't being truthful either. He was holding back.

"Yeah. Del lost a leg in some bullshit accident quite a few years back, when I was little. He lost his rank, so Van got his place." I felt my gut churn, wondering not for the first time if Trevor's douchebag dad had been the one to make Del's accident happen. "Anyway, Trevor had cornered me in the back of the dining hall, and Mama found him trying to... you know. Mate me."

"Rape you," Glen growled, and my skin prickled at the surge of fear that the sound sent through me. A male growl had only meant pain before now. But this guy noticed my reaction and took a few deep breaths to calm himself.

When he could speak, he murmured, "That's not mating. That's assault. Mating is... sacred. It's miraculous."

Unable to help myself, I snorted again. "Are you kidding? My parents were true mates, and I promise it wasn't a miracle. It was a fucking *nightmare*."

"Your parents?" He raised one eyebrow, like he was kind of interested, but I could see the laser focus in his eyes. "Where was your father when your mother was defending you from Trevor?"

"I don't have a dad." It was true; I had a biological father, but I'd never once called him Dad.

I knew who he was, or at least, I'd guessed. Mama had had a seizure every time the asshole had sex with someone else, so I'd put two and two together. But I didn't want confirmation of my suspicions, and when I'd hinted to Del, he'd warned me never to speak of it. Not that I had anyone I would tell. It wasn't the sort of thing I would brag about.

Glen flushed. "Ah, I'm sorry. Dead as well?"

"I can't really talk about it. It's complicated."

He waited like he wanted me to go on, but I sure as heck wasn't going to start braiding his hair and sharing secrets. This guy might be at events with the asshole, and he could let something slip.

"Anyway, Mama stabbed Trevor in the kidney. He healed eventually, but Mama was unranked, so..." I spread my hands in front of me. "They chucked her out for the rogues to kill. That's the way it is at Southern. If you fart in front of the Alpha, you might as well kill yourself. And he hates me worse than fleas; that's why I'm getting the hell clear of this shithole."

"You're planning to fight your way out?" Glen stood and began gathering my backpack from the bank. I could've sworn I'd seen him sneak a tampon from his pocket into the backpack, but that was crazy. Why would Glen be on his period? Or maybe shifters in his pack just carried them around, in case a girl needed one. That seemed pretty unlikely, though.

"You're entering the Games?" he prompted.

"Yeah, I figure if I can win one round, I'll be able to petition another pack to take me on as an Enforcer." I hesitated. "It is true, isn't it? That other packs have female Enforcers?"

"Not many, but some do," he said slowly, a slight smile curling on his lips. "Who told you that, though?"

"Del." I smiled. "He's the best. He trained me to fight. He was a friend of Mama's when she was alive—her only friend. He's as close to family as I have now, and I'd do anything for him." I sighed. "He did a lot for me, getting me out, packing me stuff." I waggled my eyebrows at Glen, who was not smiling now. In fact, he looked like he'd just heard terrible news. "Did you know, he wanted me to come back for the stupid mating things? He bought me a dress and left it for me before I had to split."

I shook my head, thinking about Del's awkward attempts to talk to me about trying the mating events before I jumped into the Games. I hadn't known about the dress, but it was the sort of thing females wore to those parties.

"Yeah, pretty sure it's a mating dress."

"A mating dress?" For some reason, Glen's voice was strained. "Did you bring it?"

"Sure. In fact, I was going to put it on while my other clothes dried. I mean, I'm not going to the mating things, but it's still clothes, right? And the ones I have on are soaked. Do you mind?" I spun my finger in the air, and he obediently turned around. "Not that you haven't already seen the show."

"You are not a show. You are one of the wonders of the world," I thought he murmured. But that was crazy. Almost as crazy as him offering me some unnamed favor. Maybe I should take him up on it. Maybe... Maybe he'd take me out of here. He was the Northern Alpha Heir, right? He might have the power to do that.

In two minutes, I'd stripped out of the wet clothes and slid on the dress. "Okay, I'm done." I watched his face as he turned back to me.

It was worth the trouble of changing clothes. I knew I wasn't much to look at. I had chopped-off hair, no makeup, and I'd been living rough for a few days. But the dress Del had bought me was gorgeous. Long and fitted, with a sweetheart neckline and a layer of translucent silk over the body of the dress. It was a princess dress, for sure.

"You're magnificent," Glen rasped out.

"Okay, that's a little too thick," I teased, but I knew I was blushing. "But I like it. My favorite color is this exact shade of turquoise. Del knew that, of course. I'll wear it for him someday." I ran my fingers over the dress.

"You... You love him?"

I laughed at the way his eyes bulged slightly. "Yeah, but like a father. If I get an offer from another pack, I'll invite him along. He only has one leg—three as a wolf—but he's still got so much to give. He's an amazing fighter, and a great cook, too. He's taught me all sorts of—" I quit talking when I felt Glen's hand land softly on my lips, stopping my words.

"Wills." His voice was filled with a peculiar sadness. "Flor. I have to tell you something. About Del." His angelic eyes met mine, and I flinched at the unexpected pain in them.

"No," I told him firmly, shaking my head. Somehow, I knew that what he would say was going to destroy me. "Don't say anything. I'll see him in a day or two."

"Wills," Glen repeated, his eyes filled with concern. "You won't see him again."

9
MYSTERIES AND MURDER
LUKE

I held my breath as I stood outside the pack office, listening for voices or movement. But the only sounds I heard were from the training ground in the compound yard. The Games were still days away, but the other packs had begun arriving for the Conclave, filling every spare room, even here in the Pack House. This hallway was off-limits to anyone, except the Southern Alpha, his Head Enforcer, and me.

Of course, I was meant to be hunting for Flor, bringing her to justice. That wasn't what I was doing, though. Today, I was going to bring justice down on my pack's heads *for* her. The mate I'd longed for. The mate I'd failed.

I took a deep breath and knocked on the office door. "Dad?" I called out softly. I knew he had a meeting with Van Blackside and the visiting Enforcers, but it paid to double check.

The other Heirs had arrived the day before, and I'd only had a moment alone to speak with Glen, to share the evidence I'd been slowly gathering on our pack's financial misdeeds. Glen had told me I needed more conclusive evidence of Dad's knowledge of the crimes to get the Council to remove him.

If he was gone, Flor would be safe. She could leave here, make a new life. I wasn't foolish enough to dream that I could ever court her. How could I earn her forgiveness for everything I'd done—and hadn't done—to protect her?

The place inside me that had recognized her when we were both still children ached, as always. My wolf howled to go to her, snarling that she would only be safe if I was there to watch over her. But I knew she was safer in the woods, wherever she was hiding today, and my wolf was too weak to force me to go to her side.

I focused on my task instead. The door was locked, but I had a key Dad didn't know about. I was in charge of the pack's investments, and I was damned good at it. Dad was responsible for disbursement, making sure money went to the wolves who earned it. He had divided the financial labor between us years before, though his work required him to be in the field more often. Of course, "in the field" frequently meant in his bedroom, fucking one or sometimes more of the pack's females.

Confident that Dad was nowhere around, I opened the door and stopped, stunned at the two bare desks. The laptop I used for all my pack work was missing, and so was the Alpha's. They were nowhere in the room, only the dust-free squares in the middle of the polished wood surfaces giving any hint that they had been removed.

He took his laptop to his bedroom frequently, but mine was never moved. Normally, it was hooked up to monitors, speakers, all sorts of backups. Dad was paranoid about saving information remotely, so we switched out the removable hard drive backups every other day.

But those were gone too. I slid open the topmost

drawer, suspicion lighting up my nerves. The paper files where Dad kept all of our regular receipts after I'd scanned them in sat empty. Sure, he'd talked about getting rid of those files a few times, going fully paperless, but he'd been joking. Dad was old school and didn't trust our information not to get hacked. I opened drawer after drawer, finding... nothing.

Had he done this in case one of the other packs got into the office to spy on our pack workings? Did he have a feeling the other Alphas were going to come looking around, once they saw the state of our unranked wolves? As they should.

Maybe he'd taken them to his bedroom. I jogged down the hallway, surprised to find that door unlocked. My instincts told me it was a trap. But it was also an opportunity.

I took a deep breath and stepped inside, searching through the room for either the laptops or the contents of the filing cabinets, and finally crossing to his closet. All of his clothes carried his stench—a combination of cigar smoke, sour laundry, and menthol. Holding my breath, I found the boxes our laptops had come in, and lifted them down.

They were empty, of course, but behind them was an old shoebox with my name written on it in Dad's handwriting. Baby pictures? Dad wasn't at all sentimental.

I opened it carefully, keeping an ear on the hallway outside. There were half a dozen photos of a baby I assumed was me in the hospital when I was born, and some of a French country home, but mostly the box was filled with receipts, handwritten ones. I went through them slowly. My French was rusty, but not completely forgotten.

There were a few from hospitals in France, some to an

investigator, and a copy of a check made out to Genevieve Fleuron.

Ice surged in my veins. That was my old nanny's name, the one who had cared for me from the day my parents died until my uncle's car accident. Alpha Callaway had paid her ten thousand dollars for something, almost two decades before, the same month I came to Southern. I kept flipping through the receipts, my nose itching like it had done years ago, when I scented prey on a hunt.

I found nothing else.

But then, as I lifted the box back up to the shelf, I saw a scrap of paper stuck to the bottom of the cardboard. I pried it loose with one fingernail. It wasn't a receipt, but a scrap of what looked like an invoice for thirty thousand dollars. There were rusty, old stains on it that could have been blood, though the scent had dissipated.

The feminine handwriting was hard to decipher, and the ink was faded, but I made out the phrase *mate bond severance* and the words *Florida* and *Coven*.

Witches?

At the bottom, it was dated twenty years ago, and signed by someone named V. Flock... beside another name I knew too well.

Alpha Calvin Callaway.

Holy shit. Suddenly, all the rumors I'd overheard around the older Enforcers, the whispers about Dad having a true mate who had died, made sense. Had he found his, and then killed her? Even attempting to sever a mate bond was utterly taboo. What had he done to her? And why?

I stuffed the paper into my back pocket and curled the one up from Genevieve in my fist. With anger coursing through my veins, I moved toward the door... but it was blocked. A wave of Alpha power, directed at me, weakened my knees.

"What the hell are you doing here, son? Stealing from me?" Death shone in his eyes. My death. I'd never seen that look directed at me, but I knew what it meant.

I faked shock. "Steal what, your socks? I was looking for my laptop." His posture relaxed slightly until I said, "But I found a receipt."

"What receipt?" His eyes flashed silver, like lightning.

"The one to my old nanny in France," I ground out. I wouldn't tell him about the invoice in my back pocket from the coven. "You paid her off, didn't you? To send me here."

He stayed still for a moment, then gave a short laugh. "Sure did. Those Council assholes wouldn't foster their kids with me, so I bought myself a foster. Had a nice time with that nanny of yours a few years prior, and she owed me for not telling her mate about it."

I was disgusted, but tried not to show it. Instead, I let rage color my voice. "Did you kill my uncle?"

Dad tried to look shocked, but I'd known him for too long. He was faking it. And the way he danced around the truth with his answer confirmed that. "Would I do a thing like that? That would be criminal." He frowned at whatever emotions flickered on my face. "Don't act like it ended up hurting you none. You were just one of many over there. You're Alpha Heir here. That's nothing to spit at."

"Alpha Heir," I said, emboldened by the memory of Flor's courage. "But you keep me busy doing shit any Enforcer can do. I need to know what's really happening in this pack if I'm going to run it someday."

"That's a big if," Dad drawled, crossing his arms over his burly chest. "So that's what you were doing, poking around the past few days on my laptop? Trying to dig up our dirt so you could take over?"

Ah. He'd confiscated the computers to see if I'd hidden anything on them. Probably given them to Trevor Blackside, who liked to tell everyone he was a hacker, though I wasn't sure he knew anything about computers other than how to find his favorite porn sites. Of course, everything I'd found had been backed up in files only I had access to, and downloaded onto a tiny portable drive that the Council already had.

"Take over? Fuck, no. That's the last thing I want." Dad heard the truth in my words and relaxed a little. "I just wanted to know what the hell was our play. I wondered if some of the Enforcers were skimming. The monthly accounts weren't adding up."

"Now, son, those men earned that money," he said, his arm coming around me. It took everything I had not to flinch. "We might not have followed standard protocol for disbursement, but that's not so bad." Technically, it was illegal, since it skewed the numbers we would report to the Council. He finished, "And I've been giving the men that extra for a year now. You just noticed?"

I grunted. I'd known for a while, and had been trying to get what information I could to the Council. But his Alpha commands had kept me from sharing. That is, until Finnick and Glen were close enough to hand the evidence to. "Guess I'm not as observant as I should be."

He laughed, a giant bellow, as he led me out of his bedroom. "You said it, not me. And that's why I keep giving you bullshit assignments. You need to get with the program. And today, that means finding that little murdering bitch."

I leveled my gaze at him. "It's just us, Dad. You don't need to keep up that story. We both know she didn't kill Del."

His eyes narrowed. "Okay, then I won't. I want her dead. I know you used to have a thing for her."

"A thing?" I scoffed, wondering if he knew who she was to me.

"You always were soft. Trying to keep her and some of those other nobody trash wolves fed. I need you to prove yourself, boy." He grabbed the crumpled receipt from my hand and squashed it in one fist. "You find her, and I'll think about moving you closer to some real work." He let out a sharp whistle, and his Head Enforcer jogged around the corner of the hallway, as if he'd been waiting for the signal. "Van, I want you to keep an eye on my boy here, while he searches for the murderer."

His boy? My wolf raged. I wasn't his. He'd killed my uncle to secure the heir he'd never been able to produce. It all made sense now. Of course he hadn't been able to have children. If he'd killed his own true mate, the moon would never allow him to impregnate another female. He was a monster.

And I was going to end his reign, even if it killed me. It probably would.

The coven receipt in my pocket burned like an ember as I ran ahead of the burly Head Enforcer, praying that it would be the spark that could take down the Alpha. My wolf whined, deep inside, as we ran farther from where Flor had hidden in the forest, insisting that we head her way. Not to claim her, but to warn her.

And when Van Blackside stopped watching me, running off to stop a fight that had broken out between a few of our pack's ranked males and some from the visiting packs, I listened to my wolf.

Flor had to leave Southern entirely, before it was too late.

10

THE MADNESS OF GRIEF
FLOR

"You won't see him again."

In less than a half-dozen words, the beautiful stranger utterly destroyed any chance at happiness, at peace, I had ever hoped to hold onto. I'd thought he was an angel when I saw him.

But Glen's softly spoken words were straight from Hell.

You won't see him again.

My scream was so loud, I was sure they must have heard it in the compound. I didn't care if they did. All that was left inside me was rage.

And revenge.

You won't see him again.

I lost time.

In one moment, I was being held in Glen's arms, feeling that strange wave-like thrum that coursed through my whole body. Then, not a heartbeat later, I had thrown him into the creek somehow.

The next instant, I found myself standing in the clearing, wearing the dress that was now torn and mud-splattered, holding Del's butcher knife in one hand, ready to run barefoot to the compound to kill the Alpha and everyone else I met.

I heard someone calling my last name—*Wills, Wills*—like they were far away.

I blinked and looked down. My feet burned and ached. My arms stung from cuts I had no memory of. The air swirled with the scent of blood. My own blood.

I was no longer in the clearing. I was at the very edge of the compound, but the hole in the fence had been patched. I was alone, but the words had followed me.

You won't see him again.

No. I refused to believe it. I had to find a way through, had to find... I shook my head, fighting to ground myself in the moment, before I spaced out again.

I knew what was happening, though I was helpless to stop it.

When I was little, Mama had told me in one of her more lucid moments that time didn't work for her anymore. That she lost patches of her life and couldn't remember. I figured that was good; maybe it meant she didn't have to relive her past traumas. But she said no, those stayed with her.

I shivered. Maybe I was losing my mind, like she had.

I blinked again, and my hands were in the dirt, digging under the fence, the knife half buried in a low-growing bush. What was I *doing?* I stopped digging, trying to center myself. Trying to think.

What was my plan? Del had always told me to make a plan.

Del. The name in my mind broke me open, and I clutched at my arms, scratching the skin there, like I could somehow remove the pain of his death by tearing it out of me.

"Flor?" The voice caught my fractured attention, and I

peered through the fence. Icy blue eyes met mine, short dark hair wet with sweat, his scent sweet. "By the moon, Flor, what happened to you? Your hair... your arms. You're bleeding."

Luke. What was he doing here?

"You need to get out of here." He leaned down to speak through the open wires by my face, barely breathing the words. "The Alpha accused you of killing Del."

"That toadfucker," I panted, trying not to lose any more time. I had to get a grip. "I would *never.*"

"I know." Luke's voice broke. "Van threw his body in a ditch outside the main gates, to cover up the evidence. It's gone."

"What h-happened to..." To *it.* The body, not Del. Del was dead.

"The rogues took him."

"Still... alive?" I managed to gasp.

"No. I saw Van kill Del while the Alpha watched. But he told all the packs it was you."

I tried to focus. "Did he say it outright? Say I did it?"

He hesitated. "He made it sound like they had a damned witness. But no. He just pointed all the fingers your way. Van sent the other Heirs out to the hunting grounds to find a murderer. He gave them your description. I was assigned to watch the fence in case you tried to get back in, or out."

"The Alpha Heirs?" Those assholes had found me. Why hadn't they brought me in?

"I can't stay longer; someone will notice I've stopped patrolling. There are so many wolves here, hundreds of visitors. The inner compound, the outer rings, every house is filled, every room. There's nowhere to run."

"I met them," I said, my mind spinning like a circus ride. "I met those guys."

"Those guys? Wait, you mean the Heirs?"

"Yeah," I murmured, sitting back. "One of them was spyin' on me when I was taking a bath in the creek. Northern, yeah, that was him."

"I'll fucking end him."

For some reason, Luke's declaration brought me back to now. His eyes flashed silver-blue, and fangs were poking out of his half-open mouth. *What the...?* He was wolfing out, his shirt ripping at the seams, fur spreading down from his hairline across his neck, his ears growing pointed.

"Luke? Your face. Stop, you're shifting."

It was one of our Alpha's biggest rules, to stay human in the compound. He'd never really explained why, just made some stuff up about "keeping iron control of your inner wolves." But I figured it had something to do with keeping the competition weak. Shifting made wolves stronger, and the Alpha was the only one who was allowed to shift at will, anywhere, anytime.

Luke needed a little more iron control, though. He was enraged.

"Luke, it was no big deal. Glen apologized," I said, staring as he stopped his change. "That looks like it hurts."

"Yes, it hurts." Luke panted. "And you're wrong about that fucker Glen. He will need to do more than apologize."

I let out a huff. "He did, actually. He says he and his pack owe me a debt. Something about him dishonoring them. So..." I took a shuddering breath. "Maybe I can get him to help me."

"What do you mean?"

"He could take me into his pack."

"You can't do that," Luke said, and his eyes flashed silver.

"Um, I think I can. My original plan was to fight in the

Games and get a bid." I ignored his sputtered protests. "Just now, when I heard Del was killed, I sort of... lost the thread." I pushed down the pain and despair that threatened to swamp me again as I thought of my mentor. Del had trained me to fight through pain. I needed to honor his teaching. "But you're right. I can't go in there now, I'll get murdered." I crouched down, rubbing a bleeding cut on my ankle. "I'll go back, find that Glen and cash in the favor. Maybe he'll take me back to Canada, or wherever. I'd love to stab our fucking Alpha in the heart, but I'd rather keep breathing."

Luke was staring at me, jaw dropped. "Canada?"

"What? She who runs the fuck away, lives to heart-stab her Alpha another day." Just like Del had taught me. Yeah, this was the best idea.

"Fuck, no."

Whoa. I had never heard Luke curse before today, and now he'd done it twice. In fact, I had never seen him look so... undone. His midnight-black hair was standing on end, like he'd run his hands through it too many times, and he had dark circles under his eyes.

"Come on, I can't stay. Anyone can see that." I swallowed hard. "You're not going to take me in, right?" If that was his plan, I would use the skills I'd learned from Del on his pretty face.

"Of course not, Flor. You're my... It's just, you... You can't leave with *Glen.*" He spat the name out like it was poison.

"And why not?" I sneered through the wire, gasping when one of his hands came up—a hand tipped with his wolf's claws—and tore through the wire like it was butter.

He tore two more great gashes in the fence, then stepped through, dropping to a crouch next to me. I was frozen, terrified... and sort of aroused. Strength like that was intensely hot. But he could so easily turn it against me.

"Luke, calm down. You said it yourself—I can't stay here. They'll kill me."

"They won't touch you." Luke's scent got stronger, thicker, somehow. He reached past me with those strange, clawed hands and gathered me in, embracing me like I was precious. Like I was his.

For a second, I let my eyes close, let myself feel the hum of belonging. This was what it felt to be pack. I'd never felt it before, except in short bursts, when Del had comforted me.

But the hum this time got louder, longer, until it wasn't just a feeling of safety. It was a thrumming, like a string deep inside me had finally been plucked. My soul was vibrating in time with his.

"Luke?"

His gaze delved into mine, and his hands moved on my back, on my shoulders, the strange humming spreading from his clawed hands to sing in tune with something inside me. My core itself began to respond. It felt... good. Glorious.

"Luke?" I cried out again. "What's happening?"

He growled his answer, though the word was garbled as he forced it past sharpened teeth. "*Mine.*"

My mind spun as I tried to piece together what that word could have meant, coming from Luke. "Your *what*?"

"Flor," he said, sucking in a huge breath, surrounding me with his own flame and caramel scent. "You're my true mate."

I laughed, the shock of whatever was going on dispelled in an instant. "Don't piss down my back and tell me it's raining, Luke Callaway. You're no more my true mate than I'm the Princess of Peoria. Stop messing around."

"Flor!" His hands moved to my arms, wrapping around them, and he shook me slightly. "I'm telling the truth. You're mine. You've always been mine."

I had no idea what to say to that. So I stared into his entitled, Alpha Heir, sky-blue eyes, said a firm goodbye with a friendly stab to the gut, and hightailed it out of there.

II

PUNISHED
BRAND

This day was one of the longest I'd ever suffered through, and it showed no signs of ending. Or at least, not ending well. I needed to shift, to dispel the restlessness and anger that had been growing since my arrival. But the host pack had asked us not to change inside the fenced compound, and to keep in human form as much as possible until our Alphas arrived. It would be considered an insult to the pack to ignore those requests, though they made no fucking sense at all.

I'd been appalled when I learned of it. I hadn't spent a full day in human form since the day I could shift, and I didn't understand how the wolves who lived here could bear being separated from their wolves for so long.

My pack was different. I couldn't wait to get back to it, to the forests and the mountains of Colorado. Although now that I'd met her...

"Hello, Alpha Heir Becker."

I suppressed a growl as a long, painted fingernail trailed across the front of my too-snug dress shirt. I itched to pull it off. All of it, possibly: the shirt, the fingernail, the annoying woman's finger.

Instead of attacking, I smiled. Or showed teeth, anyway. "Hello, female."

She laughed, a shrill braying that carried over the other sounds of the crowded hall. A few of the partygoers glanced her way, but kept their distance when they met my gaze. They had good instincts.

This woman had none, but she had some courage. She tossed her brassy blonde hair over one shoulder, trying to hide her nerves. "You know my name, Brand. I'm Rebecca. You've danced with me twice," she chided, but her voice trembled as she smoothed nonexistent wrinkles out of her shimmering red cocktail dress. Her hands moved around the sides of her breasts, and down her front, tracing an invisible arrow to her crotch. "I loved dancing with you. You're so graceful for such a big..." Her eyes dropped to the front of my dress trousers, and she lost track of what she was saying. It was all I could do not to snarl.

I sighed instead, and she brightened, chattering on about the party and how delightful it was to have us here. Though she'd love to see *my* packlands...

I didn't want to frighten her, even if her machinations were obvious and awkward. To be fair, she was attractive, tall with curves in all the right places, long legs exposed by the short dress she wore, and a decent face. She was, if such a thing existed, my type—a woman like many others I'd spent a few nice moments with, though I'd never brought one to my bed.

I wasn't sure anyone would believe that if they knew it, though. Or understand it. I kept it a closely guarded secret, since the female shifters I knew would see it as a challenge, even if I asked them to respect my choice. So few of our kind understood principles, or honor.

Or how deeply our wolves could love, if we waited for the one meant for us, rather than settling for an hour of meaningless pleasure spent with a pretty, interchangeable, forgettable face.

I rubbed my hand over my beard. Nearly twenty-seven, and I was still saving myself for a face I would never look away from, given the chance. Glen had teased me about finding a woman who was my type. "Don't you care at all about rank?" he'd needled me, more than once. "You know you're shifter royalty."

Royalty? Such bullshit. Too many of our Alphas believed they were set above their packs, that they deserved their titles and money. I didn't give a single shit about status. I didn't believe in the concept, and my pack didn't even use the ranking system inside our borders. The most important traits for a shifter—for a mate to have—were loyalty, bravery, and a deep connection to her own wolf side. I'd been looking for this perfect woman for a decade, not knowing exactly what she would look like.

Today, I'd learned she was nothing like I'd expected. She had slight curves, too-thin legs, short, ragged, deep red hair, amber eyes filled with rage, and she smelled like a sewer.

Possibly, she'd betrayed her own pack. She was too young to have shifted. And she would never be...

I had to stop thinking of her. "Excuse me," I gritted out, stalking away from the blonde with a curt nod, ignoring her sputtered protest.

Why did the little rogue haunt my thoughts? *Wills.* That wasn't her name. I crossed to the bar near the back of the hall, empty except for a server.

An unranked one, from the threadbare state of the white shirt and black skirt she wore, and the dime-sized metal circle that dangled from the cartilage at the top of her ear. Like a human dog's tag. Like the tag on Wills's ear.

Remembering it made me want to shift and tear out the throat of the Southern Alpha, and then start on his Enforcers. Tagging young shifters like they were property, or pets. From what I'd seen, they treated all their women that way, regardless of rank. In my pack, the women were trained alongside the men. Taught how to defend themselves and their pups, how to keep their mates in line.

What had Wills lived through in her short life, to drive her out and away from her pack? I felt a sudden urge to run back and find her, and promise her that those days were over. That from now on, she had a mate.

A mate. Fuck, I needed a drink. I placed one hand on the bar. "Whiskey, please."

"Y-yes, sir," the mousy waitress replied, careful to stare at the counter between us.

I glanced around. The music was loud, and no one was near—my grim expression had obviously scared away all but the most grasping of females. I supposed my reputation for ripping out throats first and apologizing later was keeping talkative males away too. *Good.*

"Did you know the shifter named Del?" I asked the girl as quietly as I could. "The one who was murdered."

Her eyes darted up to mine for an instant, and she gulped. "Yes, I did."

"Tell me about him."

"S-sir?"

"Girl, I'm not going to hurt you." I knocked back the whiskey she'd poured, tapping the glass for another. Her eyes flickered to the doorway that led to the main hall. *Ah.* "I'll keep it in confidence."

She remained silent, shaking.

I leaned closer. "On the honor of the Mountain Pack, I will never reveal your identity. You won't be harmed for sharing whatever you know. You don't need to fear me."

Her eyes narrowed, like she might not believe me. "The... The Alpha said that Flor killed him."

"Yes," I breathed. So Flor was her first name. "There's a hunt on for her. Flor Wills."

The servant's red-rimmed eyes gleamed. "They haven't found her yet?"

"No. They asked for our help. A bit of an embarrassment for your pack's leadership, that they can't bring in a teenage girl."

The corners of the drab girl's mouth turned up for an instant. There was the faintest hint of fire in her eyes as she hissed, "Serves them right. They won't catch her. If anyone could escape, it'd be Flor."

That seemed an odd thing to say. "Is she unusually clever? Strong?"

The girl gave a tiny shake of her head. "No, not really. Stealthy, maybe. The unmated males—and honestly, some of the others—have had it out for her since her mama... Well, for years."

"What do you mean?" What could a young shifter have done to make so many powerful enemies?

She bared her teeth. "They *hunted* Flor. Called it a game."

"Hunted her?" My teeth begin to elongate, and fur prickled on the backs of my hands.

She paused, her eyes on my mouth. "Yes. The Hunt. Flor

was the prey. Well, I suppose it used to be other girls, but it's just been Flor for about four years now."

I couldn't believe what I was hearing. "Hunting a girl? That's..." No words seemed to fit, so I settled on, "Dishonorable."

Her shoulders slumped into a posture of shame and defeat. "Don't look for honor in this pack, Alpha Heir."

"Thanks for the tip." I discreetly handed her a fifty-dollar bill, ignoring the jar in front of her. I had a feeling those tips didn't land in her pocket. She gulped again and nodded in appreciation.

I grabbed my glass and turned to go, but a whisper stopped me. "Sir? Flor would never have hurt Del. He was all she had. Please, don't hunt for her too hard. She's better off anywhere else."

I whispered back, "You know her well. Are you a friend of hers?"

Her head shook almost imperceptibly. "She doesn't have friends. She's not allowed."

It was almost impossible to keep my voice low. "Why not?"

"She's the pack reject. If anyone helps her, or even talks to her, they get punished."

"Punished?"

Her eyes filled with pain. "I gave her half my sandwich once, when we were in fifth grade." She pulled the neckline of her shirt down slightly, the gesture most likely appearing respectful from a distance.

But I saw the scars there, the burns that silver left.

Punished. For a moment, I couldn't believe what I was seeing, what she'd meant. Then her meaning clicked into place. They'd punished this unranked woman for giving a young girl a sandwich. They'd scarred her permanently.

And they'd hunted Flor. My wolf raged inside, demanding we bring justice to this tainted pack.

"Thank you for showing me. Telling me," I managed to say to the trembling waitress, though my teeth were already too sharp to be mistaken as human. "I am grateful for your trust."

She didn't answer, but gave me a solemn nod before she moved away.

I looked around to make sure no one had heard our conversation, then stalked off to find the other Alpha Heirs. As I moved through the crowd, a few of the Southern women reached out to touch me, like I was some sort of lucky talisman. As if they didn't fear me.

If this pack was as horrific as I was coming to understand, it might be worth losing a hand, if you could discover your true mate and be whisked away instead.

I didn't want to find my true mate, not anymore. The only female I wanted to see was an underfed, boyish waif whose scent I wouldn't even recognize. An emaciated warrior girl who smelled like shit and was possibly the fated true mate of one of the only wolves in the world I called brother, though it was a brotherhood built on friendship, pain, and shared secrets.

I guess I had a new type. Unattainable.

I cursed out loud, scaring the piss out of at least two young males nearby. I was losing my temper. It was time to retreat to my bunk, behind a locked door.

But on my way down the steps of the Pack House—a piss-poor, scaled-down version of the Alpha's Den my great-grandfather had built in Colorado for our pack, with none of the rugged grandeur of ours—I heard a man cursing quietly.

Then came a gasp of pain, and the smell of fresh blood.

I knew both the voice and the scent. "Luke?" I crossed through the well-lit courtyard and joined him in the shadows at the back door of the kitchens. "What the hell, Luke? Who did this?"

He was kneeling on the back steps of the kitchen, holding his hands to his abdomen, over what I instantly suspected was a seeping gut wound. He wore his black Enforcer's uniform, but his shirt was torn, as if he'd started to shift with his clothes on. Both his shirt and trousers were stained, his fingers covered with blood. The coppery scent hung thick around him.

"Damn, that has to hurt," I remarked as I approached. "Why haven't you shifted?"

"Can't," he panted. "Wouldn't help anyway."

"What?" What the hell did he mean? Wolves could heal from almost any wound.

Well, healthy ones could. I wasn't sure Luke, or any of the other wolves I'd met here, fit that description. Most of them were smaller and weaker than they should be, their scents diminished. Except for the Alpha and a few of the Enforcers, none of the shifters at Southern seemed to be deeply connected to their inner wolves.

Luke hadn't answered, but was panting slightly. I shook my head. "It's complicated, huh?"

He pressed a bloodstained finger to the tip of his nose. "Bingo. Get the door? Medical kit... in the kitchen."

I grabbed the door and wrenched the handle open. It was harder to open than it should have been. It might have been locked, but no lock was a match for my strength. Then I grabbed the bleeding Southern Alpha Heir and carried him up the steps. Well, dragged him.

"Thanks, Brand," he managed to say before he pulled away and staggered to the back of the quiet, empty kitchen. But I couldn't answer. I was frozen, transfixed by a scent.

The room smelled like old grease, food, a male wolf... and something indescribably lush and floral, mixed with a fragrant spice. I sucked in a huge breath and noticed Luke doing the same thing.

"Still smells like her. Flowers. Summer flowers on the night wind, and cinnamon sugar," he slurred, reaching for a red first aid box on the wall. "It's... addictive, that scent."

He ripped his shirt down the front, pausing for a moment, in obvious pain. It only took a moment for him to open the kit, grab the supplies he needed, wipe down his stomach with a clean cloth, and press a gauze pad to the wound. Then he pulled out the medical stapler.

"Man, are you crazy?" I grabbed the staple gun he was trying to press against his gut. "Get on the damned table."

"Done this before?" he groaned, rolling up onto the stainless-steel prep table.

"Yeah. Not on myself, but mountain life can be tough on the kids. I've patched up the ones who weren't ready to shift."

"Ready." He forced out a pained laugh. "Must be nice. How old are the kids... in your pack... for the first shift?"

"At least sixteen for males. Usually, eighteen. Twenty-one for the females." I glanced at the wound. Thank the moon it hadn't gone into his intestines. If shifting hadn't healed him, that would take a hell of a long time to fix. Wolves didn't get bacterial infections, but damage like this...

"How old were you?" He spoke through gritted teeth as I wiped the sluggishly flowing blood away with a clean dish towel so I could see what I was working with.

"I was thirteen, the youngest ever in my pack." I smiled,

remembering. "It hurt like hell, but I'd gotten into a tussle with a couple of mountain lions, and Dad said I'd earned the pain." I stopped at the grimace on Luke's face. "What about you?" I pressed the stapler gun into his gut before he could answer. I needed him to take a breath and push out the abdominal wall, and talking was a sneaky way of making that happen.

"Shit!" he screamed, then panted some more. "I was ten."

"Ten? Fuck. Were you injured?" That had to be it; there was only about a twenty-five percent survival rate for wolves who shifted before puberty. It was a good thing I'd already hit that when I shifted. But Luke had been a child. I couldn't believe he'd lived.

"Alpha said... it didn't matter... if I died." Luke's lips curled up, and I could see him fighting something internal. A memory?

"Why not?" I breathed the question.

"I'm pretty sure it's because he's never going to let me... be Alpha," Luke answered when he could breathe again. "I'm just his show wolf. His cover." He let out a growl. "Hasn't let me shift almost at all... for years. Keeping me weak... our whole pack weak."

My blood went cold. "You haven't shifted in *years*?"

"Nearly two years. I'm not sure... I could, now."

Shit. This was insane. I had a feeling Luke would never have shared this if he was in his right mind. Admitting that kind of weakness in the presence of another male shifter was unusual, outside of immediate family.

But this explained so much of what I'd noticed. I'd always thought Luke was weaker than he should be at his age. In fact, Glen and I had argued about whether he was fit to be the Alpha Heir. There were others in his pack much bigger, stronger, and more in touch with their wolves.

But I couldn't judge him for that, if it hadn't been his choice. If he hadn't been allowed to shift for years? I shuddered. The poor guy must be in constant agony. Still, something didn't make sense. I stared at the bloody gash in his gut, trying to find an explanation for it.

"Your Alpha did this to you?" I hadn't ever heard of an Alpha who could cause non-healing wounds, but maybe he'd hired a witch or something. Although the only witch I knew of in North America lived in the middle of my packlands. Well, the only *trustworthy* witch. I'd heard of some in the Keys, but I was pretty sure they'd been exterminated by Northern Enforcers decades ago.

"Nah. My true mate." Luke turned his head slightly to see my face.

I blinked, shocked again. "I didn't know you had one." No one knew it; that sort of gossip usually spread faster than pollen on a storm wind.

His smile widened, though it wasn't joy-filled, as it ought to be. He had the brass ring, the prize every shifter longed for. That almost none of us found, not for many years. "Neither... did she."

"Oooh. Tricky. Didn't take the news well?"

"I may have... chosen my moment poorly." He glanced down at his stomach, and I winced. I'd already felt sorry for the man. Now I wondered if he was cursed or something.

I was sure there was more to the story. Female shifters in my pack could be belligerent, even dangerous, with their training. More than a few of the males in my pack had been shown their place by their women, though they weren't true mates. Maybe Luke's was a great brute of a woman, with a temper to match her muscles.

At least the lack of healing made sense now. The only wound that didn't heal on a shifter was either from silver, magical, or given by a true mate. I hadn't smelled silver or magic. But what kind of a true mate would eviscerate her fated love?

Everything I was feeling must have showed because he let out another short laugh, which made more blood well out of his cut.

"Damn, who'd your true mate turn out to be? A mountain lion?"

"No," Luke grumbled. "She snuck up on me like one, though. She's fast. Sneaky." He took a breath. "Smells like her here, so good. She's so pretty. Well, not now, I guess. Cut all that... gorgeous red hair off. Why'd she have to... cut off her hair? I never got to... touch it..."

And then he lapsed into unconsciousness.

Oh shit.

12

CALLING IN A DEBT
FLOR

I felt really, really bad for stabbing Luke in the gut. Almost bad enough to sneak into the compound after him and apologize.

I didn't, though. He'd heal, and fast. I hadn't actually killed him, or even done permanent damage. He was super-shifter Heir guy, right? And it's not like he'd ever apologized to me for the lifetime of bullshit I'd lived through. I kept telling myself that, but for some reason, I wasn't sure.

Why wasn't I sure? Had I read something in Home Skills back in middle school about mates and wounds, or... *Shake it off, Flor. This isn't the time to be second guessing.*

Just because Luke had said I was his true mate didn't mean it was a fact. I mean, I definitely would have felt it before now.

The strange humming feeling during the hug started up again in my arms.

Snakeshit. What if I was wrong? What if I had just stabbed my true mate in the guts?

Why did I care? I was getting the hell out of this rotten pack, and even if Luke was my true mate, he hadn't done jack to help me over the past four years while I was being hunted by almost all the other unmated males. I'd been beaten by Van for the smallest infractions, harassed and attacked by Trevor and his group, and ignored by everyone else. I'd gone without a full night's sleep for four years. Practically starved, some weeks. If it hadn't been for Del...

I held back the sob that threatened to tear out of me. It wasn't the time to be weak. I had to find Glen and force him to make good on his promise. Then I had to get the hell out of this pack, this state, and never look back.

The dry pine needles on the forest floor crunched slightly under my sore feet as I ran, watching for tracks, although night had truly fallen and even though the moon was full, in the shadows I couldn't see for shit.

If I'd had a shifter's nose, I wouldn't have needed to watch so carefully; I'd be able to smell anyone upwind. I froze, wondering if anyone from my pack was downwind. The pervert—*Glen*, I reminded myself—had said they'd accused me of the murder. They'd be hunting me.

Crap. I smelled like *me* now. For the first time all day, I regretted my creek bath. *Too dark to go hunting for more shit to rub over myself.*

I gathered up the edges of my dress and picked up my pace, staying as low as I could when I came over the series of small rises that made up the landscape here. If I could make it past the next bigger hill, I'd be able to see farther. Maybe I'd spot the... *Glen*.

Like I'd conjured him, blond hair appeared, gleaming on the horizon in the moonlight. I raised my voice slightly. "Glenda!"

He was standing in the middle of a clearing next to the redheaded guy I'd fought, Finnick. He was still wearing his running shorts, so I figured they hadn't gone back into the compound.

They were talking about something. Well, arguing from the look of their body language, but too quietly for me to hear what had them both so worked up. But when I called out, they stopped and turned to me.

"Wills!" Glen's eyes glinted with a spark of blue, even in the gloomy evening. "You came back!" He said it like I was a puppy who'd run away.

I let out an annoyed grunt. "Yeah, sorry about tossing you in the creek." I skidded to a stop in front of them. Finnick was staring at me, bug-eyed.

"What... What happened to you? You're bleeding." He frowned, as his gaze raked my whole body, but not in a complimentary way. "And why do you have on a dress?"

"Um, news flash. I'm actually a girl."

"Maybe technically," he sneered. The frogs in the nearby creek set up a chorus that sounded a little too much like laughter.

Ouch. I was glad for the gathering darkness, which meant he couldn't see my face flush red with embarrassment. I wasn't pretty, but I wasn't horrific, was I? I had no idea why I was feeling so thin-skinned around this guy. Like his disapproval truly mattered, when none of the constant insults and disgust I'd been served every day of my life had.

I shot him the finger and turned to Glen. "Hey, Blondie. I, uh, didn't do anything after I threw you in the water, did I?"

Glen's voice was subdued. "You don't remember?"

"No." I scratched the back of my neck, wishing I had my long hair to hide behind. "I sort of freaked out. Like, I was there, then I had the knife, then I was stabbing Luke in the stomach—"

"You stabbed Luke? Why?" Finnick's tone reminded me of my own pack's Enforcers, and I took a step back.

This cocky pissant. Who was he to demand answers? "He made fun of me."

"And that's worth a gut wound?" Finnick let out a jeering laugh. "Good to know. I'll make sure to say all nice things."

"You can say nice things to your ass, I don't care," I shot back. "I'm never going to see you again after tonight."

"Why not?" Finnick ground out the words, like he didn't want to say them. I didn't answer.

"So, Glenda," I said, turning to him and batting my eyelashes—at least I still had nice long eyelashes. "You remember that favor you promised me? The one where your pack's honor is at stake, blah blah blah? The debt of honor thing. I'm gonna need it."

"You are?" Glen asked, at the same moment Finnick shouted, "*What* favor?"

I narrowed my eyes and bared my blunt teeth at the asshole redhead, even if he couldn't get the full effect of my expression. Although maybe he could; he was plenty old enough to have shifted, which meant great night vision. "None of your business, Cityboy."

Glen stifled a laugh. "What do you need, princess?" he asked, an odd lightness in his tone. "Shoes, maybe? A hairbrush?"

"Deodorant?" Finnick muttered.

"Gah!" I shouted. "I'm not fucking around. I've got a death sentence hanging over my head. I need to get adopted by your pack."

"We can't just adopt you," Glen said slowly, like he was thinking about it. "We can transfer your pack bond with your Alpha's permission, but Callaway probably won't give it." He paused for a long moment. "If you had a true mate in our pack, that would supersede your pack bonds, of course."

Something in his voice gave me a weird, dizzy feeling. "That's out, then."

Glen was making an odd growling sound. "Is it?"

Did he know what Luke had said?

"Enough," Finnick snarled.

Glen took a step toward me. "The only other opportunity to transfer a pack bond is at the Games, after winning a round. Any of the other packs' Alphas or their Heirs can bid, although none of the Alphas will arrive until Wednesday."

My heart raced. "But one of you can bid? If I win?"

He nodded slowly. "Your Alpha's permission is not required."

I let out the breath I'd been holding. *Plan A then.*

"Unacceptable. I'll petition your Alpha for your removal," Finnick said abruptly.

"What?" I wasn't certain why he thought my Alpha would listen to him. Had he not paid attention to anything I'd said? "Alpha Callaway set me up for murder, Cityboy. The only way I'm getting out of Southern is by a bid in the Games or killing that asshole."

"What a bloodthirsty little creature you are. You think you could kill your Alpha?"

"Apparently, my subconscious does." I shrugged, not at all dismayed by the names he called me. Well, maybe a little. But I'd already known that the truth hurt. "I freaked, like I said. Ran back to the compound. I came upon Luke at the fence when I was trying to re-enter the main pack grounds and murder the Alpha"—I held up a hand to stop their sputtering protests—"and then Luke tore through the wire and messed with my head." I wasn't about to drop Luke's true mate bomb on them.

"Messed with your head?" Glen said slowly. "That doesn't sound like Luke."

"How the hell would you... Know what? Never mind. I just need to get into the Games. Del—" I swallowed hard and went on. "Del was going to sign me up for the first night. If I go myself to do it, I'll be caught and executed before I even have the chance to fight." I let out a shaky sigh and squared my shoulders. "So that's what I need, Glenda. I need you to do what Del had planned, and sign me up for the Games. Try to pit me against a super-small shifter, a weak-ass boy, okay? I don't need to show off—just show up and win one round, right?"

"You, fight in the Games?" Glen let out a disbelieving chuckle. "Princess, you may have a few dirty tricks. I saw you throw dirt in Finnick's face. But I hate to tell you—"

"She can fight," Finnick growled. "She held her own against me for a while. Del trained her for years."

Glen let out a low whistle. "Is it weird that that kind of turns me on?"

Finnick let out a growl. I just laughed. "Nah, it's in character, you peeping Tom. Watching me get naked at the stream today was literally the first thing—"

I didn't get to finish my sentence, though, as Finnick had jumped on Glen in a half-shifted form and was tearing at his arms and chest.

"What the hell?!" I screamed as the quiet night exploded into violence, the two Heirs suddenly, inexplicably, trying to kill each other.

Or at least, Finnick was. Glen wasn't fighting all that hard, or shifting like Finnick had. The Northern Heir was just trying to duck and dodge the claws that kept coming. They both moved into a patch of moonlight as they fought, and the blood flowing down Glen's chest and arms glinted dark and wet.

"Stop, Finn!" Glen yelled, dancing under a blow that could have taken off his scalp. I did see a few strands of golden hair fly loose as he twisted away.

"I tell you I think she might be my mate, and you *watch* her?" Finnick's shout came out in a strange, doubled tone, like his wolf and human forms were both pissed.

Wait. Mate? Oh, I do not fucking think so. Not on his very best day, and my worst.

I picked up a rock by my foot and threw it straight at the redhead's ass. It hit, and he spun around. "Who do you think might be your mate, Cityboy?"

"No one," Finnick snapped, his jaw working like he had something else to say. He took a few deep breaths, and his fur and claws retracted, leaving the man behind. "I won't mate. Ever." He gave me a look that said *especially not to someone like you.*

Why did my stomach suddenly feel like I'd eaten a bag of rocks? "I hear that," I said calmly. "And I one hundred percent agree. In fact, I made a vow never to mate."

They both went quiet, and I wished I could see their faces clearly.

"What if your true mate shows up, and you change your mind?" Glen asked, his voice strained. He pulled off his shirt and used it to casually wipe off the scratches Finnick had given him. It seemed like they were already healing, but his chest still shone in the moonlight. His muscular, nearly hairless chest, with all those acres of moon-silvered skin...

I swallowed hard, casually watching every swipe the shirt made and wishing it were my hands instead.

Wait, what? Who's the pervert now, Flor?

I ignored his question, and Finnick's bullshit. "So, will you do it?" I asked. "Redeem your honor and get my name on the list."

Glen swallowed. "I don't want to. I think there's another way out—"

Panic threatened, and I fought to control my breathing. I didn't have another workable plan. Not one that didn't end in my death. "I don't care. This way, I get to honor Del and his teaching and get a bid at the same time. Just get me in, and I'll do the rest."

Finnick stepped up to me. His eyes widened, and he leaned closer, giving me a not-at-all unobtrusive sniff.

"I guess I don't smell like shit now, huh?" I asked, trying not to let my own nostrils flare as I took in the musk and spice that wafted off him. He smelled every bit as good as Luke had earlier, but more refined somehow. More... intentional.

I wondered if a wolf's smell revealed something about their personality. My mama had said I smelled like cinnamon the day I was born, but I'd learned in school that a shifter's scent changed as they matured. "What do I smell like to you?"

Finnick's jaw dropped. "Uh... uh..."

"Night-blooming jasmine," Glen replied, his voice a little too casual. "And cinnamon."

Finnick snarled. "Cinnamon rolls and traces of shit."

I didn't acknowledge the pissant. Instead, I flashed a smile at Glen. "That was not at all what I expected. Night-blooming jasmine, huh?"

He smiled. He had a really nice smile, all straight white teeth and strong lips.

Strong lips? What the actual fuck, Flor?

Those strong lips twitched. "What did you expect?"

"I don't know," I said, feeling strangely shy. "Like, I knew about the cinnamon. Never heard the jasmine part."

"I like jasmine. It isn't a perfume, then?"

I snorted. "Unranked wolves in our pack have to work for the right to live in the pack. They don't pay us. I never got to wear perfume. Never had enough money for girl things like that, or makeup."

"You've never worn makeup?" Finnick sounded offended. Judgmental.

"Heck, I haven't been able to afford deodorant for almost four years, since my mama died," I said, hoping it made him feel like the asshole he was.

"What do you mean, about earning the right to live in the pack?" Glen asked. My stomach interrupted, growling. He reached into his pocket and pulled out something in a wrapper, handing it to me. Holding it up to the moonlight, I read the name of what I thought was a fancy energy bar. "Here, princess. Let's walk and talk."

"Thanks, Glenda." I tried not to scarf down the energy bar as fast as my stomach demanded. "Are you asking about our pack's structure?"

"More about the way your unranked are treated," he replied.

Alpha Callaway had made sure everyone knew not to share details of our pack with anyone else. He'd even given an Alpha command at a pack meeting about it. Luckily, I had been working in the kitchen when he'd done that. So I spilled all the shitty Southern tea. "For one thing, unranked wolves here have to work inside the compound, right? They can't take outside jobs. They're all tagged, too."

Supposedly, unranked wolves might not have enough power to control their shifts, so they were an exposure risk outside the gates.

Glen cursed softly. "But they don't pay you? How do you survive?"

"I got lucky. Del got me a job in the dining hall once I was old enough. Our unranked wolves don't have pack meal privileges, except for special occasions—everyone was really excited about the Conclave since all the parties means lots of food for us."

Glen started pacing, like he needed to move or he might explode. Finnick let out a soft curse, but I ignored him.

"Anyway, twice a day, Del and I got to eat whatever the ranked wolves left on their plates, and he snuck me rice when there weren't leftovers. And taught me to hunt, of course." I waved at the trees. "I'm pretty amazing with a slingshot, if I do say so myself. I can get a squirrel eight times out of ten now."

Glen stopped pacing, balled up a fist, and punched one of the pines. Pine needles pattered all around us like rain.

"You have a pet squirrel or something?" Maybe I needed to apologize.

Glen groaned, shaking out his fist while Finnick cleared his throat. "When did you start hunting?"

"Let me think. Del took me out for the first time when I was six." I sighed, remembering those hours in the forest. They were the best moments of my life. "Mama couldn't work a lot of the time, so she didn't get rations for the two of us. Del kept us fed back then."

"Why didn't she work?" Finnick's voice was softer now. It reminded me of Luke's. Ugh, *that* asshole. True mate, my

Aunt Fanny. He'd let me go hungry. He'd seen me scrabble for food over the years. Watched me hunt squirrels.

I got back to my story, not that I was going to tell these strangers all of it. Not even I knew everything that had happened, but Del had told me that most of Mama's scars had happened when she was first mated and barely pregnant with me. For all I knew, that could be where the faint silver scars on my own chest came from; I'd had them since I was a baby.

"Our Alpha hated my mom. She was pretty unstable. She sort of spaced out for a lot of my childhood. But she was better away from the pack, and Del convinced the Alpha to let her get a job in the QwikMart outside the grounds when I was about fifteen." That had happened right before I'd been picked for the Hunt. "She was gone a lot, pulling doubles every weekend until... Well, I was glad I had Del to protect me."

"Protect you?" Glen asked.

"Yeah, from the Hunt."

"The Hunt?" Finnick rasped out the words. "What is that?"

Glen let out a soft string of curses. "I don't know if I can hear this again."

I shrugged. "Ah, it was just a stupid game the males played. They would hunt me, you know. The sort of games packs play, maybe a little rougher in Southern." I tried not to let the years of terror seep into my voice. "I got really good at sneaking around."

Finnick hissed something in what sounded like Japanese. Glen tripped on something, growling low as he shuffled through fallen pine needles.

"You okay?"

"Yeah, uh, I just stepped on a pinecone."

114

"Careful there, Glenda the Good Witch," I teased. "A strong wolf knows how to walk softly."

Glen let out a strained laugh. "You sound like Brand."

"The bear shifter? Seriously, his mom must have fooled around on the side. Wolves don't get that big."

I felt Glen's hand on my arm, and the night grew darker, warmer. In the pit of my stomach, a swirling started, like a whirlpool that was drawing me down. Making me dumb, almost needy. I closed my eyes for a second, my mind spinning.

I wanted to feel that hand everywhere. And Brand's too, his big hands... and maybe even Finnick's. He would hold me a little bit too tight, push my neck back as he... *Whoa.* Where was this coming from? Until today, I hadn't thought about any wolf—except maybe Luke—in that way. Now I was panting over three new guys?

Finnick's voice broke into my daze. "Why did the Alpha hate your mom?" I couldn't see his face in the gloom, but his voice was filled with something dangerous. Dark. "Was it because she was mentally unstable?" He hesitated. "Or did he do something to her? Did he torture her somehow until she broke?"

He was too perceptive. I didn't want to put the pieces together for these guys. Who knew what they would do with the information about where I'd come from?

"Am I supposed to have all the answers?" I replied, talking around the lie I would have to tell to deny the truth. "You know how Alphas are. Born and bred, elitist, toad-fucking butt-nuggets."

Not even a cricket interrupted the incredibly awkward silence.

"Present company excepted, of course," I finally choked out. "And your dads, I'm sure they're fine. And never fucked a toad." Oh god, did they think I was calling their mothers toads now?

Glen coughed. "Good to hear."

"Of course," Finnick replied smoothly.

They left me in the clearing where I'd found them, thankfully before I could dig an even deeper hole. It had to be two in the morning, and I was exhausted. I trudged back to my campsite, my face still flaming, and my stomach churning.

At least they were going to help me. Before they ran off, Glen had assured me that he or Finn would get me signed up for the Games. I'd asked him to use the name Will L. Rains, as a tribute to Mom, whose name was Lily Rain. It seemed fitting to give my pack a giant metaphorical middle finger on behalf of Mama on my way out.

After I washed off in the creek again, I didn't sleep that night. Instead, I watched as the nearly full moon passed overhead, fearing the coming days. Wondering how many more I would live to see.

13

MATE AND SWITCH

FINNICK

I n the end, I was the one to sign Flor up to fight in the Games.

My stomach churned as I walked to the clearing where a whiteboard had been set up against two sawhorses. I was committing a girl—an unshifted, immature female—to participate in the bloodiest battles a shifter could face, since our years of inter-pack wars had ended.

And not just a girl. My true mate. I'd known it from the moment I touched her arm.

Most shifters wanted nothing more than to find their soulmate. But I'd prayed for years that I would never find mine. Not only for my sake, but for hers.

As Alpha Heir, I was expected to mate eventually. The only Alpha in history who had ascended without one at his side was Callaway, and that aberration was only one reason Southern was seen as the worst of all the packs.

But I knew better than to hope that I would be given a choice. My parents controlled me as thoroughly as they did the lowest members of our pack. Everything down to who I was allowed, or expected, to bed.

I might as well wear a tag in my ear, for all the good my rank did me. I had to do what was required, no matter how unsavory those tasks were. No matter how degrading.

It was better for me to suffer than my little sister Tana. I would do anything to protect her, and I was the only one in our pack who would.

Like Flor, an inner voice said. *Flor has no one.*

Del had been her only supporter, training her until she could almost defeat me. At first, I'd pulled my punches in our fight, thinking she was a boy who needed a lesson in manners. Then, when I realized her skill, I'd let loose—and been knocked on my ass.

I wanted to fight her again. I wasn't sure why I found the memory of Flor challenging me in combat so thrilling, but I did. Maybe... I found myself grinning like a fool as I made a rare, impetuous decision.

I picked up a marker and read off the names on the whiteboard the Southern Enforcers had set up, as other shifters milled around behind me. I was slated to fight Patrick Hillier, Glen's younger brother, in the opening exhibition match.

Still grinning, I scribbled out his name and wrote in Will L. Rains.

The mere thought of pitting myself against her one more time, just to be near her, made me dizzy. I wouldn't claim her, though, no matter how much my inner wolf clamored for it. I'd learned to drown out his cries long ago, to ignore those instincts.

Exhibition fights were not scored as regular matches, as Alpha Heirs were outside the traditional ranking. Top Enforcers liked to have the chance to try against us, though. If they won by some freak chance, they were immediately bumped into the final rounds of fighting. It was considered brave to make the attempt, so they weren't penalized when they lost.

When Flor lost against me, she would automatically be entered into an additional fight later that night, facing the loser of a different first-round match. I double checked to make sure all the first-round fighters were low-ranked members of their respective packs, and nodded with satisfaction when I saw that they were. Some had only shifted for the first time that year. One hadn't even had his first shift.

With her skills, she would be certain to win against any of them, and then Glen could take her into his pack after her victory. Every pack would want her, once they'd seen her fight.

The thought of her so far from me made my wolf howl. Still, I knew if I brought her home to the city, to the ones who owned me, that fierce light in her eyes would be snuffed out like a match in a hurricane. But she would be safe.

The inner voice whispered a terrifying question. *What if she loses her second fight?*

The marker splintered in my hand, and the males behind me backed away.

There would be no way to protect her, unless...

If she fell to the second fighter, I would claim her as my true mate, to save her life. Even with a murder accusation against her, no one would dare to take a mate away from an Alpha Heir. If they tried, I'd tear their heads from their necks, and show them why that was so.

My mind spun with possibilities. I would never expose her to my pack, but I could call on my brothers for help. Brand and Glen. We could flee, get my sister out somehow, and seek sanctuary with Glen's family. If I could get out from under my father's command, I could tell Alpha Hillier what was happening in my pack.

Fucking Glen. What had he been thinking, spying on Flor like that? There had been something in his eyes when he looked at her, something about the way he described her scent that set me off.

Like he was thinking of her as his own, when she was *mine*.

For a moment, I let myself dream that I was free to take Flor for my own, claim her, and bring her home. She was rough, unpolished. Innocent. I would show her the city, dress her in silk gowns and lace, take her to the symphony. The ballet.

My bedroom.

I would use every skill I'd gained over the years to bring her pleasure, make that suspicious face soften with lust and longing. The thought of those fiery amber eyes lowering as I undressed her the first time, that small, pink mouth opening for me, her slender thighs parting...

What am I doing? I glanced down, shifting my weight to hide my erection, not that it helped. My damned running shorts didn't have room for me to hide the thing.

Why in the hell was I fantasizing about a foul-mouthed waif, practically surrounded by Southern shifters? Some of whom were whispering nearby.

Shit.

I threw the broken marker away from me and strode to the cabin—the hovel—Southern thought was adequate accommodation for an Alpha Heir. A few of my father's shifters nodded as I passed, one of them dropping his eyes to my shorts.

"What the fuck are you looking at?" I demanded.

"Nothing, sir," he replied, fear in his tone. As it should

be. My father had forced me to become an expert in more than one arena. I was an expert at fighting, but he'd also forced me to become the pack's torturer for a year.

My hands would never be clean.

I could never deserve to touch her.

I slammed the flimsy door to my cabin shut and crossed to the dresser to find more appropriate clothing, thinking about the one thing guaranteed to chill my ardor. Politics.

Brand, Glen, and I had a job to do beyond representing our packs here. We Heirs were also spies for the North American Council, doing reconnaissance before our Alphas arrived. The Council was extremely curious about what Alpha Callaway had been up to. Every year, the rolls in each pack were reported, and more and more of his ranked wolves were being reported as killed in accidents, or from strange illnesses.

Shifters could survive almost anything, so the death toll —including higher ranked wolves—was worrying. There had been rumors of egregious abuse as well, unranked females like Flor being forced into mating or expelled from the pack if they refused a mate.

My own parents weren't particularly concerned about the plight of the female shifters, but there had also been a marked decrease in the tithe to the Council due to the losses, and the other packs had been asked to make up for the financial loss. And if there was one thing my parents cared about, other than appearances, it was money.

So far, it seemed the rumors were true, and that some of the worst abuses had been utterly hidden. I'd even heard a whisper about Callaway having a true mate years ago, who'd died or vanished.

My father's Enforcers were already taking pictures and moving silently from shack to shack, asking discreet questions to build a case to overturn the leadership here. Brand might bitch about shifter tradition, but Luke had to step up as Alpha before more shifters died.

A knock at the door interrupted my thoughts. "What?"

"News."

Wrapping a towel around my waist, I opened the door a crack. "Report."

Hard topaz eyes met mine. My father's Head Enforcer, Torran. He'd been Eastern's wet-work man for two years, after I'd been relieved of that bloody duty. I'd always thought there was something wrong with his wolf, since Torran enjoyed torturing.

He'd enjoyed it so much, my father had recently been forced to give the job to another shifter, or risk our pack's secrets being exposed to human authorities.

"Sir, we've got more than enough on the suspect to follow through with your father's orders."

"I expected as much. Write it up, add it to the investigation's file. Make sure you use the new encryption."

"Not that these idiots would know the first thing about hacking," he muttered. "I'm not sure this hellhole even has a landline. Good thing we brought our sat phones."

"Is that all?"

His eyes narrowed. "You're expected in the Alpha's private dining room in a half hour."

"I'll be there," I replied, trying not to grind my teeth at the tone of command he dared to use. As Head Enforcer, he might be on the Council, but we both knew my wolf was stronger than his, and I was the Heir. "You take care of your work. I'll handle mine."

I shut the door and slid the deadbolt, my mind moving to the next evening, and the fight. I wouldn't hurt her. But I would test her. Anything less would be an insult to her skills, her training. I'd give her the chance to shine, like the rough diamond she was in this pack full of stones.

And then I would let the stones be crushed. As soon as Flor was safely away from this shithole, the Council would send in a massive group of Enforcers, and the Southern leadership would all suffer for their crimes.

For daring to hurt my fierce little warrior. My unexpectedly, almost unnaturally appealing mate, whose eyes had held innocence... and secrets.

The thought of her had my cock rising again, my inner wolf whining to run free and find her. *Fuck.* I didn't have time for this.

Nevertheless, I slammed the bathroom door and had my cock in my hand as I fantasized about how I would pay back my rough little mate for her dirty fighting. How I could teach her to enjoy herself, and me. I let myself dream, and feel, and wish, knowing that was all I could do to keep her from danger.

If only my life were safe enough for her, my own pack more honorable. If I were a better shifter, not stained by my crimes and attached to a poisonous family tree... I would have allowed her to taste the danger of my affection, my craving, making certain she enjoyed every second of it.

I would have loved her, with all the sharp edges of my nature, until she softened me.

Until she returned my love.

14

BETRAYAL IN THE RING
FLOR

I t felt like I'd spent my whole life waiting, so I should have developed patience by now. But the next two days were going to be the longest of my life.

Between the constant weight of grief, my ever-present watchfulness for any Southern patrols still running in the woods, and the distracting, obsessive thoughts that kept swirling in my mind about not only Luke, but Brand, Glen, and even the red-headed jerk, I was more of a mess than I had ever been.

In the distance, a twig broke. I had my bag in my hand and was up the closest pine tree before whoever it was could get close enough to sniff me. I'd been sleeping in the trees, so I hadn't left much of my scent on the ground, and I'd buried the sticks I'd used to train with under a thorny bush nearby, but paranoia was what had kept me alive. I climbed higher, into the thick branches, the scent of the pine sap that covered my arms and legs surrounding me.

A short, sharp whistle sounded in the distance. Holding my breath, I silently climbed as high as I possibly could, as the five Enforcers I hated most in the world came running in human form through the clearing.

"She ain't out here, Trevor," the lowest of the five whined. Lyndal. He was a cowardly suck-up, always sneaking out of shifts and cutting his training runs short. Ranked wolves were supposed to be stronger than unranked, but Lyn wasn't anything like Trevor, or even Grant. "Everybody else is done searching. I heard your dad say she probably took her chances with the rogues. We oughta go back and rest before the party." Lyndal was so out of breath he was wheezing, and the others turned looks of disgust on him.

"Stop bitchin', Lyn. And my dad was the one who said we had to keep looking. You know they have the Council meeting at the end of the Games. He thinks she could try and speak at that."

"Why? What can they do about it? She's Southern," Lyn grumbled. The others all laughed at him. I knew he was turning red; Lyn always did before he blew up at his friends, and got his ass handed to him.

"You never paid attention in class, didja Lynnie?" Trevor said, as they started walking away. "The Council Alphas make the rules for all the packs. And the Conclave is the only time a trash shifter like Flor could ever get the chance to bitch and moan about stuff like the Hunt. Which we all know is some twisted shit."

"Yeah, illegal as fuck. But it's fun." Lyn turned his head to the side and spat into a nearby bush. "Tell you the truth, I wouldn't even want the bitch if I caught her. But chasing her is the best part of being Southern."

Trevor grunted in agreement. "Bitin' her would be better. I like the ones that fight. And she's got more fight in 'er than ten other girls."

"I'm gonna catch her," Lyn muttered. "Catch her, and wrap that red hair around my fist, and make her suck my dick every damned day of my life."

My stomach churned, and I held my breath as Grant laughed. "You won't catch her. Anyway, Trevor's got dibs."

Lyn cursed. "I'll claim some other'n then."

"You do that. Just don't let whoever it is mark you, like Alpha Callaway told us. Then you can still fuck whoever you want, and it doesn't burn through the bond." He snorted. "Not on your side, anyway."

"Shut up, you stupid fuck." Trevor punched Grant in the gut, and the grunt was all that covered up my gasp. It was always males who marked the females in our pack. I'd never even heard of a female returning a mating bite.

If it meant her mate would be in pain when she had sex with another male, no wonder they weren't teaching that. That would make things even.

Though maybe not. Lots of our female shifters slept around. Even after they mated, some of the lower ranked women did it so they could afford food and medicine for their kids. If they couldn't get money that way, more poor shifter kids would starve.

"Why can't we fucking shift again?" Grant whined.

"Those asshole Heirs. I heard they got all pissy we were allowed, and they weren't."

"When are we handing them their asses?" Lyn demanded. "Soon as your dad gives the signal, I'm gonna knock that Northern Heir's teeth down his throat."

I froze. Why the hell would Lyn think he was going to fight Glen? Had he signed up for the Games?

Whatever Trevor said in reply was lost in a gust of wind in the leaves. Lyn's high-pitched laughter was the last thing I heard before they started running again.

An hour later, I had just started back down the tree when I heard another branch breaking on the ground.

Fuck.

I started back up, but soft laughter chased me. "It's just me, Flor."

Heart racing, I peered down. That overbearing, stuck-up Finnick was standing at the base of the tree. I'd never been happier to see an asshole in my life.

"What're you doing here?"

He didn't answer, so I sat on a branch and watched as he started unpacking a hamper full of food. A *lot* of food. There was fried chicken and green beans with ham, and... "Is that mac and cheese?" I was on the ground before I even realized what I was doing.

I used my hand to shovel the first, still-warm bite into my mouth, and let out a moan. "Fuck me," I mumbled around it. "That's the best thing I've ever had in my..." My words trailed off as I stared up at the male in front of me, who was making the weirdest growling noise. "What? This is the most delicious food I've ever eaten. I mean, that wasn't just scraps off someone else's plate." I grinned up at him, but stopped eating for a moment at his expression. It was the strangest combination of anger, grief, and... longing? "It's not your dinner, is it?" I held the bowl out to him. "There's plenty left."

"No. It's what was left that I could take without anyone noticing."

I shrugged and went back to eating. "Food's food to me. But I appreciate it." I did. Nobody but Del had ever given two shits whether I ate or not.

He sighed when I started wiping the edges of the mac and cheese container with my finger and licking it clean. "Just because we're shifters doesn't mean we must act like

127

animals." He dropped a rolled-up napkin next to me. Inside was a set of silverware.

"Thanks, assmunch," I said with a cheesy thumbs-up, which I promptly licked. "D'you come out here just to bring me food and an unwelcome lesson in table manners? Or is there some news?"

He bristled, then shook his head, like he'd lost some internal debate. "Food and to let you know that I signed you up for round one tomorrow, the opening fight of the night." The corner of his mouth twitched, and I wondered if that was his tell when he was lying.

"Swear it," I said, and was up in a flash, my arms around his thigh, the steak knife he'd supplied me with pressed against the thin linen trousers, right at his femoral artery. "Swear you're not lying."

"You dirty little..." His green eyes gleamed like emeralds, but there was amusement just behind his anger. "I swear on my honor, I signed you up, with the name you chose."

I winked and went back into a crouch by the food, tearing into a fried drumstick. "Not swearin' on the honor of your pack, huh? Glen was going on and on about pack honor."

"I know better. So should you." Those eyes went dull, and he turned away.

"Um, how's Luke?" I asked awkwardly.

Finnick let out a short laugh. "Brand found him after you stabbed him. He patched him up, though you came close to killing him."

"But he ain't dying. He'll live."

"He'll live."

"Good. That's good," I said, my gut roiling at the thought of Luke in pain. Or maybe it was just gas. Finnick shook his head at me for some reason. "Glen agreed to bid on me after I win, right?" I called at his back as he turned away. "I only gotta fight once?"

"That's how it usually works. But you and I both know you could win against almost all of the early fighters."

I tried not to let the praise affect me, but I felt a tiny swarm of shivers go down my spine. "I don't care. I'm going to forfeit the second fight. Tell him that, okay?"

"Why?"

"I don't need to show off. I just need to get out. Who'm I fighting?"

There were a lot of shifters from other packs, so it was unlikely I'd recognize the name. But if it did happen to be someone from my own pack, I'd have a leg up. I may not have been allowed to train, but I'd watched almost every Southern fighter in the training circle or the pack gym at some point. Usually from a supply closet or under a table while I was being hunted by Trevor or some other douche, but it didn't matter. I had an almost perfect memory for fighting moves, and Del had made sure I knew about the weaknesses of our males.

Finnick hadn't answered; he was walking off.

"Hey, Cityboy! Who am I up against? Someone from Southern?"

I heard his faint "No," and then he was gone. I let it go, turning back to the food.

The next morning, I moved my campsite deeper into the forest since the wind had changed a bit. I knew Alpha Callaway still had wolves looking for me, so I stayed low and didn't light any fires. I didn't have to, since Finnick had also brought me a few handfuls of jerky and some bread rolls. I ate, slept, bathed in the creek again, and trained all weekend, nervously waiting until it was time to head back.

Finally, around what I hoped was five o'clock, I packed my things and started the long jog to the compound. Thoughts of Luke buzzed through my mind like unwelcome mosquitoes as I made my way. Luke was high-ranked and strong, and the wound I'd given him hadn't been that bad. It should have healed almost instantly—I'd seen plenty of Enforcers heal from a lot worse. Everything short of amputation or decapitation.

The only mature shifter I'd seen with scars that never healed was Mom. She had explained that only the wounds left by silver, magic, or a true mate...

I stopped, feeling like throwing up. *Oh, Mother Moon. It can't be.*

He *can't be.*

Mama's voice echoed in my memory as I stood stock-still, my thoughts humming like a knocked-down wasp's nest.

"Why's your face got marks, Mama?"

"That's what happens when a true mate is bad, honey. I had a true mate, and he didn't want me. He marked me like this to show everyone what he thought. To make me not beautiful."

"It didn't work. You're still so pretty."

It was true. My mama had dark hair that spilled over her shoulders in perfect curls, and bright golden eyes that flashed when she was happy. Which wasn't often. I wanted to make her happy now.

"You're the prettiest mama ever," I told her, laying kisses on the scars that ran from her hairline to her chin and jawbone. She'd had those scars my whole life. Del had told me scars were marks of victory, not shameful like everyone else said. That they meant you'd survived and lived to fight another day.

Mama held still while I kissed her scars, but her face was crumpled up like it got before she cried, so I stopped and patted her shoulder instead. *"I'll be the happiest mama ever if you promise me one thing,"* she whispered. *"If you meet your true mate, and you even think for a second he might lay a hand on you... you run. Never let him get near you."*

"Why not, Mama?" The other girls had been talking the day before at lunch about true mates, and how it would be like a fairy tale story if they ever met theirs. They'd made it sound like it was the best thing that could ever happen to a girl, but when I'd walked over and tried to ask them how you knew who your true mate was, they'd said bad words. One of them had thrown her yogurt cup at me and splattered my clothes. Joke was on her, though. The lid was mostly still on, and I'd gotten to find out what her fancy lunch yogurt tasted like.

Strawberries, yum.

"A true mate can hurt you, cut you deeper, than any other creature on earth," Mama said, tracing the scars on her face. *"There's no way to heal when he gets his claws in you."* Her eyes went cloudy again, and I sighed. This was always what happened before she had to go into her room and cry until she slept.

I stood, bending down to kiss her cheek. "I promise, Mama. I don't care if he's the nicest man in the world. I'm never gonna mate some boy."

She had warned me. For years, I'd thought I could escape the trap of a mate, but now look what had happened.

Luke was the one. The Alpha's adopted son, the one who believed in the sanctity of the pack, who upheld every last rule like it would kill him to bend even one. He'd seen me tortured for years and not stepped in.

How long had he known we were true mates? Had he known all those times I'd been beaten and kicked, had food dumped on me, been called names and ridiculed in front of the pack? Had he known and never protected me?

Suddenly, I didn't feel guilty for stabbing him. I wished I'd stabbed him a few more times. Mama had been right, and I was going to do what she hadn't been able to.

Escape.

I found the huge gap Luke had torn in the fence and slipped through, keeping hidden behind the rows of brambles and scrub bushes. From the jabber of the girls who were walking that way, the first fight would start in twenty minutes. My fight.

Just enough time to cover my scent. I grabbed a few handfuls of rosemary from one of the fancy gardens I passed and rubbed it all over, covering my skin and the boy's clothes I wore. I grabbed the hat Del had packed and pulled it low over my face, rubbing some dirt on my face. At the last minute, I saw a garbage can so full the lid wouldn't close. *Nice.* I spent two precious minutes rubbing some greasy paper towels on myself. Much better to smell like old bacon than shit, yet equally as effective.

I ran as fast as I could to the main training yards then, slipping silently between the outermost circles to get closer, blending in with the crowd. At least one or two of the visitors had shifted, maybe to fight in their wolf forms. Their growls and yips sent chills up my spine.

I hadn't really considered the idea of having to fight a shifter in his wolf form. *But Del did*, I reminded myself. He'd made me train against him, even though he only had three legs. Whoever I was fighting now surely wouldn't be better than Del, even lame.

The shifters around me gave me dirty looks, backing away. "Damn, boy, you smell like crap," a male I'd never met said.

His friend nudged him. "That's the smell of Southern, Dave. Be thankful we only have to put up with it for a few more days."

"Same here," I muttered, slipping closer to the fight. I kept my eyes and face in the shadows of taller wolves as much as possible and leaned out to see who was in the front rows of spectators.

Alpha Callaway was there of course, dead center, seated in some sort of chair he'd had painted gold. It looked home-made, and the paint still smelled fresh, like he'd just had it finished that day. I sniggered quietly, wondering if Walmart had run a special on gold spray paint and unfinished pine furniture.

Like Glen had said, the other Alphas weren't there yet. I wondered why they hadn't come for the whole week. Then again, who would want to spend a week in Alabama in the summer?

Near our Alpha sat the Alpha Heirs, Luke by his right side. He didn't look injured, but there was something in his eyes that made me think he was hiding it. Then Brand next to Luke, and on the other side of Brand, Glen.

Where was Finnick? It seemed weird that he wouldn't be sitting with his friends. But then I saw him in the clump of waiting competitors. Was he fighting tonight? That didn't make sense. Still, I didn't think there was a rule that Alpha Heirs couldn't participate—just no Alphas, for obvious reasons. But he hadn't mentioned it.

It seemed sort of unsportsmanlike for Finnick to be there, especially if he was going up against unranked shifters. Maybe he was there to boost morale? I saw some other fighters nearby, big Enforcer types. Maybe he was supporting a pack mate.

He seemed antsy, his eyes scanning the crowd. Then I

heard the announcer shouting his name. "Finnick McDonnell of Eastern, step into the ring."

Finnick stepped under the rope that marked the area for the fights. He looked nervous, and something more. Panicked, almost.

"Will L. Rains of Southern, report for your fight against Eastern. Will L. Rains, step into the ring."

What the hell? For a moment, I looked around with everyone else, wondering where the fighter was. Then it clicked.

Oh right, that was me. I was Will Rains, for tonight anyway.

The whole crowd got quiet. "Last call for Will L. Rains."

"That's me," I said, my voice cracking.

The wolves around me laughed. "Boy, why'd you sign up to fight the Alpha Heir? Ain't nobody got that much to prove."

Oh, that chickenshit, Finn. I had something to prove, all right. I stalked forward, the crowd parting for me. I stepped over the rope, slipping my tennis shoes off as required.

"Hat, too, Stinky," the burly announcer growled. I flinched, but followed his direction. I was lucky they weren't making me take off my shirt. Finnick was only wearing a pair of gray shorts, like a bunch of the other competitors he'd been standing with.

"You rat's ass," I murmured as soon as I got close enough for him to hear. "You're trying to get me killed, right?" I felt my heart racing. There was the very distinct possibility I would lose this round. And then the Alpha would literally have me killed, probably within minutes. My chest ached, and my eyes stung. "You betrayed me."

"No, Wills," he muttered. "I've got a plan. I didn't betray

you. This is for fun. After we fight, you'll get another chance tonight for a bid."

"Huh?" He thought fighting for my life was fun? "Yeah," I purred. "I'll get my bid right after I kick your entitled, airbrushed ass." I tried to sound like I meant it, but I knew I wasn't as well trained as him. I sniffed and wiped away the tear sliding down my cheek.

I hated crying. But for some reason, the thought of Finnick betraying me, when he knew what was at stake, gutted me.

His eyes widened, a look of shock crossing his face. "No, listen, Wills. I promise I've got a plan—" But he couldn't finish, because the announcer was asking a question.

"All right, Alpha Heir chooses the form for exhibition fights. Your choice, Alpha Heir McDonnell?"

Exhibition fights? Was Finnick making some sort of example of me? Was this not even a real fight? *Oh, hell no.*

Finnick nodded. "I choose human form only."

The announcer grinned. "Right, it's an exhibition, not an execution." The shifters around us laughed.

An execution. I shivered. That's what was ahead for me after this fight. I had to win.

Win, or die.

15

ASKING FOR A BID

FLOR

"I've got a plan," the chickenshit whispered. "Relax."

I ignored him, even though I wanted to yell, to tell him to shut up. I shuddered, chewing my lip almost bloody as I tried to remember his weaknesses in our sparring match. Which were fairly nonexistent. I felt another fucking tear fall.

Finnick saw it, and for some reason, stiffened up like he'd been hit by lightning. "I mean it, Wills. Calm down, here's what's going to happen—"

But the announcer was speaking again. "First one to yield is the loser. This is not a death match, but broken bones or major lacerations are not an indication of submission, understand? You must tap out or verbally submit. Y'all ready? Three, two, one..." He let out a howl, and the fight began.

Or it didn't, really. Finnick and I just stood there, staring at each other. I was shaking, literally shaking so hard, I almost couldn't focus.

I heard someone say, "Wait, who the hell *is* that? That's not a Southern fighter. We don't have a Will Rains..."

Alpha Callaway let out a loud growl. I darted a glance at him. His voice rose over the murmurs of the crowd. "You better hope he kills you, Flor, because I'm gonna make you wish you'd died after this." And then some sort of fight broke out right around him—was it Glen, or Brand? I wasn't sure, because Finnick took the chance to dart forward with a slow right uppercut. I danced backward, my gut curdling.

He peppered a few more blows, and they connected with my shoulder, my arm, my side. All soft, like he was fighting a marshmallow.

Disrespectful. I dropped my guard and glared across the ring.

"Yielding already?" he asked.

"Fuck that," I spat. "I'm dying tonight one way or another. You may have betrayed me, but you don't need to mock me."

Those green eyes flashed with frustration. "I promise you won't die. I don't promise I won't hand you your ass in a real fight."

I raised my guard. "Big talk, Cityboy. Shut up and put up."

His eyes sparkled. "Good, this is going to be fun." For some reason, I didn't think he was talking about the fight. One edge of his mouth curled up, and he stepped back toward me. "I'm not letting you win this time, Wills. I bet you can't do it without dirt anyway."

I didn't answer. Del had warned me opponents would try to get into my head. Instead of letting the words he said sink in, I slipped into the alert meditative state Del had forced me to learn. The same quiet space I'd found whenever I was hiding from Trevor and his gang. I was silent and deadly, a shadow with fists.

I punched out, spun, dodging almost every one of Finnick's blows. A few hit me on my arms, but glanced off. I didn't even feel them. I'd been hurt a lot worse, a lot more often.

I returned the jabs and strikes, more of mine connecting than Finn was ready for, and he actually stumbled. I could see the moment when he decided to commit to the fight, to really use his advantages. His size, his strength. Those impossibly long legs, and those arms, honed and tight.

He'd spent a hell of a lot of time in some dojo or academy, getting every one of his kicks and punches perfect. But I'd spent years being beaten by the ones who were supposed to protect me. I let out a howl of rage, letting my anger fill me and fly out.

It happened again, then. I lost time. I blinked, and suddenly, I was connecting a hit to Finnick's temple. I blinked again, and I was the one being thrown back against the ropes.

Another blink, and he was down on one knee, blood pouring from the corner of his mouth. But my fists were still flying, my torso bending to dodge his returned strikes, and I was going for targets Del had taught me—not just the knee, but the testicles. Not just the temple, but the eyes and the nose.

I might break his nose and drive the bone into his brain. I didn't care. Even a shifter had a hard time healing from that.

"Stop! Stop, Wills!" Finn managed to shout.

Stop? Why? Hell no!

I went for him, wrapping my legs around him and turning him in a jiu-jitsu move so that I was under him, then on top, then holding his face against the ground, his arm twisted at an impossible angle. We both heard the unmistakable pop of his elbow dislocating.

"Yield!" I demanded. He didn't, so I smashed his head into the ground again. I could snap his neck at this angle. "Yield before I break your damned neck."

"I yield," he croaked out.

I stood, swaying. The entire crowd was silent. I held out a bloody hand; it looked like I was bleeding from scratches and cuts all over. Finnick had bled, too, though. I'd clocked him hard enough to make his ear bleed. I squinted. *Both* ears.

"Good fight," I said. "You were right. That was fun."

Finnick flopped over, staring at me like I was his worst nightmare and an unsolvable equation combined. "You... You won."

"Um yeah, asshole. That's how fights work." I *had* won, and I could get my bid now.

I kept my hand out, wondering what he was doing. Sure, I'd hurt him, but he was a mature shifter. A powerful one. He should have been healing by now.

"You're embarrassing yourself," I hissed, leaning down to grab his good elbow. He recoiled from my touch, then whimpered when the movement jarred his other arm. Ugh, I hadn't meant to hurt him that badly. "Why aren't you healing? You need me to pop it back in place or something?" I didn't know much about shifter healing since I'd never shifted, but I knew that dislocated *anything* had to be popped back in.

The announcer was heading our way, inching over like he wasn't sure the fight was done. Finnick's eyes looked weird, like he couldn't focus. "You weren't supposed to win."

I let out a sigh. "Listen, I didn't *want* to fight you. I'm sorry I got carried away. We cool?"

But he had passed out.

The next second, the announcer had my hand in his lifted over my head, practically hauling me off the ground. Two other shifters took the moment to race in and hustle Finnick's limp body out of the ring, a pack doctor already examining him.

"The first ever unranked winner of an exhibition match... is Will L. Rains, from Southern pack!"

Nobody clapped. I darted a look at the Alpha. He wasn't here. And neither was Brand. And... *Oh shit.*

Neither was Glen.

Where the hell was Glen? I needed him to bid on me for his pack. The only Heir left was... Luke.

"Shifter Rains, since you took the victory against the Alpha Heir, you will move directly to the semi-finals round tomorrow night. Congratulations."

"Wait, I don't want to fight again. Or... maybe I can fight someone else now?"

"What? No. That's not how it works. You'll need to return tomorrow night to fight." His brow furrowed. "Technically, the Alpha Heir should be fighting again tonight, as the loser. But he's knocked out."

I felt like I might pass out. "You don't understand. I can't wait. I need... I want a pack bid."

The announcer's eyes narrowed. Asking for a pack bid was the same as announcing you wanted a new Alpha. "Boy?"

"I want to ask for a pack bid," I managed to scratch out of my tight throat. *Where the hell is Glen?*

The announcer cleared his throat. "Son, I'm afraid you can't get a bid now, since the only Alpha Heir here is your own. You'll go on to the semi-finals. I'm sure another pack will bid for you if you win that one." His mouth twitched. "Might want to lay low until then."

He had no idea. "I... I have to win in the semi-finals?" I pressed a hand against my heart. "I really gotta fight again?"

The announcer leaned down, sniffing, and his eyes went wide. "Oh, shit. You're not a boy at all..." He lifted his head. "Alpha?" But the Southern Alpha wasn't there.

Where had he gone? Where had all the other Heirs gone?

Luke stood, speaking for the Alpha. "Do you forfeit the next fight?"

"Forfeit my chance to get the hell out of here?" I spat blood on the mat, scanning the crowd one more time for Glen. But he was gone.

Finnick and Glen had both stabbed me in the back. I was alone.

Good thing I was used to it.

"Hell, no," I answered, loud and proud. "I'll fight."

You could have heard a cricket fart. And then the crowd lost their shit.

16

REINFORCEMENTS

GLEN

"Fuck, fuck, what did we do? What have I *done?*" Even though my leg was on fire with pain, I paced stiffly in the cell the Southern Alpha had thrown me into an hour before.

Me and Brand, which was still making my head spin.

I knew why I had attacked the Alpha when he promised to kill Flor slowly, but for some reason, Brand had done a partial shift and gotten claws into the bastard before I was halfway there. He'd just about torn the man's ear off, leaving gashes down his neck. If Luke hadn't stepped in and hauled him away, I'm not sure Brand would have stopped until Callaway was dead.

Of course, the rest of Southern would have killed Brand then. Dominance challenges had to be announced, and just killing an Alpha because he threatened a member of his own pack wasn't reason enough to try to murder him.

And we didn't have an order for his execution. *Yet.*

Standing at the silver-plated iron door that was easily three inches thick, Brand let out an enraged growl. "Screwed up," he said, his eyes practically throwing sparks in the dim cell. "Don't worry. I got word from one of my pack's fighters before they stuck us in here. Our parents will be here tomorrow."

"I thought your dad said he wasn't coming until the last day for the mandatory Council meeting." Brand stayed silent. "And my dad was delayed because of the rogue situation at our packlands."

"Tomorrow," was his reply.

There was no way they could have arrived that soon, unless... "You called them in before the fight, didn't you? You told them about Flor."

Brand nodded once. "Right after we found her in the hunting grounds."

Relief spilled through me, quickly followed by trepidation. "Who's coming?" I sank down on a metal bench, rubbing my leg. The silver in the bars that surrounded us made shifting in this cell close to impossible, but the fracture was healing slowly. It would be back to normal by morning. "Just the Alphas?"

Brand closed his eyes for a moment, letting out a huge breath. As I stared, the shiner Luke had given him in the scuffle vanished. I was impressed, though I tried not to show it. It was the fastest healing I'd ever seen without a shift, which meant Brand might be the strongest Alpha Heir of us all. I would say the strongest shifter alive, but I'd met his dad.

Finally, he answered, "All of them except Finnick's mother." She never came to anything, other than social events and Conclaves held in their own territory.

"Oh, kill me now." I collapsed to the floor. "Mom's coming."

"What's wrong with her?" Brand rubbed at the drying

blood on his torn shirt. "Margarette's a strong, loyal, kind shifter."

"She's kind to you," I told him. "She probably wishes you were her son."

Brand leveled a glare on me. "Don't talk about your mother that way." He spat a mouthful of blood on the already filthy concrete floor. "What is it with you and Finn? Trash talking the women you ought to be lifting up." He curled his lip. "You'd fit right in down here at Southern."

My cheeks were hot. I knew he was right. "Relax, brother. I love my mom, and if anyone else said anything against her, I'd fucking destroy them. But being her son..." I let out a long breath. "You know who your dad is to you? Hard to measure up to? That's how I feel about Mom. She's legendary. If women could be Alphas, she'd be one."

"I know. She's in the history books in my pack library." Brand smiled. "The first female Enforcer in your pack. She was sixteen, right?"

I grinned. "Yeah. They had to let her graduate high school early so she could meet with the Russian pack when they tried that land grab. I still can't believe they got so far." Of course, that initial battle had only been a precursor to the much larger, far more costly war that had taken all the North American packs by surprise a decade later. "Mom was there for the first battle at Bertaud Lake. She said her parents thought it would be a safe, diplomatic venture. Mom snuck her sword into her pack."

"You Canadian fuckers. Your grandparents probably just thought they'd leave nicely if they asked with a please."

I shot him the finger. "Well, my mom sent their heads back in a crate with a lovely thank-you letter for the visit, and a politely worded death threat for the entire Russian Council of Alphas if they tried it again."

He grunted a laugh. "I love your mom."

"Me, too." I scraped my hair back, doing mental calculations as to when she might arrive. My mother had power, top-notch fighting skills, and would bring along our very best fighters. Once she arrived, even if it meant a host of other problems for me, at least Flor would be protected. Once I told her, that is. "I hope she loves my mate."

Brand's dark eyes went wide, then narrowed with something like suspicion. "She's obsessed with true mate lore. *Whenever* you meet her, if you meet her, your mom will fall in love along with you."

"Yeah, I'm not sure my true mate is exactly what Mom's been picturing."

Brand was silent, but when he finally spoke, his voice thrummed with intensity. "Who?" The question sounded like a threat. Of course, it might have been the menacing growl that came out with the word, and kept on echoing in the empty cell.

I waited a few seconds, trying to think how to say it. He stopped growling and repeated himself, louder. "*Who?* Just say it. You've met her, haven't you? Who's your damned mate, Glen?"

He sounded supremely pissed, which shocked me. Brand was the closest friend I had, along with Finnick. As close as family, and we'd fucking lived together as brothers for years, training side by side for our futures leading our packs. "Shouldn't you be happy for me, man? I mean, I just told you I found my mate."

"What's her *name?*" he growled louder, and I backed up a few inches. Brand was a solid nine inches taller than me, and we both knew he could kick my ass—in human form, anyway. Wait, was he *shifting?*

"Brand, what's the deal?"

"Call it a hunch," he snarled, grabbing the front of my shirt. "It's Flor, isn't it?"

I relaxed, feeling a stupid smile cover my face at her name. "Of course it's Flor. You think I attacked a deranged Alpha for some random girl? I don't care how brave and crazy she is, that's not the sort of thing I'd do for any unranked shifter."

He closed his eyes for a second, a line appearing between his thick brows. "I should have guessed. Does Finn know?"

"No..." I said, drawing the word out. "But he can't be her mate if she's mine. He said he wasn't certain."

Brand's shoulders slumped and he let go of my shirt as he let out a sigh. A sigh I recognized from years of friendship. His gaze speared mine, and I read everything he wanted to say, but couldn't. Wouldn't. "*I'm* certain, Glen."

It took a moment for his words to register. He was certain she was his.

My heart lurched. "It's not possible. A bond happens once, if at all. I would know; Mom made me read dozens of books on mate history. How could one girl have two true mates?"

Brand let out a shaky breath. "Try three." Then he muttered something that sounded like *or more*.

I felt my blood go cold. "No. Just... no, Brand."

"I held her shirt," he said after a few seconds of silence. "I didn't even touch her, but it was like—"

"Like electricity," I finished for him. It felt like he'd carved out my stomach with his words. "Fire in your veins."

"Not for me," he whispered. "It was the same feeling I get when I'm at my lake. Peace. Like I was home. It... scared me. At first, I thought maybe it was something else, like a pack bond thing. I couldn't scent her, under that sewage smell. But I felt compelled to protect her, to go back to her."

He shuddered, sitting on the steel bench beside me. "I wondered if she was my sister or something, a long-lost relative. She felt so *right*, as if I'd always known her. But then I went into the kitchen with Luke, to stitch him up. And I smelled her." He shifted in an unmistakable way, adjusting his jeans. "Her scent was strong there; it's where she worked for years."

My heart was aching, but I tried to joke. It was what we both needed, a little levity in this somber moment. "Is that why you had wood all day?" He threw a pebble at my face and hit my cheek. "Ow."

"Yeah, asshole, that's why. I can't help it. Her scent is..."

"Cinnamon rolls," I supplied. "And jasmine."

The corner of his mouth lifted. "I thought honeysuckle. I never cared about flowers, but now I want to start smelling them all, just to see which one is most like her."

"How is it possible?" I asked, not expecting an answer.

"I don't know. Your pack library probably has the answer, though." I chewed at my lip. I'd read almost every book in that library as part of my Heir education, but had never come across any mention of a soulmate bond with more than two shifters involved.

"I wonder who her parents are?" I mused aloud. "Her mother is dead, but her father might be alive. There might be an answer there. Three soulmates for one female?" I didn't say what I was thinking: that she would have to choose one of us. And let two of the connections wither.

I didn't want to imagine what it would be like, to know my soulmate was out there, mated to one of my best friends. Never to be mine.

"It could be more than three." He hesitated. "I think Luke might be hers, too."

"Luke?" *No.* I stood to pace again, glad my leg was healing. "He'll probably be the one ordered to kill her after the match." I tore out a handful of hair. "God, what's happening right now? What was Finn thinking?"

Brand scowled. "The fight will be over by now. She will have lost."

"Are you sure? Finn said she was skilled."

"He won't have planned to throw it. That would be dishonorable."

I scoffed. "No, that would be the entire Eastern Pack. They're no better than the human mafia."

"Finnick's not like that."

I nodded. It was true; Finn was practically the only ranked shifter I'd met at Eastern who wasn't a complete sociopath. "But after she loses, she'll be forced to fight a second time."

He nodded. "Right afterward. Tired and already hurting."

We both cursed aloud. I made a mental note to beat the shit out of Finn the very next chance I got.

We sat in silence, straining to hear anything from outside—cheers, or applause, or howling—until Brand finally said, "Maybe he *did* throw the fight. He knew that if she won against him, she could get a pack bid."

"Not from us." I ground my teeth, feeling the sharp edges of my canines against my tongue.

"Finn will bid for her. He won't let her die." I wasn't certain, but the tips of Brand's ears looked like they'd gone furry. I knew how he felt. At the very edge of control.

I paced back and forth, my wolf fighting to emerge, to

attack the silver and iron compound bars that held us here. That kept me trapped, away from my mate.

I hated to think of her as part of Finn's fucked-up pack. But if I could get out and prove she was my mate—hell, if Brand could do it—she'd be allowed to go to whichever pack she chose.

Brand's words had settled my wolf a bit, though. "You're right. Finn can be a stuck-up jerk, but he's not an idiot."

He raised one thick eyebrow. "Wouldn't go that far."

"Yeah, he's pretty dumb sometimes." I laughed. "Remember the water snakes?"

He snickered as well. "City boys like him think every stick is a snake."

I shrugged. "Yeah, but you actually carved a bunch into snake shapes, Brand. With eyes. And dyed them to look realistic. And hid them everywhere."

We both slumped down on the bench, waiting, remembering. We'd spent almost every summer together growing up, me and Finn and Brand. Luke had joined us once, but he hadn't quite clicked. There was something about him. I'd always thought it was because he was European. Brand said it was because he was raised without honor.

From what I'd seen in this pack, he wasn't wrong.

"What happens next?"

"Best case, our parents get here soon, we apologize to the Southern Alpha, and Finn... Finn gets to live with her in New York." After a moment, he went on. "She might like the city. Fancy dinners, operas, that sort of thing."

I shook my head. "Brand, you met her. She'd be way better off in Ontario with me—or in Colorado with your pack. She's scrappy, a fighter. Take no bullshit, take no prisoners." I swallowed. "She might choose one of us."

Brand's scent went slightly bitter. "You know how this'll turn out. Your mom's gonna meet her and kidnap her for you."

I hoped so. Suddenly, having my overbearing mother descending on us didn't seem so bad. "We have to make sure what happened to her down here goes before the Council. Southern can't abuse their females like this. We're losing too many shifters each year as it is."

"Not enough are being born."

"You know Mom thinks it's because fewer true mates are being found. She's going to lose her shit entirely when she meets Flor."

Brand turned his head slightly, and I felt his gaze bore into me. "You going to tell her about me, and Finn? And Luke?"

I sighed. "Not Luke. Flor can't stay here, or come back, ever."

"Agreed," he muttered. "Anywhere is better than here." His lip curled again. "If she's smart, she'll pick me."

"She can't mate a dead shifter, Brand. You know my mom will probably murder you and Finn both to make sure I get the girl."

"You're not wrong. By the moon, I can't wait until we get out of here."

"Me neither."

17

UNEXPECTED HONOR
FLOR

I wouldn't have bet more than a nickel I'd live more than a few minutes after that clusterfuck of an evening.

But as it turned out, the competitors I'd seen hanging around Finnick were more decent shifters than the ones in my pack. They were mainly Mountain and Northern wolves, although one of them, Joaquin, said he came from a small pack in Mexico, just south of the border with Texas. I hadn't even known there were packs down there—other than the main four packs, there were only a handful of smaller packs. Supposedly, those had weaker Alphas who had sworn allegiance to one of the big ones, so I wasn't sure they even counted.

But Joaquin didn't feel weak at all; his power made my arm hair stand up when he came close, though it stopped like a faucet cutting off when I shivered.

He kept to himself, though. He was the only one in the group wearing real clothes, jeans and a black shirt. Everyone else had on the gray shorts, easy to strip off for a shift, or fight in as a human. A few of them had on t-shirts as well, but most of them were bare-chested.

The others had gathered around me as soon as I was ushered into the small area where the next rounds were being announced. All the winners were supposed to stay there until the end of the night for some winner ceremony thing.

For some reason, Alpha Callaway still hadn't shown up to kill me.

"You're amazing, kid," a guy with curly red hair on his head and his chest stated, holding out a hand. "I've never seen fighting like that. How the hell did you beat my Alpha Heir?" He didn't seem mad.

"Um, I didn't know I'd have to. He was supposed to sign me up to fight a nobody, so I could get a bid from Glen."

Another one of the winners interrupted. He looked slightly like Glen, with the same blond hair and straight nose. "Wait, you know the Northern Alpha Heir? Glen said he'd bid on you for our pack? Hell yes, we want you."

I let out a shaky laugh. "Hate to tell you, but as soon as Alpha Callaway gets back, he's gonna kill me. Like, literally."

"Why?" The quiet solo wolf from the border spoke up. "Because you're a female?"

Every guy around me went still, except for nostrils flaring, taking in my scent. I guess the rosemary and old bacon had worn off. Then they all started talking at once.

"No way."

"A girl?"

"There's no possible—"

I held up a hand. "Guys, yeah. I'm a girl. I'm an unranked female in Southern, and long story short, your

Alpha Heirs were supposed to help me get a bid so I wouldn't be put to death. My Alpha accused me of murder."

"Oh, shit, you're *that* girl." The blond Northern wolf growled a little. "They say you killed Del Talbot."

"I didn't. I was set up," I growled back. "Del taught me every damned thing I know about fighting and honor. I know who did kill him, and when I get the chance, I'll take what Del taught me and get justice." I had a quick, gratifying mental image of me slicing through my Alpha's neck with a giant sword. Or a chainsaw. I'd use whatever came to hand.

The muttering died down, none of these wolves having much issue with me calling my Alpha dishonorable. They'd been here long enough to see the rot, I supposed. The one who looked like Glen asked, "How can we help?"

You could have knocked me over with a feather, I was so shocked. Males who wanted to help me, not hunt me? I'd lived in a pack my whole life and never had a single shifter my own age stand up for me. I had to be dreaming.

"Whatever you need, little shifter."

I swallowed the unfamiliar lump of emotion and rasped, "I have to live until tomorrow night's fight, right? I'll be up against one of you, I guess—or the guy that wins the fight that's going on now." In the background, we could hear snarling. "I can't shift, so I don't think there's any way I can win."

Someone in the group growled. "You want one of us to lose on purpose?"

"Hell no," I shot back. "I'll win it fair and square. Just give me a chance? Fight me in human form." I didn't expect them to; no male shifter had ever helped me before. Except Del.

Maybe these guys would be like him. Hope curled in my belly like a tiny green shoot.

The blond raked his gaze over me. "I can't believe you won against Finn in either form. He's one of the best." The guys all looked at each other. "All right, so we'll fight you in human form. Right?" They all grunted in agreement.

My eyes were stinging, and I wiped them with the back of my arm. "Wow, that's decent. I never thought..."

"Of course you didn't," one of the guys said, patting me on the back with a hand that felt as heavy as a sandbag. "You were raised in Southern. We need to get you out of here."

"If she stays in this compound overnight, without protection, she will die," the solo wolf said, commenting casually on my death in a voice that sounded way too caramel-honey sexy for the topic.

Focus, Flor. "Actually, I know everywhere to hide. My scent is mostly covered."

"Hard to hide with blood on your clothes," one guy said, sniffing my shirt. "And you smell delicious, little female. Like bacon and cinnamon."

Instantly, the solo wolf was there, holding one of the sniffer's arms behind his back, and dragging him off behind some of the others. I heard a short yelp and the unmistakable sound of a body thumping on the ground.

"Can I, um, borrow a shirt? I'll leave this one. I have a few hiding places the jerks in this pack never found over the past few years. I'll get to a bolt-hole and stay there until tomorrow."

"That's... crazy," the blond guy said.

"What's your name? I can't keep calling you *blond guy* in my mind."

"Patrick," he said, holding out a hand. I shook it.

"Okay Patrick, call me Flor."

He laughed. "You look more like a Will than a Flor right now."

I winked at him and said in my best Southern drawl, "Yeah, but I clean up real nice."

"I'll bet you do," he agreed. "All right, I'm going to give her cover so she can get away. Who wants to fight me for a distraction? Joaquin?" He motioned to the solo wolf, who had returned alone to the inner circle of shifters.

Closer now, it was almost impossible not to stare at the stranger. He wasn't massive and burly like some of the Enforcers, but he had an aura that was every bit as dangerous. He radiated a sort of cold awareness, and I shivered.

But he didn't frighten me, though I couldn't meet his eyes, which was odd. That had never happened before, not even with my own Alpha. I could feel his midnight gaze on me, though, taking in every detail of my appearance. But not judging me. Not condemning my appearance, my smell, or my lack of rank, though his lip curled as he took in my ear tag.

"Joaquin?" Patrick repeated. "When the time comes, will you help me distract everyone?"

"Gladly," he answered, and gave me an odd, courtly bow. He moved so fluidly, it was like gravity didn't have the same hold on him.

Somehow, then he'd closed the distance between us and was holding my hand in his. He smiled, dark eyes flashing red for a split second, and leaned over my hand, giving it a soft kiss. It made my insides feel... strange. Not necessarily in a good way. But not completely bad either. My whole body felt cold, except for my core, which burned with a peculiar fire. I clenched my thighs together, and the heat intensified.

What the heck's going on with me?

Something in those eyes told me this wolf knew. "Do you have food for the day, little one?"

I pulled my hand free, shaking it out slightly, though some of the weird feeling stayed with me. "No, but I've gone a lot longer without food. Unranked, remember?" I tapped my ear tag.

"Unranked. Yes." Joaquin turned away, and I tried not to let my disappointment show.

Patrick let out a soft curse. "So they do starve the unranked here. I've been asking around, but no one was willing to spill."

I shrugged. "Lots of our unranked wolves don't have enough to eat. Food rations gotta be earned, and there aren't a lot of jobs inside the fence."

"That's bullshit!"

"That's Southern. Worry about the kids, not me. I can hunt. I get squirrels, rabbits, all sorts of critters."

Patrick frowned. "But you can't shift."

I frowned right back. "Doesn't mean I can't hunt."

"I heard of some sort of Hunt game," Patrick said, his words slow. "I was supposed to check it out. They say they hunt females."

"Just one," I muttered. "Me."

The group got quiet, the air filled with a dangerous tension. Someone in the group murmured, "What the actual, inbred, redneck *fuck?*"

"Guys, one problem at a time. I need to get to my hiding spot."

"You sure they won't find you?" a giant shifter asked through his enormous beard.

"They haven't for four years," I joked.

The man growled louder. "Four *years?*" Rage began to

swirl like an invisible hurricane in the group. "You were just a child." All I could do was nod, stunned to have so many males nearby who seemed to care.

Joaquin was back in front of me, watching me again, his dark eyes moving over my face like he was trying to memorize me. Like I was some sort of treasure. "What have they done to you, little one?"

I sighed. "What haven't they done?"

His brows furrowed, and a strange, low rumble started in his chest. In fact, all the shifters around me had started to change, their teeth lengthening, eyes flashing.

"Did they... Did they dare?" Joaquin hissed, and suddenly, it felt like all the air around us was bristling with danger. With rage. "Did they ever...?" His mouth was changing shape, the teeth growing sharp behind his parted lips.

Patrick was the one who finally asked. "Did they ever catch you, Flor? Did they... force you?"

18

NIGHTMARES AND MEMORIES
FLOR

Acurrent of rage swept the area, and I froze in place. But then it dawned on me that they were angry on my behalf. Not at me.

I looked away, not certain how to respond to compassion.

"Flor?" Joaquin's gaze caught me, and I shook my head one time, slowly.

"They caught me once," I said, forcing each word out. "One of them did. He was going to... He touched me. But he didn't do more than that." I shivered, remembering Trevor's hands on me, his breath on my face. "He would have. But I got away."

"How did you escape?" Joaquin's voice was almost too kind. No one but Del had ever spoken to me like that, with gentleness.

"My mother saved me. Attacked him, which gave me enough time to get away. And they killed her for it." The area exploded with soft curses and growls.

Joaquin stepped up to my side. "Give me a name, Flor.

Just a name, and no girl in your pack will ever have to worry about him touching them again. I'll tear his hands off for you, my sweet little one, and give them to you to burn."

"That's the nicest gift anyone's ever offered to me," I said with a weak smile. "I might take you up on that." I sniffled, hoping I wasn't going to cry again.

I wiped one hand over my mouth to hide my wobbling chin, then felt something being pressed into my other hand. One of the chestnut-haired wolves—he was almost as big as Brand and looked a little like him—had handed me an energy bar. I thanked him. "I bet you're related to Brand."

"Second cousin," he said. He shoved a shirt into my hand, then looked away as I stripped off my bloody one and changed. "Time to run."

He was right; the fight was breaking up. Alpha Callaway was still gone, but I saw some sort of movement near the Pack House entrance that made me think that wouldn't last.

"Right," Patrick yelled loud enough for the sound to carry past the group. "Joaquin, you piece of shit. You shouldn't even be *here*. The Games are for pack members, not half-rogue trash like you."

Joaquin's eyes glittered, and he answered in Spanish. They rushed each other, fists connecting with far less power and far more noise than normal.

"Now," Brand's cousin murmured, and he and two other shifters circled around me, hiding me as I moved as quickly as I could into the shadowed part of the ring. "We'll get you out of here, one way or the other."

"You've already done more than anyone in my pack would have," I whispered, then ducked down as a huge roar came from the crowd. I didn't look back to see what was happening. I was already across the compound yard and running for one of the few places I thought might keep me safe.

Behind the first row of houses was an old storm drain. It smelled horrific and was only one step above hiding in the latrines themselves. But it was perfect for what I needed.

I unscrewed the two bolts I'd worked loose a few years before, pulled the heavy metal grate away, and slipped inside. This was the tricky bit. My fingers were bigger than they had been when I'd first found this spot, and I had to snake them through the wire mesh and screw the bolts back in from behind.

In the dark. Silently. While I was panicking.

I dropped the bolts twice and had to hold my breath as I heard footsteps nearby once. Eventually, though most of the skin on my knuckles was torn, I managed it. I picked up two handfuls of muck from the drain interior and smeared it on the bolts, just in case my scent had rubbed off. Then I walked, bare feet squelching quietly in the warm mud, listening for snakes and other more dangerous predators.

I counted my steps. When I reached one hundred, I stopped, hunkered down, pulled the energy bar out, and let myself eat.

Then, after another count of a hundred, I let myself cry. For Del, for myself, for my mom, and for the unexpected kindness the other fighters had shown me. At least those final tears were happy ones.

I leaned my head up against the side of the cement pipe and whispered one last prayer of thanks that there were some honorable shifters in the world, even if none of them lived around here.

Then I slept.

THE THING about my nightmares was it was almost impossible to tell if I was having one, or if I was awake and remembering. My nightmares were almost all things that had happened to me in real life. Memories that I couldn't escape, once my eyes were closed.

It was nearly dusk, and gnats buzzed in swarms around my face. I probably still had food in my hair. Trevor Blackside had dumped his mashed potatoes on my head at dinner, saying I'd spit in them.

He hadn't been wrong. But I'd been spitting in his food for months, so I assumed it was a lucky guess.

The entire pack was gathered outside the Pack House, milling around, buzzing with gossip. I knew better than to draw attention to myself. Mama already did plenty of that, with her raving and the seizures she had. But today, she was at work at the QwikMart, and I was on my own since classes had been canceled.

A few of the nearby males gave me long looks, though, and I crossed my arms over my chest and tried to slump lower. My clothes were too small, and my boobs had started to show. I wished they hadn't, but I was fifteen—even if I was the very last female in my grade to hit puberty. At least Mama had helped me find a bra someone else had outgrown in the pack rag bin. It was only a little big, but I'd grow into it soon, she said.

When no one was looking, I dared a small wave at Mindy Pearson, who had been the teacher's helper in my homemaking class the year before. She'd been picked as the focus of the Hunt the previous year, and she'd been caught after only four days by Jackson Billings, who was a huge, good-looking Enforcer. The other girls at school had been jealous, but Mindy was on her own right now, in the back of the crowd. Hiding, like I was, maybe. From the skittish way Mindy's eyes moved over the crowd and the fading, finger-sized bruises on her upper arms, I knew being caught wasn't anything to wish for.

Even if the one who caught you was hotter than the sun. Speaking of which... My own gaze moved like a magnet had caught it as soon as Luke Callaway stepped out of the front door of the Pack House. He'd cut his hair again, buzzed close to the scalp, and I wanted nothing more than to run my fingers over the stubble to feel if it was soft or prickly.

Although I'd settle for running my fingers over any part of him I could get.

"Stop drooling, Flor. You'll get your shoes muddy."

"I'm not drooling, Del," I snapped back, though I knew my cheeks were flaming. I moved over, making room next to the tall pine so Del could lean against it. We weren't allowed to sit down, not when the Alpha was speaking.

"You know what this is about?" I whispered, as the rest of the Enforcers poured out of the Pack House and stood near Luke, whose face was pale and weirdly expressionless.

"It's... bad, Flor. Be ready to run," Del choked out as the Alpha stepped out, with his Head Enforcer, Van Blackside, next to him. Alpha Callaway stared down at the closest female shifters, who preened and flirted wordlessly under his gaze. Blackside's eyes moved over the crowd. Scanning, searching, and finding.

Me.

I froze, holding my breath. After a second—too long, I was being careless—I dropped my gaze from his.

"Go on, Van. Give the good news," the Alpha said with a curt nod. He crooked his finger at one of the preening shifters, and she stepped up next to him, the two of them vanishing back into the Pack House.

Shit. *Callaway had turned the meeting over to Blackside?* I started to move away, so slowly I thought no one would notice. But Del had one hand on my shoulder, the other pressing something into my hand. I didn't look down; Blackside had started speaking about traditions and their importance in our pack.

But Del had handed me what felt like a length of rope. He breathed the words so quietly, I could have imagined them. "Take to the trees. Stay high, out of sight. Remember everything I taught you."

Blackside's voice broke through my focus on Del. "Enforcer Billings caught his prey—sorry, his mate—in four days. I challenge all of you young males to beat that record in the new Hunt. Which starts tonight!"

My ears were buzzing, ringing, and I kept creeping back, crouching low.

"Rules of the Hunt are as always. The shifter who succeeds wins not only his mate, but a place on my Enforcer team, as well as the housing and increased food allowance. Remember, no hunting in the Pack House, no weapons but teeth and claws. Anyone found breaking the rules is automatically disqualified, and earns a lashing with silver." He chuckled, as if that consequence was amusing. "Now, normally we wait for our target to reach eighteen, but as we have fewer young females to choose from this year, the Alpha and I decided to change that to a female who is showing signs of sexual maturity."

The crowd started buzzing, with excitement and concern.

I was almost behind the pine when I heard the words I'd feared. "The new prey in our traditional Hunt will be Flor Wills!"

The crowd broke into shouts and mocking laughter. Derision and disgust filled every voice.

"The pack reject? Who'd want to mate that?"

"She's filthy!"

"I'd fuck her in the dark. She'll be grateful."

I was frozen in place, until I heard Luke call out, "She's a child! Still in school. She's years away from—"

"Alpha decreed it," Blackside interrupted. "You know pack law."

Luke's voice shook me free of the fear that had hobbled me. I spun on one heel, my eyes meeting Del's for a moment. He had tears on his face and a hand filled with what I knew was pepper, already sprinkling it over the ground where I'd stood.

He was trying to obscure my trail. Fighting to protect me. But no female had ever been able to fend off the Hunt for more than a few weeks.

Without the meat I brought in from my own hunts, Mama would starve.

Without my help in the kitchens, Del would suffer.

And I sure as fuck wasn't going to mate one of these asshole mouthbreathers.

Howls of the chase followed me as I ran faster than I ever had before. I'd always been fast. Light on my feet, and running had been an escape.

But I knew this time, when I stopped, I was as good as dead.

"Stop running, little queen," someone whispered in my ear. "Your mate is here. I will keep you safe."

I whirled around and saw a midnight black wolf, with sparks of red and blue in his eyes, staring at me, his teeth bright in the nighttime.

"Stop running," he said, though he didn't move.

"Never," I replied, and suddenly, my shiv was in my hand,

thrusting up and into the wolf's belly. "Never," I cried as the beautiful creature died at my feet. Then I looked down, and it wasn't one dead wolf there, but five.

And the knife was in my chest, plunged between my breasts, right through my silvered scar.

19

TOO LITTLE, TOO LATE
FLOR

I woke up quickly as always, though this time I felt an unusual pain in my chest, right under the scar centered around my heart. The dream came back to me then, and I let myself wonder about its meaning. Why was I dreaming of killing wolves? Wolves besides the assholes in my pack, anyway.

I heard something shift in the tunnel. Water, maybe. Or a rat. For a moment, I held my breath, listening.

Silence.

Then I inhaled deeply, silently, scenting the air with my blunted human senses.

I was alone. I couldn't hear, see, or sense anything in the darkness of the storm sewer. I kind of liked it, feeling cut off from everything. I'd heard people in big cities paid good money for that sort of experience, floating in tanks of water or something.

But I had no idea how long I'd been out. It could be morning, afternoon, or evening; there was no telling. I was still exhausted, but my nightmares made sure I never felt truly rested. I was hungry, but that was my normal state.

I crept closer to the entrance to try to make out voices. I wasn't that far from the center of the compound, so I had to be careful not to make a sound. But as I got closer to the metal grate, I realized no one would have heard.

Outside was chaos, as far as I could tell. Everyone and their uncle was awake and tearing up the compound. From the light that was filtering in, it wasn't long past sunrise.

A woman with a strange accent was cursing a blue streak, and her voice pierced through the general din. "What do you mean, you incarcerated my son? He is an Alpha Heir, and if you've harmed one hair on his blessed head, I will tear you Southern fuckers apart into pieces so small, you'd have to hire a thousand witches to reassemble your ugly asses."

I was dying to meet this woman. I hoped whoever she was cussing out wasn't higher ranked than her.

She kept going. "So you say he attacked you, Calvin. Well, I say he had a reason to—look at this cesspit you call a pack! Look at these children, starving. I might attack you now on principle."

Holy shit. This woman was dressing down Alpha Callaway. I held my breath, letting each word soak in like rain in the desert. Hoping she didn't start whimpering when he used his Alpha mojo on her. Or set his Enforcers on her for her disrespect.

"And your pathetic Enforcers are out of shape. By the moon, they wouldn't pass a human military physical! You should be ashamed."

Alpha's voice came next, blustering, "Listen here, Margarette, you can't come in here and talk to me like that. Your idiot son jumped me—" A sound of a hand cracking on skin shocked me. Had she *slapped* him?

Oh shit, she was going to be killed. I wanted to run out

to save her, but I held still when I heard an impossibly low, gravelly voice. "You lay one finger on my wife, Calvin, and you won't ever get to use that hand again."

I had no idea what was going on out there, but I was dying of curiosity. I forced myself to breathe slowly. One thing at a time. Staying alive was my priority. Meeting some badass shifter woman would need to come much later.

If I survived this day. And won my next fight.

By midafternoon, I was so thirsty that I was considering licking the walls. Of course, I wouldn't. The water on the ground was stagnant, and the seep was most likely from broken sewer lines. I was just weighing the relative hazards of dehydration versus intestinal illness when I heard something that made my blood go cold.

The sound of a bolt being slowly, meticulously loosened. *Snakeshit.* Someone had found me.

I scrambled as quietly as I could backward in the pipe. If they came down with flashlights, there was no escaping. The other end of the drain ended in a grate right outside the main hall of the compound. There was no way out of that one, either—it was welded shut.

I waited, my heart pounding in my throat, for at least a half hour. Then slowly, I crept back toward the opening. No one had come in, and when I got close enough, I saw the drain cover was still on.

Something glinted in the dim light that filtered in the wire mesh. Water. A bottle of water and two more energy bars.

Someone out there knew where I was. And whoever it was wanted to help me.

I reached out one trembling hand, hoping against hope

it wasn't a trap. Slowly, I grasped the water and the bars, and scuttled back a dozen feet.

And that's when I heard it, a beautiful tenor voice singing in Spanish. Was it the sexy solo wolf, Joaquin? I wasn't sure.

"Thank you," I whispered. The voice stopped, and I backed up another dozen feet and ate and drank in the dark, praying that he hadn't drawn attention to my hiding place.

I didn't hear him again, but for some reason, I had the feeling he was still around as the day passed, watching. Protecting me.

When night fell, that feeling vanished. In the distance, I heard shouts, the sound of fighting, and I knew it was time.

Getting out was easier than getting in since whoever had left the water and snacks had also left the screws half done. It didn't take long before I was at the edge of the compound, staring into the mass of bodies gathered there.

The energy was different tonight. There was a sense of anticipation, like a storm approaching. I supposed one had already arrived—the Conclave itself was such a change, and knowing our Alpha would have to at least pretend to follow basic rules of conduct at the event tonight gave me a small sense of hope.

Hope that I carefully extinguished. Hope had never got me even a stick of gum. Plans, on the other hand, had kept me alive for years.

My plan for the night before had been solid. Tonight's was less so. I just prayed Glen or Brand or someone actually showed up—or one of the Alphas.

Fucking Finnick. This could have all been over if he had done what he'd said and signed me up to fight a no-name wolf. It had been sort of fun to hand him his ass again, though. I'd be sure to tell him that, if I lived long enough to see him.

The fighters for the evening were gathered in the roped-in corral, and they'd shoved their chairs into piles on the side so they could have more room to stretch. I saw Joaquin, Patrick, and the others immediately. I was scanning the group, thinking about the best way to cross unseen to the corral and wondering who I would be fighting tonight, when I saw a wolf I hadn't expected.

Trevor. Of course, he was one of the only Southern fighters to make it into the semi-finals. Maybe the presence of the other wolves would keep him from trying anything.

Maybe Christmas would come early, and I'd get that fifty-pound wheel of cheddar cheese I'd always wanted.

The announcer's voice rose over the crowd, calling out names I didn't know, announcing the first match of the night. I hadn't missed my fight then.

Making sure not to stare into the lit areas and lose my night vision, I prepared to make a break for the corral, when I heard a voice. "Who's that? Show yourself."

Shit.

A Southern Enforcer I'd seen before—although I'd never interacted with him—started striding across the open space between me and the corral. I got ready to sprint, but a familiar voice called out. Luke.

"Enforcer Victor, they've seen a suspicious female in the inner circle!"

The Enforcer motioned to the shadows hiding me. "I saw someone here."

"Go. I'll check on this one," Luke told him. "I have to stay by the fighters—Alpha's orders."

With that, the guard left, and Luke jogged over. "Stand

up and walk casually," he said from the corner of his mouth.

I pinched myself, just in case I was imagining him helping me. Maybe he wasn't. "Walk where? To the cells under the main hall? To the whipping post?"

"Stop talking," he rasped out. "You're fighting third tonight."

"I'm shocked, Luke. I for sure thought you'd turn me in to Alpha Callaway. What if he finds out you helped me?"

His brow furrowed. "He won't." I gave him a friendly punch to the side, and he almost collapsed. "Damnit, Flor!"

I smelled copper on the night air. Blood? "Luke, what's wrong?"

His eyes glittered in the reflected light from the fight ring. "My true mate stabbed me," he said, each word precise. "I get to heal at human speed."

A wave of guilt rolled over me. "I'm... I'm sorry. I didn't know you, um, thought we were mates when I did that." I laid my hand on his arm, feeling that strange shivery feeling move up my arm. "Forgive and forget, etc.?"

One corner of his mouth twitched upward. "If you live through this night, I'll consider it."

His low voice sent shivers up my neck. I wanted more of it, more of his buttery, warm scent to surround me. I found myself closing my eyes, luxuriating in the feeling, until the words he was saying sunk in.

"—you'll be fighting Trevor."

All the good feelings evaporated. "Trevor? What happened to the guys who said they would fight me in human form? The other fighters and I had a plan," I explained. My whisper sounded panicked, because *of fucking course* I was panicking. Trevor's dad had trained him personally, for years. Trevor was a walking piece of shit, but he and his shitstain of a father could fight better than anyone in our pack.

"Our Alpha overrode the scheduled fight. He asked earlier today if there were complaints with the final lineup. You didn't speak up—"

"I was hidin' in a storm drain!"

"The one by the Pack House. Yeah, I figured that's where you'd gone."

"Wait, you knew about that spot?"

I felt fingers, soft on my neck, stroking gently. It felt... glorious. My eyes fluttered shut for an instant. "I know all your hiding spots, Flor. I know you think I didn't protect you—and I *didn't* protect you the way I should have. But I did what I could."

I wanted to feel angry, needed the burn of rage in my veins for this fight. But I couldn't muster the fire when I saw the despair in his eyes. I could speak the truth, though. Whether or not he'd meant well didn't matter.

"What you could do wasn't enough."

20

CATNIP FOR SHIFTERS
FLOR

hat you could do wasn't enough. My harsh words hung in the air between us.

"I know," he acknowledged at last. "I don't expect you to agree to be my mate. I... I wouldn't want you to settle for someone like me. Someone with so little honor."

I rolled my eyes. "Luke, it's true, you may not be much. In a pack like ours, though, you're super fucking honorable. You want me to forgive you? If I live, if I get away from this place, you have to try harder. Not just for me. For the kids who aren't getting enough food. For the other females who get caught by toadfuckers like Trevor and can't get away."

"I will." He let his hand fall from my neck, and I wanted to grab it and set it back on my skin. "And I'll make sure you get through this night, if I have to give my own life to make it so."

I huffed. "I'm not some damsel, Luke. Get me in the ring with Trevor. I'll kick his ass, but then you gotta make sure that Glen or Brand or someone makes a bid. Someone has to bid for me. I..." My voice broke. "I don't know if I can hide again. I've been hunted for so long, I got a feeling my luck's dried up."

"You won't be hunted again." Luke's voice crackled with something—passion, or conviction, or maybe just exhaustion like mine. "I'll make sure you're not. Somehow."

I sighed. *Somehow.* That wasn't a plan. That was just a hope. I took a breath to tell him not to bother with empty promises, but he was gone, and I was under the rope in the corral and swathed in tall, hot, male bodies.

For a moment, I was able to see the humor in it. Pretty much every other female shifter in my pack would give their right boob to be this close to so many males. Of course, they wouldn't have wanted it if it meant they had to fight in the Games.

And I wouldn't have had it any other way, I reminded myself. I didn't want to be a mate to any of these males. I wanted to be their equal. I forced a grin as some of the fighters moved in, hiding me in their circle.

"You made it," Patrick said, his tone conveying relief and surprise.

"You thought I might not? You underestimated how badly I want out of this pisshole." A few of the shifters around me laughed softly.

"*Querida.*" Joaquin stepped directly in front of me, and I fought to keep my expression calm, though my pulse hammered in my throat for some reason. "I wish I could have brought you a proper meal."

"Thanks for the water," I said quietly, ducking my head. "And the song."

He lifted my chin with his hand, and a strange, icy cold wash of sensation flowed through me, like his hand was a cold mountain stream. His dark eyes flashed. "I will sing for you every night, my love."

What. The Fuck. Is happening?

Had I turned into some sort of sex goddess? I wrenched away from his gentle grip and ran my eyes down my body. Disgusting filthy bare feet?

Check.

Boy's clothes, baggy as hell, and dirtier than the storm drain had been?

Check.

Ratty hair that still smelled like a latrine, a creek, a fight, and a sewer?

Check.

Skin covered with the remains of garbage and who knew what else?

Check.

"What the hell is going on here?" I muttered. "How am I suddenly catnip for shifters?"

Patrick leaned in next to me, pulling me away from Joaquin with a look. "You're literally the most badass woman I've ever met, except for my mom." He chewed his lip. "In fact, you're a lot like her. Smaller, though. A lot smellier." I punched him in the arm. "Don't worry, short stuff. I'm not going to declare you as my mate." He gave me a quick hug, braving the stench apparently. "My big brother would probably beat me to it, anyway."

"Big brother? Wait, you *are* Glen's brother then?" I had suspected, with the blond hair and blue eyes.

"Yeah," he said. "And Margarette is my mom. You'll meet her after your fight, and she's already asked me to tell you she's got your back. Don't worry about the politics. Beat the crap out of this douche, and then you're coming home with us."

Right. Trevor. I had to beat him first. I peeked around. Why hadn't he come over to give me a hard time?

Then I realized a few of the other fighters had made that impossible. They were walling him off from my side of the corral. He glared at me through their wide shoulders, his hair glinting with some sort of greasy hair product, it looked like. Or maybe just grease. He kept calling out angry threats, but I just stretched to limber up, trying to ignore him.

Trying to ignore Joaquin's gaze, which felt like an icy hand stroking me, was much harder. I shivered, but I wasn't sure if it was from anticipation of the fight... or other things. I would have sworn I felt him tuck a stray piece of hair behind my ear. *How is he doing that?*

"Cut it out," I muttered without turning my head. He must have heard, since the feeling stopped.

I sort of missed it. *Stupid Flor*, I chided myself. *Stay away from the smoking hot males until you get out of this mess.*

Wait, I meant I'd stay away from the males *forever*. I wasn't planning to mate with any of them. I was going to get out and find my own way in a new pack.

"Florida..." The oily voice that haunted my nightmares intruded on my thoughts. I met Trevor's eyes across the ring. He had on a pair of shorts, a fake smile, and nothing else. "It's time to pay the price. I'm gonna tear you up in there. But I'll leave enough to fuck later."

Then he grunted, like one of the other shifters had punched him.

I ignored them all. The truth was, I was terrified. I'd watched Trevor train from a distance, and seen him in action more than once. He was brutal, efficient, and fast—a worthy heir to his dad's seat as Head Enforcer.

And he fought dirty.

I gritted my teeth. I'd have to find a way to fight dirtier.

The announcer's voice called out for Trevor Blackside,

then for Will L. Rains. I followed him, ignoring the murmurs of encouragement from the shifters around me, ignoring everything except the beat of my heart.

After a few breaths, I slipped into my focused state. Del had made me concentrate and meditate for years. He would pepper me with small missiles—pebbles, sticks, even a few spoons in the kitchen—and browbeat me if I reacted in any way. Once he'd hit me with a stick in my eye.

I closed my eyes, allowing myself the snippet of a memory from when I was twelve.

My right eye watered and stung as I backed away from Del, who was half-laughing at me. "Do I have your attention now, Flor?" He lifted his chin toward the fence, where a split second before, I would have sworn I saw Luke Callaway staring through the wire, watching me fight.

Well, more like watching me sit still and try to dodge the shit my mentor was throwing at me. Luke wasn't there now, though, and Del was in a mood.

I held a hand to my eye, letting go of my own temper. "What the hell, Del? This is stupid. You aren't teaching me to fight. You're teaching me to what, take a beating? I know how to do that—I get beat on almost every day. I need to learn to kick and punch, not to sit still and ignore their shit!"

He gave me the look I despised most, one dripping with disappointment. "Girl, I'm telling you now. Your whole life is gonna be a fight, but most times, you won't be allowed to use your fists or your feet to engage the enemy. If you can find this place, this stillness so that you can think, and learn, and win against your opponent mentally? Dodge the blow before it lands, find the perfect moment to duck so they fall on their own ass instead of handing you yours? You'll be unbeatable, in the fighting ring or out. I promise I'm not wasting your time."

"But when will I learn to fight?"

"*You are learning to fight.*" He shook his head at me. "*You just can't see it yet.*" When I slumped down, he walked over and ruffled my messy hair. "*This is the gift I would have given my own children if the moon had seen fit to give me a mate. This is my legacy, the only way to win every battle you'll fight. I can make you unbeatable, Flor. Just focus.*"

The announcer's voice brought me back to the present. I tucked the memory deep inside and let everything else go as I stepped into the ring.

21

LOSING THE FIGHT

FLOR

Quickly, I scanned the fighting ring. There were no weapons to be found there, not yet. No divots on the surface of the packed ground to trip an unbalanced foot, nothing but emptiness.

And when I looked up, the laser focus of hundreds of shifters was on me.

Shitshitshit.

I dropped my eyes back to the tamped-down earth, ignoring the Alpha on his spray-painted throne, although I could feel his heavy gaze on me. Not just his gaze—his power, hammering into me with physical force. It had been a long time since I felt his Alpha mojo aimed solely at me. I'd almost forgotten how it sapped my strength.

My legs grew weak, as disapproval and rage emanated from that side of the stage, the insistent demand to kneel clawing at my mind. A few of my pack gasped and fell to the ground, catching the edge of it, too. Even Trevor fell to one knee and glanced up at the stage, confused and off-center. I could see the question on his face. Why was I still on my feet, if he couldn't stand? I was unranked. I was nobody, the pack reject. Prey, as far as anyone knew.

But I could stand under the Alpha's power.

That made me smile. Trevor had fighting skills, but his whole shining life had been given to him gift-wrapped. Everything he'd wanted was his to take, with the approval of the other ranked wolves. I'd had to claw my way just to survive, and I'd never relied on the Alpha's approval to stand on my own. I sure as fuck wasn't going to kneel to him, or anyone, now.

I sent a mental thank you to Del. The focus he'd taught me from the time I was six kept my mind clear of outside influences, even my own Alpha's.

The oppressive power lessened, and the announcer cleared his throat and began speaking, asking what form we would take. Trevor had the choice since he was ranked, and he shouted, "Wolf form!"

The crowd grumbled. They all knew I hadn't shifted yet. They could see it in the fading scars I wore on my arms, could smell it in me. Hell, I probably looked like I was twelve; I'd been starved for so long, I really didn't measure up.

Near the Alpha, the woman's voice I'd heard before protested. "This is the sort of match your pack finds acceptable? A child, a girl, fighting a shifted wolf? This isn't a game; this is a punishment."

"She deserves it," Alpha Callaway growled back. "She killed one of our own."

There was an outcry near the Alphas. I refused to look, taking one calm breath, then another. But the announcer asked me a question. "You have never shifted?"

I shook my head.

He exhaled heavily. "This sort of match, an uneven

fight, has only occurred once before, sixteen years ago." His face was stone still, revealing nothing. "The immature shifter was killed. In order to keep such an event from recurring, a new rule was put in place. You are allowed a weapon."

I heard my Alpha yell, "New rule? What the hell's he goin' on about?"

I let his words wash over me like a rush of hot wind. My heart was swelling, bubbling, and I fought the surge of giddiness. I had a chance. "What kind of weapon?"

The announcer's eyes went dark. "It must be something you have trained with as part of your pack duties or schooling. No guns, no explosives. Your pack must provide it. You cannot leave the ring or you forfeit."

Aw, hell. I let out a calm, slow breath. "Does anyone in my pack offer a weapon?"

No one answered. I shrugged at the announcer. "Unranked shifters in Southern aren't allowed weapons anyway. Or formal training."

The announcer's eyes widened in shock. "You've never had any formal training?" Where was this guy from again? I shook my head. "The way you fight made me think... You're a wonder, girl."

"Thank you," I said, bowing. The announcer bowed back to me, lower than he should have, considering my lack of rank.

The crowd was growing restless. Someone with a Southern accent shouted, "Murderer!"

Another voice called, "Liar!"

But then Luke sauntered up the edge of the ring, holding something. "She's not lying. She spent all her time in the kitchen. Her only training was in cleaning and cooking." For some reason, his voice didn't sound mocking when he said that.

The wolves in the crowd from the other packs let out disbelieving sounds.

"I swear it on the moon. She has never taken a single lesson in fighting from any ranked wolf in this pack. This is the only tool she was allowed."

The visitors in the crowd roared with shock, disbelief, and anger. I almost smiled. They'd seen me fight. And now they knew I'd done that without any formal training. Even if I died today, I had made my mark on the greater pack. Maybe one of the other Alphas would hear this and see what they were doing down here. Maybe someone would help the other girls like me who needed to learn how to defend themselves, but didn't have a Del to make it happen.

Luke threw the thing in his hand into the ring. I leaped forward, catching it, grinning as I did.

It was a mop.

"Is this true?" The announcer sounded flabbergasted. "You had no training in weapons, but you had pack duties that required training in the... mop?"

"Yep," I answered, sort of loving the disbelieving look that flickered over his impassive face. "I have years of experience with this baby."

"I will allow it," he conceded. Then he backed up, announcing the beginning of the fight.

Trevor had already stripped off his shorts and was almost fully transformed into his monstrously large wolf form. Quickly, I rotated the mop head off the sturdy wooden handle. The cloth could be bitten or torn from me too easily, and all I needed was a staff. I chucked the head into the crowd and settled low into my fighting stance, holding onto the calm that came with each breath.

Trevor ran at me like a flash of dark lightning. His wolf was black and gray, mottled. His coloration made his bunching muscles difficult to see in the flickering lights, harder to gauge his next move.

If he was smart, he would feint, use a series of attacks to wear me down. I was exhausted already, and while he might have some respect for my fighting skills after last night's bout with Finnick, anyone could see I didn't have the reserves for an extended fight.

Trevor was a lot of things. A bully, a would-be rapist, an entitled cockmuffin with a tiny dick—I'd had the misfortune of seeing it more than once when he shifted. He was a decent fighter.

But he sure as hell wasn't smart.

He came at me, enraged, in a full-on frontal charge. Like water flowing around him, I moved to the side, letting the end of the mop swing around in a sharp arc to connect with his back leg.

The sound of the bone breaking filled me with a deep satisfaction. I hadn't even put much effort into it; his own speed had injured him. Growling furiously, he turned and ran at me again. Seeing his limp, I almost let my meditative state slip.

He was a three-legged wolf now. The only type of shifted wolf I'd ever fought before. I knew exactly how to bring him down, the way I'd done to Del in practice. I spun the mop around in an unpredictable pattern, forcing Trevor's eyes away from me and to the metal end, as he tried to avoid my weapon until his back leg could heal. I darted in, dropping low, and swung it again, hitting the leg I'd broken again, close to the same spot.

I was a little slow, and he ran a claw over my arm as I slid back out and away. Blood dripped down my arm, and something was happening in the crowd—some sort of ruckus near the Alphas—but I shook it away like a horsefly.

His leg wouldn't heal now, couldn't. The bone had pierced the flesh, and unless he set the bone and shifted, it would stay broken.

Or worse for him, it would start to heal with the bone protruding.

I could end this faster than I'd thought. I settled back into my stance as Trevor circled, limping on three legs, fury shining in his eyes. I tried a few more attacks, but he hopped away in time. If only I could get my staff to contact his nose—the one I'd broken a few days before. It would still be damaged internally, most likely. Easy to break again. Normally, a broken nose was nothing, but if I could hit it hard enough, maybe send some bone fragments deep into his skull, it could take months to heal. I could really get my revenge and laugh while I did it.

Plan made.

I moved my hands on the wood, changing my grip as Del had always told me to do before a strike. "It's a wakeup call to your tired muscles," he'd told me a thousand times. "It tells your body something important is about to happen. Makes it use slightly different muscles and tendons, too, so if you're injured, it's an edge."

The blood from my arm was making my grip on the mop slippery, and I fought to maintain the new hold. Trevor ran around my side, then darted in, reaching out not with his jaws to bite, but a claw again.

And hit the injured spot on my upper arm. I screamed out loud, the fire from his hit racing through my body. He'd damaged something inside my arm. A long, deep cut that might have nicked an artery, judging by the blood that was pouring down my forearm, maybe sliced through tendons as well. I had no grip.

I held tight to the mop handle with my other hand, refusing to look at the wound that was making me slightly dizzy from pain and blood loss. I had to end this *now*.

But I couldn't find a move, any move, to make it happen.

"Yield," some spectators were urging.

The announcer nodded. "Yield," he muttered.

Trevor was moving in and out of range, wearing me down now as he should have in the beginning. Waiting as I bled out on the fighting grounds.

The best I could do now was die with honor. Force him to kill me.

Between a clean death in the ring, and a long torturous one at the hands of my Alpha, I knew which one I would take.

"Come on, Trevor," I hissed. I needed to enrage him to the point where he would break the rules. Where he wouldn't demand I yield, but would deliver a killing strike. "You know why?" I panted. "Why I never let you catch me in the Hunt?" I let out a laugh. "I saw your tiny little dick... so many times. And I knew." I dodged a clumsy swipe of his paw. He was making guttural sounds in his throat that I'd never heard a wolf make. "I knew... I wasn't a good enough actress... to pretend I could feel that little puppy dog's tail... if I let you touch me."

He let out a crazed howl and rushed me, no style, all killing rage. I dropped the mop and stretched my neck out. I fought to keep my hands from flying up, to keep from defending myself. I had to let him kill me.

It was the only way.

I felt his teeth tear into my scalp, one scraping alongside my neck, but not finding the artery. For a second, a strange giggle wanted to burst out. Did I have to draw him a map? Then I felt his jaws closing, crushing my skull.

Okay, I wouldn't bleed out. He'd tear my head off. That worked, too.

I lost consciousness, wishing I'd been able to kick Trevor's ass. It would have been cool to see Ontario. To meet that woman.

To have a first kiss with one of the guys. Okay, maybe more than one of them.

But as I slipped into the darkness, I knew it was too late now.

22

CHALLENGING THE ALPHA
LUKE

Rage and shock coursing through me, I retook my position by my father's side at the platform by the fighting ring, like a good little Enforcer. He lounged in the gold-painted chair, while the Alphas of the other packs stood on each side of us.

As soon as I was close enough, he snapped out a question, thick with Alpha command. "What the hell did you do, son? Get over here." I shuffled closer, feeling the eyes of the other Alphas on us.

The crowd's buzz rose in pitch as my mate unscrewed the mop head and threw it into the throng. The announcer was speaking to Flor, bowing to her, and I marveled at her poise. Her outward calm.

I fought to hold onto my own as my Alpha gestured for me to kneel at his side, and gripped the side of my neck with one hand. The skin broke under his lengthening nails, blood flowing freely from the deep punctures in my throat, and I swallowed hard. If he squeezed a little harder, dug those nails just a bit to the side, he'd hit my carotid. With my existing injury already weakening me, I wasn't sure my wolf's healing could ensure I'd survive an arterial puncture.

"You gave her a weapon, boy?"

I forced a sneer. "A mop isn't a weapon, it's an insult. The other packs needed to hear she's nothing. A pack reject, not some secret warrior." I tried not to flinch at the low growls from the other visiting shifters who heard me.

"You need a lesson in leadership," he snarled, but let go of my neck.

"Yes, Alpha." I kept my gaze lowered as I stood, but his expression promised a world of pain as soon as we were alone.

Glen's mother Margarette stood next to her mate Bradley, who was the Head of the North American Council. Bradley frowned at me, but Margarette's deep blue eyes were filled with compassion. I'd stayed at Northern years ago for a few days, and for that short time, she'd made me feel like I had a mother again. Until I'd been driven to return home, to Southern.

To Flor.

Margarette opened her mouth now to speak to me, but I shook my head slightly.

Not an hour before, I'd slipped Glen evidence of my father's crimes, hoping he would give it to his parents. Not just indications of financial mismanagement, which would only merit an investigation, but a new scrap of evidence I'd found earlier that week that pointed to worse. It was proof of one of the most hideous crimes one of our kind could commit. A death sentence for any shifter, Alpha or not.

To my surprise, Glen had slipped me a torn page from a recent Northern American Combined Pack Law book that spelled out the recent loophole to provide Flor her makeshift weapon. I'd studied pack law, but we didn't have the most recent editions in our Pack House library.

"That young woman could kill a grizzly bear with a mop," Glen had suggested, snarling when I demanded an explanation. "I'll leave one near the ring. You need to get it to her."

Everything was balanced on a knife's edge now, my wolf raging louder than it ever had. The crowd howled and gasped and jeered at my mate as she defended herself. It was all I could do not to run into the ring, and proclaim to all the assembled packs that she was mine, my mate. I didn't care about my pain. All I cared about was her. Flor, the woman who was holding her own against one of the strongest and most corrupt shifters in our pack.

She was so small, so thin. A miracle.

I was powerless to truly help her, as I had always been, even with shifters here for once who might be allies. If Margarette read what I passed on, though—if she put it together, shared it with the other Council members... it could save us all.

Save *her*.

The night before, I'd run by the storm drain I knew she was in, to make sure her scent wasn't detectable to any other shifters. I could always scent her, even when no one else could. I'd assumed she'd try to stay close enough to hear when the fights were starting. She hadn't used that spot often enough for her scent to gather at the entrance, and it was by far the most secure.

She would never know how often I'd scented her and diverted the other males away from her hiding places. How often I'd come up with stupid tasks for the unmated males to complete far away from the compound, to keep her safe.

Even before she was declared the prey in the pack's

Hunt, I'd done everything I could to keep her safe. It had worked, mostly. I'd even been able to throw the other Enforcers off her trail for those first few weeks after the announcement.

Of course, most of her success was her own. I found myself smiling as she used the mop to break Trevor's leg in the ring a second time. A compound fracture, one he couldn't heal without help. Only the sound of my Alpha and his Head Enforcers cursing hid my cackle of laughter.

Good girl. Don't let up.

She was so much faster and sneakier than any other shifter. Stronger, in the way that mattered in the long run. She might be small and underfed—how often had I left meat on my plate when I was still hungry, knowing she would get it when the meal was over?—but she was tougher than a shifter had any right to be. Harder.

Trevor was the only one besides the Alpha that she truly feared. I had smelled the acrid stench of terror on her earlier, and wanted to tell her she had nothing to worry about.

But she'd been cornered by the fucker years before, when I was away leading the younger male shifters on their first pack deer hunt, and that day had broken her.

I'd redoubled my efforts to protect her. But even if she knew, she would never forgive me. I was to blame for her mother's death—one of *them*, in her mind. I'd parroted the Southern leadership's laws and rules, even when I suspected they weren't being followed by the ones who ruled.

And while I'd spun my wheels trying to find a lawful way out for both of us, she'd suffered in ways I couldn't prevent, and had never anticipated. I remembered the empty room in the dorms, the bare shelves, and pressed my hand to the stapled wound she'd given me. I deserved her hatred. I'd failed my mate so many times.

The air filled with the scent of her blood as Trevor managed to claw her arm, pulling a piercing scream from her throat.

"Yield!" voices from the crowd urged.

Next to me, Margarette muttered, "This is atrocious, Callaway. She could be killed."

Killed. My blood went ice cold. If she died...

"Fuck this," I growled and tried to step forward, but Bradley's hand on my arm stopped me.

Not yet, he mouthed. He let go when I nodded, understanding. He knew. They knew, and were going to move.

Relief mingled with terror, and I swayed on my feet, wondering if I might pass out. I hadn't eaten a real meal since Flor had stabbed me, and I hadn't healed. If I'd been allowed to shift, maybe I could have. But Van and Dad... No. Not Dad. I wouldn't call him that ever again.

The terrible knowledge I'd gained—that he'd murdered the uncle who had taken me in after my own parents died in a pack boundary dispute, then stolen me—blazed like a wildfire in my heart as my wolf tried to convince me to rip out his throat.

It would mean my death. The Alpha and his other Enforcers were allowed to shift weekly, and that had made them grow stronger over the years. I'd been forbidden to shift for so long now that some of the unranked wolves in the visiting packs were probably just as strong.

The one I loved surely was.

Only a dozen yards away, my fierce, perfect mate insulted Trevor Blackside in the ring. Then she spun and struck at him, fearless and faster than any unranked shifter should ever be. I forced myself not to react when she took a hit, and tried to hide my fierce smiles when she landed punishing blows on him.

But then the battle turned. Flor was tiring. Worse, she was bleeding heavily, her arm sliced open. But instead of backing away, she taunted the asshole who was healing quickly. Trevor was going to charge, and she changed her grip on the mop handle I'd given her. The visiting shifters standing nearby cursed softly, and I felt their eyes move to my father.

He would never help her.

The crowd roared, and I shifted my gaze to the ring, just in time to watch my little fighter drop her weapon and stretch out her neck, as if she wanted to give Trevor a better angle.

He took it, clamping his jaws over her head, his teeth gouging into her neck and shoulder. It would have been a mortal wound for any shifter, and she had no power to change forms and save herself. I felt my teeth begin to lengthen, my hands prickling as the small bones began to move, even under strict Alpha command not to shift.

"Don't you dare, boy," the Alpha muttered, and I felt his power stop my shift. "Don't you move." I was frozen, though my beast began to tear at the invisible bars that trapped us.

I heard howls from all around me. The other Alpha Heirs shifted spontaneously and raced into the ring, savaging Trevor. The announcer yelled for quiet, but the crowd was turning into a riot.

I needed to run to her, but couldn't move. Only one man could save her now.

"*Quiet,*" our Alpha's voice boomed over the crowd. "Be still!"

All of the Southern pack instantly quieted. The visiting

wolves didn't; they were still outraged, shouting and kicking their way through to the ring. The fighters in the corral were already pouring in, pulling Trevor away, forcing him down.

"Be still!" the Alpha yelled again, and the visiting wolves looked up at him, expressions ranging from shock to revulsion.

The announcer called back, "The wolf Trevor did not ask her to yield before delivering what would be a mortal blow. He has broken the first rule of the Games and forfeits the match. The winner is Will. L Rains."

"There is no such wolf," Callaway said, a smile curling over his face. "The wolf there is a wanted murderer named Flor Wills." The crowd noise swelled again as I felt the bonds that held me still begin to fray.

"Has there been a trial?" Margarette called. "The Council would see proof this child committed the crime."

"Nah," he snickered. "I'm sure we would have gotten around to it. But apparently, the moon's judgment is already upon her."

"Callaway," Bradley broke in, stepping up to his side. "She's not dead. Compel her first shift so she can heal, and then we can have a trial. It's proper protocol. As a member of the Council, you know that."

"Hmm." The Alpha faked a concerned expression. "As a Council member, you should know that the decision when to compel a pack member's first shift is the sacred duty of one Alpha alone. She is Southern—she is mine to discipline, mine in every way that matters. And I have decided... not to force her to shift."

His Head Enforcer let out a grunt of agreement. "Not much of a loss to Southern. Let her bleed."

A snarl escaped my lips, but the sound was lost in the

cries of shock and outrage as Alpha Callaway stepped up to the edge of the ring. The near-feral wolves there turned to face him, forming a circle around the girl.

It wasn't just Brand and Finnick and Glen who had shifted and surrounded her now. Another wolf, a smaller black one, also guarded her fallen form, and quite a few of the other fighters, including Patrick, looked close to shifting. The other shifters on the Council stepped forward to join Bradley and Margarette in the ring.

The Mountain Pack's Alpha—Brand's father, Samuel—rumbled a question. "You mean to say..." Every shifter around him quieted. Samuel almost never spoke. There had been a rumor he'd stayed in wolf form too long when his true mate had died, and he'd forgotten how. "You will let this child die, rather than seek justice?"

Alpha smiled, like he was delighted with the thought. "Yes. It's my pack, my choice. No one can claim her."

"I can," an accented voice called, and the small black wolf—who'd just shifted back to human form faster than anyone I'd ever seen—stepped toward the Southern Alpha. He was stronger than I'd thought, lean and muscled like a professional fighter. "I am known as Joaquin Villalobos, an Alpha from the Borderlands, and I claim her as my true mate." His voice rang with truth.

Two questions raced through my mind: *True mate?* and *The Borderlands has a new Alpha?* Shock rippled through the crowd, while a zip of fear ran through me. I knew the stranger wasn't her true mate. But *he* definitely believed it.

There were a few shifters from the smaller packs at the Conclave, who had been invited to join us in hopes of finding true mate bonds. But an Alpha from the Central American Pack, who hadn't gained permission from the Council to attend?

At best, it was a diplomatic misstep. Something wasn't right, though I couldn't hear the lie in what he'd said. I heard a few mutters about rogues and contested claims.

"You haven't been recognized as Alpha, boy," Callaway called around a toothy smile. "And only an Alpha or Alpha Heir's mate claim supersedes her own Alpha's edict... so, tough luck. Hell, she wouldn't survive the mating, and you'd probably die with her. I'm doing you a favor; she'll be dead very soon. You can try for another mate someday."

The Alpha command was loosening, and I stepped toward him, blinded by anger. But Van Blackside clicked his tongue and sidled between us.

The stranger lunged forward as well, as if he would fly across the intervening space and tear out Alpha Callaway's throat, but Patrick caught him and whispered something in his ear. The crowd began muttering, moving. Preparing for something? Perhaps a riot.

The other Heirs howled and threw themselves into their transformations faster than was safe. Brand shifted first and shouted, "The hell she'll die. I claim her as my true mate."

His tone thrummed with honesty, and I swallowed. *How?*

Not a second later, Glen joined in. "I claim her!" To my relief, he didn't say she was his true mate... but his eyes blazed with rage and desire.

"What?" The Southern Alpha whistled loud and long. I could tell he was reveling in the attention and power, even though the others were shaming him. "All y'all are her true mates? Maybe nobody ever explained how true mates work."

"We know how they work, Alpha," Margarette purred,

stalking toward him. "How they're supposed to work. Give her to my pack. We'll take her off your hands."

Bradley let out a growl when my Alpha sneered openly at her and drawled, "Wish I could, dear lady. But she killed a dear friend of mine—and yours, if I remember correctly. Del Talbot. Tore his throat out right there in the yard behind the dining hall. It was brutal, bloody."

We all heard the lie. A few shifters named it out loud, calling, "Liar!" and "She didn't!"

"Tore out his throat? But she's never shifted," Margarette replied, her smile a weapon. "How could she do such a thing?"

The Alpha purpled with bluster and rage at getting caught in the lie. "She mighta used a knife."

"A knife?" Finnick glided up to join Margarette. "You mean you can't tell the difference between the marks left by a wolf's teeth and a steel blade?"

The Southern wolves nearby shifted nervously.

Bradley wrapped an arm around Margarette. Not because he was supporting her, I realized. But because she looked like she was about to rip my Alpha's throat out. "If you're lying about a crime, Alpha Callaway, you'll be the one facing a Council investigation."

He laughed nervously. "What, Brad, you want her too?"

Bradley recoiled, and Margarette growled, her features shifting slightly. "Watch it."

"If I'd known one of my pack members had a magic pussy, I'd have capitalized on that a long while back." Callaway scratched his chin. "I'm so sorry, but now there are multiple competing mating claims. And I'm being accused of fabricating evidence, or some such. We'll need to take this to a formal meeting. Let's set that up for... tomorrow morning sound good?"

He let out a dark laugh as Margarette cursed him in French.

In the circle of fighters, Flor's breathing slowed. Something began to tear inside my chest. As I clutched at my heart, I saw Finnick, Glen, Brand, and finally Joaquin, stumble and drop to their knees.

"She's *dying*." Margarette's voice was shrill. "She needs to shift!"

The Southern Alpha grinned. "Too bad. I'm not doing it, and it won't take if any of you try." He turned to the crowd. "Everybody get on home. The show's over."

A small group of Southern Enforcers, Trevor's friends, darted through the crowd, hauling him out of the ring and off to somewhere else. My wolf wanted to chase him down and finish the job Flor had started, but saving her life came first.

The Alpha turned to leave, taking a few steps across the ring as he moved toward the Pack House. It couldn't end like this. With Callaway and Trevor walking away, and Flor dying.

But the fucker knew his pack law. He was right. The only way Flor would live long enough to see a Council meeting and resolve the claims was if the Southern Alpha died.

There was only one way to challenge him. If a ranked member of Southern and the Alpha were both standing in the fighting ring, and the challenge was made formally in front of a quorum of Council members.

No one had challenged for Alpha in decades, and the last night of the Conclave was the traditional place for such a thing. It wasn't the final night, but all the other parts were there.

I raced behind him and spoke before his foot cleared the

ropes to exit the ring. "I challenge you, Alpha Callaway, for leadership of the Southern pack."

He actually stumbled, then turned slowly. "Boy?" His voice was soft and sharp as a whip. "You stupid fuck." I'd felt his whips and belts on me for years, but his voice now cut just as deep, fueled by his power. "Don't do this, fool," he ground out. "I will kill you."

"I know. But I'll take you with me." I raised my voice so the shifters around would hear. "If you die with me, the Interim Alpha is Bradley Hillier, Head of Council. He'll be able to force her shift then, won't you, Alpha Bradley?"

"Yes, son, I will."

I heard Glen whisper, "I never knew Luke was that brave."

Finnick answered. "I did."

My heart beat a little slower, knowing there was one wolf here who thought I was worth something.

Callaway stared at me, like he'd never seen me before. "What's your game, son? You're not doing this for that girl? You're throwing everything away."

"You've been stealing from our pack for *years*, Alpha," I shouted, so that every wolf there could hear me, even the unranked in the back. "We made four hundred thousand dollars in profit last year in the stock market, and almost as much the year before. You told the pack we had a loss, and that's why there wasn't money for food or medicine. But really, you spent almost half of that gambling in Atlantic City, right? Yeah, I saw *those* receipts, too."

The Southern shifters were all listening now, even the Enforcers. Van looked unsurprised, but some of the others looked pissed. Their houses weren't as nice as the Enforcers in the other packs; they'd seen that at past Conclaves.

"Do your Enforcers even know?" I called, hoping to

insert a little more doubt in there. "You spent the money the Council sent us for battle training, not on trips to make pack connections, but on prostitutes and vacations. Unless by pack connections, you mean sexual hookups with fourteen-year-old Russian shifters."

Now even Van looked irritated. That money had been earmarked for Head Enforcers to distribute.

"Shut up, boy." Callaway stripped off his shirt and pants, and I realized it was the first time I'd seen him without clothes in over a year. He was as broad and burly as ever. But his muscle tone was weaker than it should be, and he had a small spare tire around his gut.

The shifters around us laughed out loud when they saw it. Someone called out, "I think he's been spending your pack's money on Twinkies."

The Southern ranked shifters were enraged. The visitors acted like it was funny, but I could see them reaching for their weapons, casually unsnapping pockets where they must have stashed knives, even though the Conclave accords required visitors to leave all but one small weapon at home.

Our Enforcers sensed the change in the crowd, and their hands settled on the hilts of their own daggers.

Callaway began his shift, and I did too, fighting through the pain. The staples flew out as my abdomen curled and slimmed, and my wounds tore open. The best thing about shifting was it sped up healing—not that much for me, though. I sighed, knowing I'd earned my wound... and my death.

I hadn't been allowed to shift for so long, the change hurt more than it should, and took more out of me. I let my wolf feel the muggy breeze move through his fur, let him sniff the air that held her scent, and the harsh iron tang of her blood.

Mate, he whined in my mind.

Yes, I answered. *Mate.*

I felt a sudden rush of strength from my beast. I just hoped we were strong enough to kill the Alpha for her so she could live.

We had to be.

The last moment of the shift settled into my bones. And then, we were at war.

23

THE SHADOW THAT KILLS
JOAQUIN

A battle raged in the fighting ring, Alpha Heir against Alpha.

A more dangerous battle raged inside my chest, the magic I carried burning to be released, to protect my mate. If I didn't control it, there was the chance it could kill every single shifter gathered here, and would kill indiscriminately. There were many here who did not deserve death.

Though many deserved more than death, and I itched to deliver it to them slowly, painfully. I pushed the urge to kill to the back of my mind. I had other work to do, and I could sense time had almost run out.

I slipped to the back of the crowd, my slight stature helping me to avoid notice. When I'd first found my wolf form, I'd regretted my size, so much smaller than others when I shifted. Even in my human form, I was nowhere near the size of shifter males, though I was taller than many females. Taller than my Flor, though her spirit towered over every other shifter I'd met.

She lay beside the ring, crumpled and motionless,

though I couldn't let myself look at her, or my control would break. She was so thin, starved. Old and new scars marked her skin, though I knew they should all vanish at her first shift. Flor was a marvel. Strong, fast, and fierce, with a deep well of honor and kindness, but so close to death. She might even die while the Heir fought for her.

The darkness inside me roiled, roaring a soundless *no*. She had to live, or I would set my own magic ablaze and take the entire rotten Meridion pack with it.

Not Meridion. Southern. I reminded myself that the packs on this continent were no longer called by their original names, the ones I'd first seen written on my father's hand-drawn maps hundreds of years before. Meridion, Oriens, Boreal, Occidens, Centralis... I'd repeated the names of the places that had seemed distant and exotic over and over as a child. What a disappointment to visit Meridion, once a great pack, and find *Southern* in its place.

I'd changed my name as well, of course, long before I traveled to this Conclave. I'd been drawn from my home far away to this continent years before, but not known where I would find what I sought. Who I sought. I'd spent two decades looking for her, not finding any trace.

Had I known she had been here all along, suffering... I stifled the rage that threatened, and I glanced back at the ring once more, at Flor.

While the corrupt Alpha and the others had spoken, I'd slipped through the wall of protectors and made sure Flor's wounds were bound tightly. I'd tried to send a small trickle of magic into her, but encountered a strange resistance, my power only connecting to a small part of her spirit. It had helped, but her blood still flowed too freely.

Those bandages were now blood-soaked, and my little mate was growing weaker.

My mind spun with possibilities. I couldn't unleash my magic, bite her against pack law, heal her, and reveal myself. Not unless all was truly lost. Some among the Council would surely recognize my power and try to kill me. Others would do worse, especially if they knew how I was connected to Flor. I glanced at the Eastern Alpha, one of the most corrupt. He wasn't the strongest here, but his spirit was the most twisted. I couldn't risk him discovering my presence and hurting my little mate.

My little mate was strong; she would survive these wounds. There was a greater danger to her I needed to address.

I used the small magic my mother had taught me when I was a child in St. Petersburg to stay unnoticed as I slipped away. While they watched the fight, I moved unseen through the crowd, doing insignificant things. I spun hobbles of magic thread around the knees of the Southern Enforcers. I slipped blade after blade out of their scabbards and pockets, even some guns, tossing them into the storm drains and ditches nearby. No one heard the splashes of the weapons hitting the water.

No one paid any attention as I disarmed the Southern shifters, spinning minor illusions so they would still feel their weapons nearby. Small confusions, my mother had told me. She had made a game of it for me, a child's amusement. Take the object, leave the false memory of forgetting their weapons at home, in the dining hall, elsewhere.

The largest Southern Enforcer was too alert and guarded for me to approach without his notice, his mind too strong, but the others were soft and weak, especially the younger ones. They would have been cast out of my father's pack, fed to the new moon as sacrifice. They weren't warriors; they were meat.

My little queen, though, was a warrior. A goddess. Even with her short hair and her camouflaged scent, I had recognized what she was.

A thorn bush, pricking the unwary and unworthy.

A sharp blade, tempered in the fires of agony and despair, shining in the darkness. Ready to be used to remove the rot from our world.

Why the Moon Goddess had seen fit to gift Her little shadow with so many mates was a mystery. Maybe she had a need for more protectors. Maybe she had a need for more love.

There was something intrinsically magical about her, that reminded me of the sacred places near my childhood home. A deep stillness, like she knew how to go to the well of the moon and harvest its power.

I had watched her do it, in her battle with the coward wolf. Watched her sink into that space, slowing time. Did she even know she was using magic? Who had taught her that? The shifters on this continent had done all they could to stamp out any magic that didn't come from their own wolves.

Movement in the darkness alerted me to the presence of a group of shifters. Southern, from the smell. They did not bathe often enough and revealed themselves by their stench, as well as their clumsy footsteps.

A few dozen were sneaking away, shadows moving along the ground to the west of the ring. To the armory? Yes.

Of course, they were planning to attack their guests. The rumors had been widespread in the Borderlands, where I had spent the past few years. Southern was weak and could never overcome the others in a fair fight. But if they gutted the heart of the Council and worked with the dark witches as I had heard they did... then, yes, they could make a hole wide enough in the combined North American pack's fabric to tear a larger chunk free for their own greed.

Hidden by the shadows of tall trees, I followed the noisy footsteps to the armory door. I'd found this place earlier and picked the lock to see what they had for defense. The blades were decent, although I had a feeling the current Head Enforcer hadn't been the one to purchase them. They were fine old weapons, but left to rust, not taken care of for at least a few years.

When all but one of the Southerners had disappeared inside to collect their weapons, I slipped behind the guard and slid a blade into his neck. With a thrust and three twists of the blade, my other hand firmly over his mouth, he was dead, his head falling with a quiet *thunk* to the earth below.

"Thank you for your life," I whispered, spooling his glowing energy onto my knife. "I accept the gift on behalf of my queen."

The smell of blood would alert the others, so I made quick work of the door handles, using the dead man's blood to mark a rune that would erect a wall of silence around the place, then another rune to lock the exits.

Mother had warned me not to use blood magic often. It unbalanced the spirit of one's wolf. But I felt my wolf and I were aligned in our purpose tonight. We both knew that even if Flor survived long enough to shift and join a new pack, these cowards were already under orders to kill all outsiders. They would have taken her life at the order of their deranged Alpha.

Deranged. I had been called that many times. Insane, unstable. I didn't understand. I had only ever killed those who needed to be removed from the world to keep the balance of light and darkness.

Was it my fault there were so very many who needed killing?

I had doubted myself, at times. When I had taken more pleasure in the slaughter than my mother would have approved. When I had made beautiful sculptures of the bones of the fallen, lapped up their spilled blood after I followed the Moon Mother's call to do Her justice.

But now I knew. If I was broken, it was for *her* good. My Flor, my brilliant, sparkling mate. She was light and fire and all that was good in a weeping world. For her, I would be the darkness.

I would be the shadow that killed without hesitation.

24

FIGHTING FOR HER
LUKE

The flickering lanterns that surrounded the training ring added their light to the full moon, throwing shadows across the dusty ground as I fought for my life.

And for hers.

My little mate lay unconscious at the side of the ring, though the scent of her blood was thick on the air. Blood and dust, fear and rage, and the faintest hint of jasmine and cinnamon swirled around me, distracting me at inopportune moments as I battled the Alpha who'd tortured me for years.

He was enormous, his wolf form oversized from years of shifting regularly and eating bigger and better meals than anyone else in the pack. My own wolf was weak and slow, and the only thing that kept me from getting my throat torn out in the first few seconds of the fight was my father's overconfidence. Well, that and his complete lack of respect for me and my wolf.

He sent waves of his Alpha dominance toward me, trying to force me to submit to him. Instead, I backed away, head low, ears back. In my human form, I was nowhere near capable of standing against him. He'd made sure of that by preventing me from training with the other Enforcers long enough, by forbidding me to shift for longer and longer periods.

He lunged again, at my flank, and I leaped up, avoiding his teeth at the last moment, weariness setting in as he continued his efforts to drown me under his dominance. The staples that had held my wound closed had torn free when I shifted, and I was bleeding sluggishly from the wound Flor had given me.

My vicious, phenomenal mate. All that kept me from faltering was her presence and the knowledge that if I failed, she would die.

She had no friends in this pack, but the shifters from the other packs were protecting her, shielding her from the Southerners who would take advantage of her weakness. I had no real friends either, in or out of the pack. The unranked wolves didn't trust me, of course. The ranked ones didn't respect me.

The worst of those, Van Blackside, yelled from the side of the ring, "You can't beat your father, boy. Give up now."

I snarled, dodging another blow. Father? My wolf had never seen Callaway as a father. He'd killed my uncle, and for all I knew, he'd killed my parents as well. I growled at the thought, as Callaway darted in, jaws wide. I met his attack, my teeth tearing skin on his muzzle, though his did far more damage to mine before we both withdrew.

Blood splattered the dirt below us, and I noted with some satisfaction that he was tiring as well. He came at me again and again, and I met his attacks with more speed, more brutal counters. Was I winning?

Van shouted from the ringside, "You stupid little fuck. Just die already!" and a memory was unleashed.

Except for the Alpha, the entire pack had gathered for the full moon run, all the mature shifters standing in the center of the clearing still in their human forms, and the younger ones—though there weren't many of us—off to one side, with a few Enforcers close by to keep us in line. It wasn't necessary. The young shifters knew to stay still, stay quiet, and stay low when the rest of the wolves were getting ready to run.

But the moon was already high, and the pack was growing restless since the Alpha hadn't arrived to start the run. We all knew where he was and what he was doing. We could hear the grunts and moans, and smell the odors of sex filtering through the screened windows of the Pack House. Farther off, we could hear the muted screams of another woman.

We all ignored those, except for one of the youngest of us.

"Mama!" The little girl, Flor, was no more than a toddler, skinny legs and arms attached to a belly, and ratty red hair tangled around a dirty, blackberry-stained face. "Mama hurt!"

She was right. It was her mama screaming. I wanted to go to her, pick her up and comfort her. But as the Alpha Heir, I had to stand with the other children of ranked wolves, waiting at attention until the run began, no matter what.

"Mama!" The toddler broke free of the teenager who'd been holding her arm, and flung herself across the ring, just as Van Blackside stepped backward. She collided with the back of his legs, and he tripped, falling over his own legs and over her. Someone in the crowd laughed.

Flor squealed and tried to get away, but he grabbed her by the arm and was shaking her so hard, her head flopped back and forth. "You stupid little fuck! You'll pay for that."

I was too far away to stop what came next, though I called out, "No!" as Van took off his belt and began beating the toddler, his arm rising and falling again and again. I stepped out of line, and suddenly, the mature Enforcers on both sides of me had my arms in unbreakable holds, while I struggled.

"Not worth it, Luke," one of them grunted when I kicked his shin. "He'll kill you. Your dad ain't here to stop him."

Flor was screaming louder than the far-away woman now, though, and her cries pierced my heart as the belt fell faster and faster, Van's eyes lit up with an unholy glee.

No one stepped in. No one could stand against him. But every blow that fell on the little girl felt like it was piercing my heart. She struggled to crawl away, but Blackside kept beating her.

"Stop," I croaked. "Stop hurting her!"

Van's lip curled up, and he adjusted his grip on the belt, letting the metal buckle hit her back, breaking the skin. Her tiny face turned, and her eyes met mine, gleaming gold in the moonlight.

"Just die already," Van muttered, and I saw acceptance in those tiny eyes.

She was about to die. Something deep inside me broke... and something else was made whole.

"Mine," I whispered. I let my muscles go slack, and the Enforcers released me. In seconds, I was across the ring, my body draped over her small, bloody form, the blows Van was raining down on her hitting me instead.

He didn't stop. In fact, the blows came faster, harder. There was no way for me to carry Flor to safety, no time to do anything but take the punishment intended for her. My skin burst open on my back, my own blood mingling with hers as it fell.

Mate, I realized. This little girl would someday be my mate.
If we lived.

That had been the same night I shifted for the first time.

It had been both a punishment for daring to question the Head Enforcer, and a last-ditch attempt to save my life.

My father had appeared in time to stop Van from killing me, and the concern he'd shown that night had fooled me into thinking he might truly love me. I was his son, after all. He'd forced my shift to save me... or so he'd repeated often over the years.

I'd tried to believe he loved me, but he had never felt anything of the kind. He was rotten to his core. And so was his wolf, I thought, as I noted his reflexes slowing. I was exhausted, in pain, and had begun the fight wounded, but the Alpha was growing sloppier and more desperate as the fight wore on.

Was I stronger than him? Maybe not, but my love for Flor was. My need to get her free of this pack, to protect her from him and all the others like him, was a force as strong as the moon. I would do anything, give anything, to secure her freedom. To make sure she had the chance to flourish and run free.

I feinted left, rolling under my Alpha's legs, causing him to stumble, and in a flash, had his throat in my jaws, my teeth piercing his fur... No, his skin.

He was shifting. Why? Confused, I gazed around the ring, as my opponent did the one thing I wasn't ready for.

He begged for mercy.

25

KEEPING HER ALIVE
BRAND

"May the moon have mercy on her," my father murmured, echoing my thoughts. "May Her justice be done tonight." He kneeled below me, his hands keeping pressure on Flor's wounds, one ear pressed every so often to her chest, as I stared out at the ring where Luke fought against his Alpha.

I didn't feel merciful. I wanted to charge into the ring and slaughter the Southern Alpha myself. I would kill him slowly, and as painfully as I could, to punish him for all the harm he'd done to my little flower. But I had a more important task: keeping her safe.

"I need to touch her, Dad," I muttered, though he'd asked me to watch his back while he guarded her. Neither one of us trusted her pack not to take advantage of her current weakness. A few feet away, Finnick and Glen were guarding as well, along with an assortment of fighters and Enforcers from the Mountain and Northern packs who circled us. "I have to protect her. I can't—"

He settled a hand on my leg, squeezing a warning. "You're too close to the edge, son. I can sense it. You'll shift, and your wolf will be out of control. The rest of the Council is watching; we have to follow their rules. And our own tradition."

I didn't need the reminder. I knew the Southern and Eastern members of the Council would jump at the chance to discipline us. Our pack, the Mountain wolves, were seen as a threat. We had greater numbers than the next two packs combined, and our wolves were enormous, almost as if we were an entirely different species.

I'd asked Dad once why we were different, and he'd explained that it was only because we lived in harmony with the land. We followed the old ways of the Moon Goddess, and for that She rewarded us with great strength.

Dad never went to Council meetings anymore, and I wasn't sure he was wrong to avoid them. The corruption that I knew ran through some members of the Council was shocking. They had even begun to hold their meetings in New York of all places, and Dad would never leave our packlands for the city, unless he was forced to. Like this Conclave.

"Breathe. Be patient; she's holding steady. This little one's a fighter."

"You have no idea what she's gone through here," I rasped. "The males hunted her for sport, to force her into a mate bond, from the time she was fifteen. Every night, every worthless male that lives here, chased her, for years —" I broke off, and concentrated on fighting off my shift. Dad cursed softly as I struggled.

"They'll pay for that." He hesitated. "She's Luke's true mate?"

"I'm sure of it," I replied.

"Then why...?" I wasn't sure what he was asking. His gaze darted to Glen and back to me. I knew he wanted to ask why we'd all spoken for her, but I wasn't sure how to explain. He would have heard the honesty in our claims. He knew that at the very least, I believed her to be my mate.

And my wolf was sure as fuck acting like it.

"The fight will be short if Luke is as injured as you say." When he spoke, his lips hardly moved. I think that was where the rumors came from that he had gone mute—he didn't look like he was talking when he was. Mainly, he only spoke to me and Dean, the one the other packs knew as our Head Enforcer.

I nodded. "Where's Dean?"

"Getting ready to challenge Callaway when Luke falls."

I just grunted. Dean was a beast of a shifter, deadly, ferocious, and nearly unbeatable in a fight in either form. There was no doubt in my mind Dean would wipe the floor with Southern's Alpha if he needed to.

And he would almost certainly need to.

I cringed at the scent of blood in the air, and Luke's jerky movements as the fight progressed. Losing Dean would be brutal for our pack. He was one of the only shifters in our pack with a true mate, and he and his mate had two teen boys who were going to be every bit as powerful as their parents. We would lose them all when Dean took the position as Southern Alpha.

But losing Flor to death would be far worse. I glanced at her again. Had she stopped breathing?

"Don't look," Dad grunted. "She's holding on. I'm listening to her heart."

I didn't doubt him; my dad's hearing was the best in any pack. Shifter scientists had traveled from near and far just to study him. He usually sent them away, but last fall, one scientist had stuck around for a few months. I had a feeling she'd wanted to study more than Dad's hearing.

My gut twisted at the thought of Dad finding a girlfriend. Mom had been dead for seventeen years, though. It was time.

What would I do if Flor died? Would I survive as my father had, spending the rest of my life pining for her? Would I try to move on? I had only shared a few words with her and watched her fight. But watching her in battle was like seeing the sun rise over a mountain lake. Like a wonder of the world—every move precise, every movement graceful and clean. Sharp and deadly, like a shining blade.

How had any of us thought she was a male when we met? I almost smiled, remembering her response when she'd first seen my size. She was so genuine, honest in her reactions. I longed to experience more of them.

I had to believe she would make it. She was perfect for me... though I wasn't certain she would be thinking the same when she healed. She had to heal.

Inside, my wolf paced and snapped at invisible foes.

Dad growled, distracting me from my whirling thoughts. "Watch the Southern pack. They're up to something."

"What?"

"I heard whispers. A coup, perhaps. All the Council Alphas are here. And not nearly enough of their Enforcers." He was right. While the Alpha was fighting would be the perfect time for the Southern Enforcers to get armed and set up a trap for the outnumbered visitors.

From the corner of my eye, I saw a flicker of black. It was Joaquin, the Borderlands wolf. It was almost impossible to see him in the shadows. He was doing something odd—tying people's shoelaces together? No, something else. I watched threads of silver-blue light glimmering near his hands.

Magic. He was doing magic.

Fuck. He wasn't just a wolf. I almost shouted a warning before I realized he was doing it to Southern wolves only.

I relaxed slightly when he took their oblivious Enforcers' weapons and chucked them down the nearby storm drain. He kept at it while Luke fought, finally vanishing around the corner, following a group of Southern Enforcers who were leaving.

Leaving their own Alpha's dominance fight? Yeah, they were up to something, even if Joaquin was stopping them.

That wolf made the hairs on the back of my neck stand up, though. He was quiet but strong, and his power was hard to gauge, which made sense if he was using magic somehow. Forbidden magic. I knew better than to fear all witches the way most shifters did now, but this one was an unknown. And an Alpha. He was too dangerous to allow near my mate.

I turned to tell Dad what I had seen, when a sharp, painful howl from the ring caught my attention.

Luke's wolf was weaving with exhaustion and pain. Honestly, I was amazed he was still on his feet with that brutal gut wound. I reminded myself not to piss off my little mate, unless I wanted to see my own intestines up close.

But Callaway wasn't looking much better than Luke. He was panting like a human who didn't even jog. How did an Alpha let that happen? His whole job was the Protector of the Pack. That meant he had to be at the pinnacle of physical fitness.

As I watched Luke snap and snarl, reaching out with claws and teeth and connecting at least twice as often as the much larger Alpha, I had a thought. "Dad, you remember the rumor Finnick reported—that Alpha Callaway tried to kill his true mate? Glen whispered that there was more proof. Maybe he did kill her, to break the bond."

Dad let out a rare curse and nodded. "Do you think it weakened him? Look at his wolf."

"Big," I muttered.

He grunted. "But slow. Look at his response time. Luke is practically dead. But his Alpha is..."

"I know. Weak." Any other Alpha would have torn the head off his opponent in seconds; they had the combined strength of the entire pack's energy to draw on.

"Could be," Dad said after a minute. "Might be cursed by the Moon Goddess."

I nodded, knowing what he meant. In the old stories, wolves who committed grave offenses against the moon usually went mad and died. In the ones Dad had read to me, the dishonored wolves were often eaten by carrion crows. I hated crows to this day because of those stories.

Dad was all about the old ways. The tale of Flor's background would have shocked him, but discovering she somehow held more than one soulmate bond? I wasn't sure if he would be able to wrap his head around that. Accept it.

I'd already accepted the possibility. Sure, it bothered me that she might not be only mine, but not as much as it should. Except for Luke, I was close to the other Alpha Heirs. I saw their worth and had fought with them long enough to know their honor. Even Finnick was solid, deep down, once you got past the sushi and symphonies.

His family, though... They were a different matter.

And that Joaquin? *No.* I would not allow her to be endangered by his presence. Shifters did not do magic. At least, not that I knew of.

"Dad, when the Russian wolves invaded Northern, did they have any shifters who used mag—"

The crowd let out a shout, cutting me off. In the fighting ring, Luke snarled and faked a hurt leg, drawing his Alpha's attention to his hindquarters. It was a decent ploy, but fairly obvious. Any Alpha worth his salt would see it for what it was and refuse to be drawn out.

I blinked when this Alpha *didn't* see it. He stretched out his neck, his most vulnerable zone, to reach for the supposed injury. However, he never got the chance to lay teeth on it, since Luke had whipped around—the much smaller wolf using his size to his advantage to avoid the hefty Alpha's clumsy maneuver—and wrapped his jaws around his Alpha's throat.

"Thank the moon," my father muttered. "Finish him, Luke."

We all knew what had to happen next. Alpha Callaway would die with honor in the fighting ring, and Luke would take his place. I should have relaxed, but some instinct had me holding onto my tension.

"What's the kid waiting for?" My dad's voice was strained as we all stared at the gory scene, where something unusual was occurring.

Instead of two wolves in the ring, there was one. And a mostly shifted, human Alpha.

The whole crowd was waiting for the fountain of blood, for Luke to finish the kill, and take his place. But it didn't happen. Alpha Callaway had begun a fast, painful shift, possibly the instant Luke had gained the upper hand.

What is he doing?

Luke's wolf kept hold of the Alpha's almost-hairless neck, but seemed as confused as the rest of us. This couldn't be happening.

"I yield," the Alpha shouted, his voice raspy through a

partially crushed windpipe. His beefy, bloodstained fist pounded on the dirt floor of the ring.

"What is this madness?" Dad growled, his eyes flashing. He stepped forward, over seven feet of enraged Alpha. "There is no yielding in an Alpha challenge."

I wasn't sure about that, but then again, there hadn't been an Alpha challenge in decades or longer. If anyone would know, though, it was Dad.

Luke obviously had no idea what to do. It was considered borderline dishonorable for a wolf to fight a shifter in human form, which was why so many had jeered Trevor earlier. But to change in the middle of a fight, to yield verbally? Normally, a wolf would roll over and show its belly, a typical submissive pose, or make obvious sounds of distress.

Once a wolf had yielded, it was against all the rules of a normal dominance challenge to continue. The defeated wolf would take his new place in the pack, and the winner would move into the top spot.

But Alpha challenges had to be different. An Alpha could no sooner be integrated back into the pack as an Enforcer or lower, than an unranked wolf could suddenly become Alpha.

Dad seemed certain that what was happening in the ring now, with Luke backing off, and the Head Enforcer of the Southern pack helping the Alpha limp out of the ring, was against pack law.

"Is this illegal?" I wondered aloud.

"No, but it's wrong," Dad growled. "If that Alpha leaves, Luke won't be able to step up until after the Council appoints him."

"What?" My blood went cold.

"The Alpha position will be in limbo. The pack connections will not pass to Luke."

Dad, tell Luke! I almost called out, but the crowd was milling about, screaming, confused and angry. Luke had collapsed, and healers were surrounding him. It was too late.

We needed the Council Alpha to call an emergency meeting, *now.*

I scanned the crowd, finding Bradley. I had just taken a breath to call for his assistance when Margarette screamed. "The girl!"

Dad gripped my leg again, hard. "Brand. Her heart has stopped."

I felt my own heart stop beating for a moment, and for the second time that night, I lost my balance. My mate was dying, and even though we hadn't secured the bond, I felt her pain. Saw her darkness.

Dad turned me to face him, his eyes wide with shock.

"No!" I pulled myself away and dropped to my knees next to her, knowing there was nothing I could do.

What could be done was already happening. In the absence of a declared Alpha for the Southern pack, there was no Alpha of Southern.

Bradley leaped into the center of the ring, where the ground was stained with the Alpha's blood. "Council, a quorum is present, and a meeting is called. I request that the powers of Interim Alpha of Southern be transferred to me as Head of the North American Council."

Voices shouted out around the ring—Margarette, Dad, Dean. "Aye!"

Two voices murmured, "Nay." Finnick's father, and his Head Enforcer, Torran. But we had a majority.

"Thank the moon," Margarette breathed.

Bradley moved over the still form of my mate as I watched, unable to move, even to blink. I felt rather than saw Finnick and Glen step next to me. My head swam. I would lose my perfect, fierce mate before I'd ever held her, kissed her.

She was the only one. The only voice I wanted to hear each morning, the amber eyes and mischief-filled smile I wanted to see reflected back in my children's faces.

Please, Mother Moon, I prayed. *Please. I will give anything. I will give everything.*

My life, my heart, my pride, my strength. Take it. It is yours. It is hers.

Bradley shouted, "Shift!" in a baritone voice that had a few of the surrounding shifters dropping to four paws in response.

My tiny, bloody mate lay motionless, though.

If she dies, I will too.

I didn't know I'd said it out loud until I heard Glen and Finnick's soft answers. "Yes."

"Son?" Dad's voice was raw.

"Yes," I answered, all of my heart in that word. He understood. His hand reached out, crushing my arm, squeezing it like he could hold me to this world if she left.

Then Bradley leaned down, grasping Flor's pale arms in his hands, and shouted once more, directly into her ear. "*Shift!*"

And my mate's broken body began to move. Began to change.

I cried as I watched. It was the worst shift I'd ever seen, slow and bloody. Bradley chanted into her ear, each syllable infused with power, his command to keep going, keep changing, keep *living*, acting as a spiritual shock to her whole system.

I felt her agony in my own bones, reached out with my own spirit, and accepted it into me gladly. I felt blood begin to pour from my own nose and splatter the ground.

When Bradley had finished, when he'd forced her to change to her wolf, she lay motionless. I couldn't tell what color she was. Her fur was so bloody, she shone red-black in the dim light.

"Why is she still unconscious?"

"She's not healed enough," Finnick gasped.

She had to shift back to human form to continue healing. But her heart was slowing again.

"She's still dying," I groaned.

The realization swept through everyone gathered around, but before anyone could begin the mourning howl, Bradley thundered again, his command inescapable, "Shift!"

And somehow, she obeyed.

Her fur receded, her limbs reformed, arms and legs thickening until she was pale again. Finally, she was human, without the gaping wounds that had stretched her open. Her heartbeat was sluggish and weak, her lungs rattling slightly as she breathed.

Finnick darted forward, startling me. I growled, but he was just pulling off the cloth that had bound her wounds. The skin underneath the red-soaked bandages was clean and clear. He rolled her over, double checking that all wounds were gone. His hands moved over her skin as if he had to feel every inch of her, to make certain.

"Healed," he whispered. "She's healed."

She was, but by the moon, she was thin. Like a prisoner, each rib outlined, each muscle protruding in a way that showed she had never eaten enough to develop the softness that other girls had. The only curves she had were those of the tight, lean muscles that defined her body.

I didn't care. She was alive. I would feed her every delicacy she ever wanted, starting with the hearts of her enemies, if she would let me kill them for her. Still kneeling, I wondered at the way the moonlight shimmered over her skin.

First shifts had the effect of erasing all injuries in a way later ones did not. She was as physically perfect now as she would have been at birth.

Which was why it was odd to see the five silvered marks that stretched from her left shoulder across her chest to her waist on the right.

A birthmark? I didn't care. She was perfect in every way.

Thank you, Mother Moon. Thank you for whatever part of her is mine to care for, to protect, to worship. I will never hurt her.

26

DREAMING OF DEATH
FLOR

Pain tied me up, stuck a sock in my mouth, and dragged me down a gravel road that seemed to never end, cutting into my insides and pulling me apart as it went.

My throat was pulsing with agony, my head split open by razor blades dipped in acid. My lungs were filled with what had to be blood, but my mouth was dry as sand. I'd never imagined this kind of pain was what I'd find in the fighting ring. If I'd known, I would have run from the Southern packlands and taken my chances with the feral rogues.

Why wasn't I dead? Hadn't Trevor killed me?

I wanted to die. Before I remembered that the moon had never answered me, I prayed for it. *Let me die. Take me now, before I break.*

She didn't answer me now, either. But someone did.

Buried in the gritty rockfalls of pain, Del's voice was a gentle touch. "Trevor? Kill you? That boy couldn't wipe his ass with both hands, girlie. Millie over at the laundry told me as much."

I wanted to laugh, or cry, or jump for joy, but I could barely manage a whimper.

"Del?" I whispered into the darkness. "Are you all right?"

"Sure," he replied. "But don't worry about me right now. I need you to focus, or that useless piece of shit will win after all. Focus on slowing your blood, slowing your breath. Hear me? The boys are fighting for you now. Give them the time to save you."

The boys? Save me? What was going on in the world outside the ocean of pain I was in?

"Focus. Slow everything down. Now."

Del was dead. I knew that, so I knew this couldn't really be him. It was my subconscious, or something. It just felt so good to hear his voice, I almost wanted to ignore his instructions. But he'd kick my ass in the afterlife if I didn't at least try to hold on.

"Del, say hi to Mom, will you?"

A strange silence slid around me like a cold embrace. "Sure, kid."

The pain didn't stop, but the feeling of isolation, of being lost to everything but agony, receded. I began to hear sounds. Whispers that turned into shouts. It sounded like a battle.

After a while, the battle ended, and the pain began to fade. *Good. No pain is good,* I thought.

Del's voice came again, louder. "I said slow your blood, your breathing, you squirrely girl! You've got shit to do. Focus!"

FOCUS!

I tried. I honestly did.

But it was so hard... and then it got harder. A deeper voice called out to me, a command I couldn't resist. *SHIFT.*

For a moment, I wasn't sure what that meant. But my body knew. It meant pain.

I felt myself begin to tear, as if all my limbs were connected by loose seams that had suddenly lost the binding threads. My legs tore away from my torso, bending, breaking, followed by my arms. My nose and mouth and chin split, and I tried to scream, but my throat had torn in two, and was regrowing in a new shape. My ears stretched, grew, lengthened, heard more. Breathing, voices I knew, surrounded me.

God, she's beautiful.

Smallest wolf I've ever seen.

She's not healing.

She has to shift back.

Now!

The deep voice boomed again. *SHIFT.*

The tearing reversed, the strings reappearing around my limbs and stitching me back together with threads of fire, of lava. Melting my whole body into a shape that felt like it was too small to hold the pieces that had been torn away. I tried to resist.

SHIFT.

Shift yourself! I wanted to yell. I didn't know who that goatsucker was, but if I ever got to meet him, I would punch him in the jaw so he couldn't torture me with this shift nonsense.

I wanted to curse. Instead, I felt my mind twist, as if it were trying to exit through my ears. Then the places on my neck and skull that Trevor had savaged began to burn like acid had been poured on them.

Toadfucker probably gave me rabies. Goddamn motherfucking cockmuffin. I'd tear off his tiny little limp dick and stuff it in his nostril, if it wasn't so small it'd fall out...

I panted, wondering why I could hear laughter.

Laughter? Was someone laughing at my pain? I didn't care if I was dead, I wasn't going to lie still and listen to that.

I opened my eyes and saw the moon shining, heavy and full, above me. I wasn't dead. Lifting a hand to my face, I felt for my nose, my chin, all the parts I was sure had been taken from me.

I was whole.

I staggered to my feet. I was drunk, too. Or something like it. I tilted to one side, watching the ground rush toward my face. But it stopped when something caught me.

Something that thrummed and surged with energy, heat. I grabbed hold of it, leaned to smell it. It smelled like the ocean, and citrus... exactly how I imagined those beach cocktails I'd once seen in a magazine might taste. I licked my lips, suddenly thirsty. Maybe I'd died and gone to paradise.

If it was Heaven, the cocktail would be real. I gave it a lick to see. Yummy as fuck.

Yep, this is paradise.

Laughter again. I swung out with one arm. "Who's laughing? If that's Trevor, give me a damned second and I'll... I'll..." I had no idea how to finish that sentence.

The ocean citrus arm that had been holding me pulled me in tighter and spoke into my ear with a voice that gave me chills. "You'll tear off his tiny dick and stuff it in his nostril, right?"

I blinked, and suddenly the world came into clearer focus, although everything was too sharp somehow, and my face was turned to the ground so all I saw was dirt. But every single particle of dirt was outlined, like I was viewing it through a microscope, somehow.

A dream. I was dreaming this. That's why I could smell everything—like all the delicious scents around me—and could hear breathing and even the pounding of the hearts nearby.

This was an amazing dream. Or a drug trip. Had I done drugs? No, I knew better than that. I could never let my guard down.

But this was what everyone had said being drunk or stoned felt like. Moon drunk, was that a thing? It felt like I had moonlight coursing through my veins, emanating from the hands that were holding me up.

I let my fingers glide up the muscular arm, then followed my hand with my eyes. At the top of the sun-bronzed shoulder was... Glen, smiling at me, though his face was wet, and it looked as if his nose had been bleeding.

He was holding me with those delicious arms, looking at me as if I was the most beautiful creature in existence, like I was ice cream and all-you-can-eat macaroni and cheese and a two-hour soak in a hot bathtub all rolled into one. I knew I was dreaming when I thought that; those were the exact ingredients of the dreams I'd had for years, except Luke had been in the bathtub with me.

Maybe this dream would be like the fantasies I'd had, even without Luke. I licked my lips and tried to make my voice sexy. "Hey, Dream Glenda."

The world filled with laughter again. But Dream Glen hadn't laughed.

"Hey, Dream Girl," he answered, his voice raspy with emotion.

Wow. His voice had made my nipples tight. What the hell was that? Dream Glen blushed for some reason. *Blushed.* That was perfect.

I leaned in, whispering, "You know, at the stream?

When you were watching me touch myself? Do you remember that?"

His eyes went wide. "Um, Flor, maybe this isn't the time—"

I pushed a hand over his soft lips. "This is my dream, and I can say what I want." He nodded, blushing even harder. "I never thought I'd have an o-orgasm. But I always wanted one. But not alone. Nobody wants to come alone, right?"

"Right."

"So even if you did sneak up on me, I don't care. I'm glad you were spying on me."

His eyes were bugging out now. I could hear a weird growling in the background, but ignored it. He wasn't staring at me with hearts in his eyes now. He was glaring. *Dream Jerkface.*

I scowled. "Just because I shouted your name doesn't mean you were the only one I was thinking of, so don't get cocky—"

Suddenly, a hand was over my mouth. Not Dream Glen's hand. This hand was soft. Smooth. Smelled like fancy perfume. Who the hell else was in this stupid dream?

"That's enough for now," a woman's voice murmured.

Wait. A woman?

"There's only room for one woman in this fantasy. And that's me," I grumbled once the hand was removed. I tried to focus on the arm, then the face, then the whole person.

"I think we need more women and fewer men right now," the person disagreed. Her face swam into view. She was a tall stranger, with dark brown hair pulled back into a braid. Her form-fitting outfit was almost all black, like she was cosplaying an assassin dominatrix, with a shit ton of gold jewelry on her neck, and enough mascara on her eyes for three women. Super sexy, but probably twice my age. It was hard to tell.

"Okay, you're gorgeous. We may circle back around to this. But if you don't mind, I kind of want to try out the Alpha Hei—"

She gently placed her hand back over my mouth, and spoke over my head in a soft but powerful voice. "I'm going to ask every male here to keep your eyes to yourself, and your ears as well. I'll take the newest member of the Northern Pack back to her room." I wondered who she meant. "Someone from Southern—if there's anyone left here? Please show me the way."

As she spoke, I took deep breaths. I was breathing. I was not dead, not dreaming.

And I was stark naked.

"Holy *shit*."

"Yes," the woman agreed, her blue eyes dancing. "If I take my hand away from your mouth, can you promise not to talk?" I nodded, and she waited a second. "Good." She let her hand fall, and I took a second to admire her nails. Long and bright red, and—my gaze swept over her again—they matched her shiny red combat boots perfectly.

"I'm not dreaming, am I?" I waited, and she shook her head slowly. "Because this is a lot like a dream I had, where I was naked in the dining hall, and this guy Luke was—" Suddenly, the hand was back over my mouth.

"No more talking," she demanded, her eyes flashing to someone I couldn't see.

I gave a thumbs up. Talking was overrated anyway. I was just going to float on the moonlight inside me.

"Moon drunk indeed," the woman murmured.

Laughter sounded, farther away.

I felt a blanket being folded around my shoulders, and

Dream Glen moved away as the woman took me from him, carrying me without any problem. I took a breath, scenting blood. A lot of blood. I craned my neck to see whose it was.

"Don't look back," she instructed. So I didn't.

As she carried me away, my head began to clear. "That was Glen, right? The real Glen," I whispered.

"Mhmm," she said, her lips twitching. "My son."

"I said all that stuff out loud to him."

"Mhmm." We were following another shifter, an unranked girl who looked vaguely familiar.

"Did I... Did I lick him?" *Oh, please let that part have been a dream.*

No such luck. "Mhmm."

"Can you do me a favor and kill me when we get back to the dorm?"

The woman let out the least feminine laugh I'd ever heard, snorts and all. More of a guffaw than a giggle. "Oh, sweet girl, I would never do such a thing. Keeping you alive is my number one priority."

That was nice, and not at all the reaction I usually got. "So... I'm not sure what happened while I was passed out." I waited, but she didn't speak. "Is it correct to assume Trevor kicked my a—I mean, defeated me?"

"Yes."

This made no sense. "And my Alpha didn't kill me?"

Her red lips curled up. "You don't have a Southern Alpha right now."

"How is that possible? Is he dead?" *Please let him be dead.*

"No," she spat, her tone scathing. "That's the problem. Luke challenged him, defeated him, but didn't kill him for some reason."

"You're not allowed to kill in dominance battles," I

inserted. I didn't like the way she was second-guessing Luke's decision. Without him bringing me that mop, I wouldn't have lived through the first minute of the fight with Trevor. I was just moon drunk enough to tell her that.

She shook her head. "Yet another strike against your former Alpha. He didn't teach pack law?"

"Oh no, he did, all the time. He read it out loud." Him or Van Blackside. Every fucking dinnertime, and at lunch on Sundays.

"Honey, if he did, then he left out a lot. Or changed it to suit his needs." She sounded certain.

"So why isn't Luke the Alpha now, if he beat him?"

She kept going, carrying me as she walked and answered my questions, not even slightly out of breath. "When the old Alpha dies in a dominance challenge with another shifter, the power of the Alpha naturally moves to the winner. Unfortunately, until his death, your old Alpha is still in charge."

I froze. "Is he... loose?"

"No, he was taken to the cell he'd had my son in."

"Super thick silver-plated bars, close together," I muttered. "Not even I can get out of that one. Trust me, I tried."

She sucked in a breath. "You spent time in that dirty cell? But you're a child!"

I shrugged. "I'm nineteen." I had been a child when he'd thrown me in there, but I didn't want this strong woman to think I was the sort who complained.

She let it slide, but I could see she wasn't forgetting it. "In any case, Luke will be Alpha as soon as my husband—Bradley, he's the Head of the North American Council—gets it passed in the meeting."

That seemed too good to be true. "He can transfer the moon's blessing?"

She laughed, like I'd said something hilarious. "No. He just had to get permission to execute your Alpha. Don't worry—it'll happen, and soon. After the battle, we thought the other Southern Enforcers might try to stage a coup, but for some reason, they didn't. I think they were too shocked Luke won, especially as he was already visibly wounded."

"Huh," I said, equally shocked. "I knew Alpha Callaway was an assho—a jerk, but I didn't know he was that weak."

She hummed in agreement. "Luke will be the Alpha by tomorrow, after he heals enough to regain consciousness."

"Wait, he's still out? How hurt is he?"

For some reason, my heart started pounding. I needed to see him. *Crap, is this that mate bond thing everyone kept going on about?* I stuffed the feeling down. "Is he safe? Van or one of the other Enforcers will definitely try something. They're a bunch of rat bastard, trash panda fuc—I mean, uh, they have no honor."

"Well, he's not Alpha yet, so it wouldn't do any good. We sent a Council guard to surveil the armory, just in case anyone gets ideas. I can ask Bradley to place another guard outside Luke's room until Calvin is dead."

"Great. So is anyone planning to kill me right now? I mean, you should know they probably are." I was wanted for killing Del. It wouldn't be the regular Hunt; my whole pack would be after me. "Wait, what about Trevor? Is he... He's alive?"

"Not for long, if my boys find him," she muttered.

I knew better than to depend on a possibility. If Trevor was alive and free, so were his buddies. And those shifters would never stop hunting me.

Never.

The whole pack could be hunting me right now.

My pulse raced, knowing the clock was probably already ticking. "Listen, thanks for the help, but I have to get to a safe place. Can you put me down?" I wasn't sure I could walk, but I had to go.

My mind spun with the possibilities. The storm drain was out. I was too weak to climb a tree. Maybe the potato cellar behind Mary Quick's old place...

But the woman was talking. "Even if someone is looking for you, they won't get through me." I gave her what must have been a *what the fuck* look, because she stopped walking.

"Lady, I hate to say this, but you and me against my whole pack? I don't hate those odds; you seem pretty fit. But I think we might want to run." I wriggled. "Please let me go. You don't understand. I have to run, *now.*"

Gently, she set me down. "No more running, Flor. And it's not me and you. It's us. You, me, and our pack. You're my foster daughter now," she said softly, helping me to balance on my own feet. "My name is Margarette Hillier. I am the mate of our Alpha, and I adopted you into our pack."

"I'm... I'm not Southern anymore?" I asked, my breath coming fast, I clutched her arm, sure I would fall over if I couldn't stop gasping for air.

"No," she said slowly. "Not if you don't want to be. We had to make a decision after Callaway was defeated. I know we didn't ask you, but you were, well, mostly dead all day."

I giggled. "Say it again."

"You were mostly dead?"

"No, the other part."

"Ah." Her smile was fierce as she raised a hand and stroked my short hair back from my face. "You're not a member of the Southern pack anymore, and you've been granted probationary status at my pack, Northern. You're free. You can leave. If you don't want to stay at Northern—" She kept talking, but I couldn't hear her over my sobs.

I crumpled on the ground and felt myself lifted into her arms again. "Thank you, thank you," I chanted, holding onto her as tight as I could. "I'm free. Del, it *worked*."

It might have meant almost dying, and I may not have won the fight against Trevor, but I was going to get out of this hellhole and run free. Free of fear, free of pain, and free of the males who'd chased me and tried to chain me to them.

Free.

27

OBLIGATIONS TO THE PACK
FLOR

I t took me a while to stop crying, but by then the woman—no, *Margarette*, she'd told me to call her—was crying, too, so it didn't matter. It had surprised me when she stopped walking right in the middle of the gravel road and just rocked me for a while, like a mom, her own soft sobs moving her chest under my head.

I'd cried even harder then. But she never told me to quit, or hushed me, or acted like losing my shit right out in front of the unmated shifter dorms was anything out of the ordinary.

I wasn't embarrassed. Well, not until we wiped our faces, walked inside, and Patty, the unranked girl on duty, led her into my dorm room. It hadn't changed since I'd left, but even Patty seemed shocked at how bare it was.

Margarette set me down on my narrow, broken-down cot and whirled around to Patty with a snarl. "What the fuck is *this?*"

The unranked shifter bowed so low, I thought her head would hit the ground, too terrified to answer. Margarette's power seemed to suck the air out of the room, making it hard to breathe.

I straightened, pulling the blanket around me. "Margarette, she's no one to worry about. Just a girl who lives here. She's not one of the bad ones." Patty's eyes met mine, and she blinked in shock. Margarette closed her eyes for a moment, clearly trying for calm. I nodded toward the open door. "Patty, you should go. Tell the others to steer clear for tonight."

Patty smiled slightly. "Thank you," she whispered. It was the first time she'd ever spoken to me, though I was almost positive she'd been the one to leave a half-full box of tampons in my trash can a year before.

Once we were alone, Margarette stalked through the room, opening the three drawers and cursing when she saw the meager contents. I was shocked that no one had taken the stuff I'd left. Of course, I had almost nothing.

I pulled on a ragged pair of shorts and a stained t-shirt as she went into the bathroom, still cursing. She poked her head out a moment later. "You live here? Full time?"

"Until a few days ago, yeah. I've been in the woods since... Thursday, I think."

"Ah." This seemed to make her feel better. "Did you take your belongings out there?"

"No." Where was she going with this line of questioning? "I mean, I have a few things. A toothbrush, a canteen, and a knife. But this is all I have."

"Excuse me." She walked around the corner to the bathroom, and I heard her punching the wall, shattering one of the tiles. Her voice filtered through. "All she has. All she fucking has."

"Um, sorry I don't own more stuff. I'm unranked. It's

sort of like being a monk, except the vow of poverty isn't optional," I tried to joke.

She stormed back into the room and sat on the bed. "I am *livid*," she growled, then took a deep breath. "I am livid that a treasure like you has been wasted on a pack like Southern. I'm beside myself at the thought of any girl being forced to live in a room with nothing, less than what home-less humans have." She grabbed my hands. "And I'm enraged that the girl I saw fight a shifted wolf harder and better than almost any Enforcer in all of the packs just apol-ogized to me for not having 'stuff.'"

I wasn't one hundred percent sure about this woman. She was coming off as a tiny bit unhinged, and I could tell for sure she had anger issues, but lots of shifters did. At Southern, though, the female shifters weren't allowed to show it.

I inched away from her slightly, and she winced, her voice softening. "Ignore me. You can't stay here; I won't hear of it. I'll find you a room near mine—one that doesn't smell like piss, and make me want to burn this whole pack to the ground and salt the earth."

Definitely anger issues, though the burning and salting had a certain appeal.

She rubbed the spot between her brows, like she had a headache. "I'll pack for you. You rest, Flor."

"Thanks," I murmured, trying not to feel even worse when all she could find to put my stuff in was a plastic grocery store bag. She stomped back into the bathroom.

A shriek suddenly drew my attention to the doorway. "You little murdering slut! I swore if I ever clapped eyes on you again, I would beat the evil outta ya!" The dorm mistress Holly was already halfway across the room, her hair half in pins and half out, the day's mascara smeared around her eyes in a raccoon mask. "You shamed our whole pack, you little whore!"

I would have laughed, but I was too tired to move, and she had a hairbrush in her hand, already raising it to hit me. Closing my eyes, I tried to curl up on my side. I knew from past experience that her brush hurt a lot less on my back and butt than on my face, but the blow never landed.

"Wha—!" Holly shrieked again, a sort of gurgling sound, and I opened my eyes to see Margarette holding the dorm mistress off the ground with one hand wrapped around her skinny neck.

"Who the hell are you?" Margarette asked, shaking the dorm mistress like a dog would a squirrel it had caught, and with as little effort.

I was pretty sure Holly was trying to answer, but there was no way she could talk. Or breathe, for that matter.

"Flor, dear daughter of mine, who is this trashy person?"

I sat up, the pain in my abdomen still awful, though I wasn't sure why. I'd shifted, right? But I suppose I had been mostly disemboweled. It'd take time, maybe. "That is Holly Grier, the woman in charge of the unmated shifter dorm."

Margarette tilted her head, her ice-blue eyes glowing like a wolf's now. "In charge of discipline?"

"Among other things," I said with a look at the hairbrush. "Pretty sure that was the part of the job she worked hardest at."

Margarette nodded at the fallen brush. "Hand me that, dear?"

I did, and watched in awe as she used her free hand to crush the hairbrush like it was a brittle twig, before dropping the pieces to the floor.

"Holy crap, you're strong," I breathed. "I've wanted to destroy that brush since I was fifteen."

"She's hit you with it before?" Margarette demanded. Her long nails were piercing the sides of Holly's throat now, and the hot tang of fresh blood joined the odors. I nodded, and my rescuer growled. "She'll never hit you again, darling. Not with that or anything else." She whispered in Holly's ear, "You need to have hands to hold a weapon, don't you?"

Holly went still in Margarette's grip, the sobbing dorm mistress's terror filling the room with a sour, acrid stench. Well, her fear and the urine that was now staining the legs of her jeans.

Margarette purred her question again, holding the other woman up like she weighed no more than a loaf of bread. "I asked you a question, shifter. You need to have hands to hold a weapon, don't you?"

"Y-yes, ma'am," Holly whimpered. It was all I could do not to do a fist pump and cheer. Margarette was obviously slightly psychotic, but I was a hundred percent here for it.

Her gaze was calm when she turned to me, though. "Is she the one in charge of making sure the girls who live here have the basic necessities? Clothing, bedding, toiletries?"

"Yep," I said, loving the desperate, bloodshot glare that Holly sent me. "That's her job."

At last, Margarette dropped the bleeding shifter on the floor, and we watched her wheeze for a moment before she glared up at both of us. "I don't know who you are, lady, but my Alpha is gonna tear your tits off for daring to touch one of his own—"

"You weren't at the fights then," Margarette said with a cool look. "You have no idea who I am."

"Who are—" Holly's words cut off as Margarette stepped down on her neck with one red combat boot.

"I am the Head Enforcer of the Northern Pack, and the mate to the Northern Pack's Alpha, who happens to be the Head of the North American Council. And the girl you were trying to assault is the newest member of my pack." I swallowed hard, still wondering how my luck had changed in such a short time.

Holly made a gurgling sound.

"Help me understand, Holly, why this room had nothing, if you have the job of seeing to the needs of the residents? No blankets, not even an extra roll of toilet paper. What I really want to know is if you weren't provided with those things to distribute, or if they are—I don't know—stockpiled somewhere? Perhaps providing a little income on the side?" She stepped off Holly's neck, so she could answer.

"There might be a few rolls of toilet paper in the storage," Holly rasped. "I've got some canned goods in my room, cereal and some bottles of juice. Not much. Alpha Callaway ain't sent supplies in for a good month now."

"Hmm," Margarette said, tapping a long, manicured nail on her chin. "I really want to kill you. But my new daughter is tired. Flor? I'll leave it up to you. Would you like me to rip her throat out?"

I stifled a giggle when I realized she really meant it. But I shook my head. "Make her give the supplies and food she's hoarded to the unranked girls. Share it out evenly."

"As you wish, sweetheart." Margarette kicked Holly over, toward the door. Then she spoke in a voice that resonated with power and anger. "Holly, you will leave this room and give everything you've hoarded to the girls that live here. You will empty out your own room until you have no more than what Flor has at this moment in here. If you try to disobey, I will kill you. If you keep back even a scrap of food, no matter if you think you'll escape me, I will find you, and keep you alive as my wolf feasts on your innards in retribution. Then I'll give your remains to the vultures. Are we clear?"

I wasn't sure if Holly was going to pass out or not. She went an odd shade of red, and the shaking her head was doing might have been a nod. Margarette allowed her to crawl out of the room as I stood to watch, wishing I had a camera to record this on.

Margarette took me by the elbow and moved me back to the bed, her voice soft and sweet again. "Well, that was unpleasant. And I thought I asked you to rest?"

"I've been dreaming of that woman getting her just desserts for a long time. I needed to see it." We both laughed, and I decided maybe both Margarette and I were the same kind of crazy. While she bagged up my belongings, I gathered my courage and asked the question that had been burning my tongue. "So you're really my foster mom?"

She hummed her assent. "For now, yes. I'll also be your bodyguard. There are too many angry Southern assholes looking for you. Don't worry, I'll be driving us out of this cesspit as soon as possible."

"Amen to that. And you don't need to pack my stuff. I don't want anything, except to leave this place and never look back."

She turned halfway to face me. "Throw it away?" I nodded. "Oh, thank goodness. We'll get you all new." I laughed, but stopped when she went on, too casually, "You don't think you'll ever want to come back for... Luke?"

"Luke?" I tried not to react. "Why would I do that?"

She dropped the half-filled bag into the trash can. "He's your true mate, Flor."

"I truly don't give a rat's ass," I stated baldly. "If he is— and I'm not sure he's not making it all up—then he lost the right to be my mate when he let Southern use me as their whipping girl. When he let them..." I almost said, "hunt me," but I wasn't sure I was ready for the questions that would bring. "When he let them treat me like shit."

Margarette's brow furrowed. "Flor, true mates are Mother Moon's greatest gift. You only get one. You should feel compelled to mate with him. Don't you want to have children?"

The thought of being a mother made me cackle with laughter. "Hell to the no, ma'am," I finally managed. "Baby-making? I've spent years running from that trap. And I'll keep on running. Anyway, Luke's no such thing."

Margarette frowned. "But... we witnessed his wounds. The ones you gave him. The moon has called you both to be together. All shifters have obligations, Flor. Especially since the war—we lost almost one in three wolves at Northern. All of the packs suffered, and are still struggling to rebound. Those of us who are left have a duty."

"Um, to who?"

"To our species," she said, her tone gentler. But I didn't trust it now.

"I don't want to offend you, Margarette, and if you rescind the pack adoption, or whatever, that's fine." *It is not fine,* my inner voice chanted, but I wasn't escaping one cage for another. "I'm not interested in a mate, now or ever. And I sure as hell won't bring children into a world where they could end up property of an Alpha like Callaway. Or in a pack like Southern."

She tilted her head, an odd gleam in her eye. "No, never

here. And if you don't feel the pull... maybe your true mate isn't Luke." I wasn't sure I liked the direction of her thoughts. "You will eventually choose a mate, though. What about my son Glen—"

"No!" Fuck that. I knew what came next. Being tied to a future Alpha, who would treat me like a doll or try to kill me, depending on his mood. I would be powerless again. Owned. "Let me go." I stood, shaking her hand away.

She stood, too. "You need to calm down, Flor," she said, giving me that Enforcer stare, like that would make me listen. Make me stay. Her voice was filled with command as she said, "Sit down."

I scoffed, ignoring her shock as the command rolled off my back. I should have guessed she would try that shit. Her son was the guy who hadn't respected my right to privacy.

"I ain't going to Northern with you, or anywhere with any asshole who thinks I'm gonna belong to them. I've been in a prison for my whole life, and I ain't leaving this one just to go to yours."

If she'd had pearls on, I knew she would have clutched them. "My pack is not a prison. We're not criminals like the shifters here at Southern."

"Your son isn't all that different. Except when he pulled his shit, he took responsibility. He didn't try to roll me with his dominance." I sneered. "Maybe it takes a few more years for the integrity to fully wear off at Northern."

She gasped, and her eyes glowed again. I shifted my stance, taking in the things I could use in the room as a weapon. My shiv was back in the mattress where I'd put it. I could use the wooden shards of the hairbrush, maybe the metal trash can. I was ready to fight, ready to kick my way out of the window if I had to, to run. Even though I knew I wasn't strong enough.

But then, just when I thought she would attack, Margarette dropped to one knee, her eyes on the ground. "You will not die, sweet child. You have nothing to fear from me. Flor, you have my deepest apologies," she went on, still not looking up. "My son dishonored our pack, and now I almost did the same. We owe you a debt, and you owe us nothing. You are welcome at Northern. More than welcome —wanted. Your presence would be a gift."

I didn't change my stance, still wary. "I won't have to mate some guy? Start shooting out pups?"

"You misunderstood. You will not be forced to mate anyone; no one would have done that. I swear it on the moon, and on my honor."

I didn't think I had misunderstood one fucking bit, but I let it go. I had to; I was about to fall on my ass with exhaustion. "I accept your offer to stay at Northern. As a visitor. For now."

Her lips curved upward. "You honor us, Flor."

I hated to tell her, but I was no prize. She'd learn.

In the meantime, I would get the hell out of here. "Know what? There is one thing I want to pack. My mop handle."

She wrinkled her nose and rose. "The one you fought Trevor Blackside with?"

I grinned and limped toward the door, keeping my side turned to her, just in case. "It's the only weapon I was allowed."

"We'll get you real weapons at Northern," she promised. "And real clothes." She tugged on a lock of my butchered hair as she strode past. "And a real haircut. I hate to say it, but yours is *awful*."

"It wasn't by choice."

Her eyes narrowed as she stared down at me, and it felt

like she was seeing straight into me. "Darling girl, I don't think much in your life has been by choice, has it?" Her voice thrummed with sympathy. It sounded genuine.

I didn't know how to take her words. Had she forgotten that only moments before, she'd basically been threatening to take away my choices herself? I tightened my lips so I wouldn't start crying—or worse, point out her hypocrisy.

"Well, from now on, all the choices are yours." She rubbed her hands together as we strode down the hallway, the shouts of the other residents following us. "Starting with dinner. Steak or chicken?"

"Do I have to choose?"

"Of course not." Her smile was almost too wide. "Not tonight, anyway."

28

DINNER WITH THE COUNCIL
FLOR

Less than a day after I'd thought I would die, I stared at my reflection, wondering who the girl in the mirror was.

She couldn't be an unranked shifter. She had on a new, clean, powder-blue skirt and a sleeveless cream-colored silk top, and her short hair had been cut into a cute pixie style. Her long lashes had a coat of mascara on, and her lips were pink with gloss. Even her nails were buffed and shining.

How could she be me?

I touched my cheek and watched my too-thin reflection move as well. Far too thin. I was still starving—literally, it felt like. So not everything had changed.

I lifted a hand to my ear, to the tag that Margarette had insisted I have cut off immediately. I would have agreed, but I was just petty enough to want all these fuckheads at Southern to see me leave through those ugly razor-wire-topped gates, unranked and still wearing the tag they'd put on me, and let them choke on their jealousy. So I'd told her I'd wait until we got to her packlands.

Anyway, the small weight of it there kept me focused on my surroundings, forced me to pay attention, and to remember that not everything had changed. The fear that had always thrummed in my veins was still there.

Trevor and his guys were still out there somewhere, though no one had seen them since the Alpha challenge.

My skin still itched with the need to hide, especially as the hours for the Hunt drew closer.

Yeah, some things were the same as always.

Margarette had escorted me to a room in the guest quarters that smelled a lot like Glen, though I assumed he'd been shoved somewhere else for the remainder of the night. After I'd barricaded the door with furniture, I'd slept like the dead until a few hours before, when she'd shown back up with another female shifter from Northern to help me get ready for dinner.

Margarette's pack member had only been a few inches taller than me, and nice enough. The skirt they'd brought in smelled like her, but fit pretty well, and she'd loaned me matching blue sandals that were only a little too big. It was thoughtful, but I'd have rather had my mop handle and a cheese sandwich.

My stomach echoed the wish for more food. A knock at the door interrupted the growling. "Flor? It's Margarette and Alpha Hillier."

I opened the door, already smiling. The Northern Alpha stood with his hand at his mate's waist, but his light-blue eyes on me. "I'm glad to see you still breathing, young shifter," he said, offering his other arm to me as I stepped out of the room. "Margarette, you did an amazing job! Won't Glen be pleased."

As we walked, he exuded waves of Alpha power so strong, I could feel it moving from his arm to mine, though I wasn't sure he was even aware of it. His jovial nature was the farthest thing from "Alpha" I'd ever seen.

I smiled, too flustered to speak and slightly nervous about his comment. Why would Glen's approval matter? I had a sinking feeling I knew. While Margarette had been making me over, she'd broadly hinted at the Glory of True Love and the Deep Satisfaction of Having a Mate about a dozen times. Once I'd threatened to climb out the window, though, she'd mostly stopped.

Still, she'd already tried to use her dominance to make me accept Glen. If this guy did that, I'd be bitten, claimed, and pregnant before I came out from under the command. I pulled my arm out of his.

"Really, you are a vision, Flor. No wonder my son clai —" He went silent when Margarette shot him a hard glance. "Nevertheless. I am so glad to see you looking better. Are you hungry?"

My stomach answered for me, and we all smiled. However, I was surprised when we didn't go into the pack dining hall. "Where are we..."

Turning a corner, we entered a room I had never been in. Well, not with anyone's knowledge. I had hidden under the vast mahogany dining table once during a particularly tricky Hunt. The Alpha's private dining room had a table that could seat at least thirty running the length of it, with ostentatiously carved chairs padded by maroon velvet cushions.

The Alpha Heirs and some of the Head Enforcers from the other packs, about sixteen in all, were seated at the other end of the room, but rose when we entered. Something in my gut yanked me toward the guys, but I stopped when I smelled dinner.

Three sideboards that ran the length of one wall were

practically groaning with food. There were slabs of rare steaks along with boats filled with sauces, stuffed chicken breasts oozing cheese and topped with crispy greens, some sort of fried things that smelled like shrimp, and more platters of vegetables than I knew existed.

"Am I dead?" I wondered aloud.

"I think you're just starting to live, sweet girl," Alpha Hillier replied gently, then squeezed my shoulder and took a seat next to some other strangers.

Margarette guided me to a chair next to one of the Heirs. Brand, who smelled every bit as delectable now as ever. When he rose and bowed to me, for some unknown reason, his piney, wild scent made me want to rub myself in his shirt. *Maybe in his pants, too,* I thought, taking in how the tight cloth clung to his massive thighs.

"Flor," he said in a bass murmur. "I'm glad to see you well."

I didn't know what to say. "Brand," I finally muttered. "Backatcha."

"You can call me Bearman, if you prefer," he teased. My eyes flew to his dark gaze, and I saw something in his face I'd never seen before. Wonder? Awe? As if I were something worth staring at. "You look good," he said at last. "I'm glad you…"

"Didn't die?" I joked. Something primitive flickered in his expression, and for a moment, he almost seemed to expand, growing wider and taller. "Bearman?" I whispered, my mouth suddenly dry.

Someone down the table cleared their throat impatiently, and I practically fell into the chair, the soft velvet almost swallowing me. Cheeks burning from all the attention focused on me, I dropped my gaze to all the forks and spoons spread out on the white cloth. Why would someone need more than one spoon? Or one fork, for that matter?

I noticed Brand rising and moving away, but my mind was spinning. What was I doing sitting here, in this room, with the most important shifters in North America? When was someone going to yell out that it was all a trick, a hoax?

An unranked servant stood by the door that led to the kitchens. Was he there to serve us? Maybe to keep me trapped in this room when everyone was done eating and ready for their after-dinner entertainment. For all I knew, they'd be hunting me.

I forced my breath to slow before I hyperventilated. I had to stay alert.

"Flor?" Brand's deep voice interrupted my growing panic. "I made you a plate." I didn't look at him, but a plate piled overfull with steak, only steak, landed in front of me, splashing the tablecloth with juices.

For a moment, his massive form blocked out every other diner in the room, and I could pretend they weren't there. That I was safe.

"You don't like steak?"

He sounded so distressed, I grinned up at him. "I haven't ever had a whole one." I gestured at the plate; it was enough meat to feed me for a month, easily. "And that's a lot of steak for one gal."

He grumbled and sat in his chair, which creaked like it might crumple under his bulk. "You need feeding up. As much steak as you can manage. You can go back for green things later, right?" He sounded so awkward, uncomfortable. I watched him hesitate over the forks, like he didn't know which one to pick up either. I dared a longer look at him.

He was seven feet tall, wearing a too-tight dress shirt

and a tie that both looked like they might pop open at any moment. His long dark hair had been pulled back in a rubber band at his nape, and he was blushing red above his short, trimmed beard.

He was adorable.

"Thanks," I told him, and gently laid my hand over his. A strange warmth moved through me, like a heater had come on right behind our chairs. My skin warmed where our hands met, and the smell of him—pine and woodsmoke and wild berries—enveloped me. I closed my eyes, confused, and let myself breathe it, taste it. I moaned, wishing that there was some way I could hold that scent inside me forever, that I never had to exhale.

"Um, Flor?" Brand's deep voice had gone oddly squeaky.

My eyes popped open. *Oh, Mother Moon.*

I'd moaned.

At the dining table.

I shot a terrified glance at the rest of the guests. Glen and Finnick were grinding their teeth, for some reason. Margarette and Alpha Hillier seemed concerned, staring at their food like it was a physics problem.

Down the table, though, a colossal giant of a man who could only be Brand's father was looking right at me. His long beard was messy and much thicker, his dark eyes far less warm, and he was probably the wildest shifter I'd ever seen. You could sense his wolf, as if he was ready to shift at any point—wanted to shift, even—and would tear out as many throats as he needed to get back to the wilderness.

I watched, mortified, as one corner of his harsh mouth turned up. And he winked.

"I'm so sorry," I whispered, whipping my hand away and stuffing a small piece of steak into my mouth. I figured

I should eat fast, since someone would almost definitely ask me to leave after my show of unranked table manners.

"Don't apologize," Brand's father boomed. I noted that, unlike the other well-dressed guys at the table, he had on a plaid long-sleeved shirt and jeans. They probably didn't make suits in his size. "I like a girl who appreciates her food."

With that, he had given me an out, and I took it. "That's me, super hungry." For some reason, that made a few of the Enforcers cough, and Finnick blush as hard as Brand had. *Whatever.* "I've never had meat like this before, though. It's amazing." I sawed off a huge hunk of steak and shoved it in my mouth. There. If I couldn't make sounds, or talk, I couldn't embarrass myself any further, right?

Next to me, Brand wasn't eating. He just sat there with a ridiculous grin on his face, running his fingers over the spot on his left hand where I'd touched.

"You okay?" I asked through my chewed-up steak.

He just nodded, eyes glued to his food like he was memorizing it. His blush had gotten even deeper, moving down his neck under his too-tight collar. My hand itched to touch him again, to feel that heat, whatever it was.

I kept my mouth shut for the rest of dinner—shut and filled with amazing food. I had a feeling the others were covertly watching me, but I was too hungry to care. I should have eaten slowly, but I couldn't. Who knew when I would ever see this much meat again? If only I could take it with me.

Wait. A thought bubbled up. I might not be able to sneak steak out—any shifter would smell it and steal it away—but I might be able to get away with something else.

When I was sure no one was watching, I slipped a

sturdy steak knife under my shirt, tucking it into my waistband at the back. With that one movement, I felt safer, even here in the Pack House.

Silverware didn't count as a weapon at Southern, so I didn't feel too bad. I wasn't sure who in the Alpha's house I could trust, and I wasn't sure how long it would be before Margarette took me away.

Hell, I didn't know if the Hunt was still on. I wouldn't put it past Trevor and his gang to use the other packs' presence as a distraction. I needed to go.

"Thanks for the meal. It was an, uh, unexpected treat to get to sit with all y'all... Wait." I peered up and down the table, suddenly realizing Luke was nowhere to be seen. "Where's Luke?"

"He's healing. He's... having a difficult time, with his existing injury," Brand answered, and weirdly, a sob suddenly worked its way out of my throat.

I had no reason to feel guilty, but I had a feeling running away from this room would be easier than escaping the raw emotions that scoured me inside as I stood. "I gotta go."

A reject like me didn't belong here.

Or maybe anywhere.

29

EAT AND RUN

FLOR

"Y ou can't go!" At least three voices complained at the same time, but I took a breath to keep the dinner knife I'd stolen securely in my skirt's waistband, and nodded to Margarette.

"Thanks again for the meal, and everything. The saving my life and giving me a home stuff."

"You're welcome, Flor," Margarette murmured. "I'll have them box up another plate for you for later." If she hadn't been across the table, I would have hugged her.

"Flor?" From the far end of the table, a man I hadn't talked to, sitting next to Finnick—an older version of him, minus the gorgeous green eyes—addressed me in a voice so cold, it stopped all the conversation in the room. I cleared my throat and leaned around Brand, craning my neck to see who was speaking.

The first thing I noticed was that the man wore glasses. That was super strange to me; shifters all had perfect vision, unless they'd lost an eye. I knew our Alpha had plucked out more than one pack member's eye for discipline over the years.

I shuddered, trying to focus on what the guy was asking. "Yeah?"

"Your name—it's Spanish for flower," the older man said impatiently. He peered down over his glasses, like I was a bug under a magnifying glass. "Do you have Latin shifter heritage somewhere?"

"Nope," I said, catching a curled lip and eye roll from Brand. "I'm not Flor, actually." I didn't miss the confused sounds the guys made, Finnick included. But it wasn't like my name was a secret. Well, not all of it. "My real name is Florida."

"Florida?" Margarette smiled. "I may like that even better. What's your middle name?"

"Um, no middle name," I lied.

The man scoffed. "You would lie to our faces? To members of the Council?" He shot Margarette a glance. "I thought you said she had skills and honor. Margarette, I can't believe you'd let this one step foot in your home."

"Father," Finnick interrupted. "Please."

His father's voice dropped so low, I imagined he thought I wouldn't hear him. "You spoke about her like she was some sort of Valkyrie. She's ill-bred, unattractive, and her accent is like nails on a chalkboard. Son, if this is what you admire, we need to recall you to the city so you can be around shifters worth knowing."

"Father, enough." Finnick stood, his heavy chair toppling to the carpet.

His father laughed in his face. "Why? You can't possibly be attracted to her. She's an unranked female from Southern. They pass them around like after-dinner mints. You can play with them, but don't ever think of bringing trash like that home."

Finnick growled. "Father. Stop talking." The waves of

Alpha energy rolling off him were alarming, and his father was shivering under it for some reason. That was so odd. His father had to outrank his own Heir. But the way he was almost cowering under Finnick's display made it clear that something wasn't right.

"You dare?" Finnick's father hissed. "You'd risk everything for a Southern slut?"

Growls were now rising from all over—Brand, Glen, Margarette, even Alpha Hillier.

"I said, *stop talking*." Finnick's tone was all Alpha bark.

Everyone at the table was stunned. "A-are you challenging me?" his father sputtered.

Suddenly, the room was thick with emotion. Rage, concern, fear, anticipation. Amusement? I sniffed in Brand's direction.

"Finn's balls just dropped," he breathed. "He's about to be Alpha. About damned time."

"Don't stir the shit," I replied, thumping him on the shoulder. That weird warmth emanated from his dark hair, and I almost buried my fingers in it. "Why do you smell so good, Bearman?" I whispered aloud without meaning to.

The growling got louder, and Finnick's eyes swung to me. He was growling now, too.

At the other end of the table, Brand's father let out a coughing laugh. "Girl has good taste." He shot a condescending glance at Finnick's father. "Aidan, apologize for insulting my son's... friend." I heard Margarette curse softly, for some reason.

It was time to show Finn and the others I fought my own battles and won. "Everybody calm down. He was right."

"What do you mean?" Glen demanded.

I shrugged. "You were right, Finnick's Dad."

"Alpha Aidan McDonnell," Brand whispered.

I winked at him. "Like I said, Alpha McDonnell, you're right. I mean, not about the slut part. But ill-bred? I'd have to agree with that; my sperm donor was a rat bastard, for sure. I know my accent's thicker than flies on shit, and I ain't much to look at." I ignored the muttered protests from the guys. "I did lie to you. But I mean, haven't you ever had something you didn't want to announce at the dinner table?"

"I wouldn't be afraid to say my own name," he shot back. "I was told you had courage."

"I was told you Easterners had manners. Even I know you shouldn't confront a fellow dinner guest and talk shit about her under your breath. Or out loud." I waved at his glasses. "And isn't *that* a lie? Your glasses, I mean. There's no way you need those."

He huffed, and Finnick spoke up, picking up his chair and sitting again. "Yes, you're right. My father wears them around humans to blend in. It's common practice for those who work in the human world. Many shifters in the city wear them."

"Gotcha." I sat back down and chomped on a small piece of cheese to keep my hands busy. "Sorry, I wouldn't know about human stuff. I've never been outside pack grounds."

"Never?" Brand murmured the word. I shook my head, then felt his warm hand cover mine under the table.

A tense, fraught silence swamped the room. Someone had to speak, and it wasn't going to be me.

"So, Florida..." Brand's father surprised us all by beginning; he didn't seem the type to make small talk. "You said you are nineteen. When did you finish high school, this year or last?"

I swallowed. "Yeah, just Flor, thanks. And I didn't. Finish, that is. I had to quit going to school when my mama died, back when I was fifteen."

"Why?" Margarette demanded.

I felt my face burning. "It was either quit school and take up pack duties, or be cast out along with Mama for the rogues to kill."

"When you were fifteen?" Alpha Hillier ran his hands over his beard. "I can't believe we didn't know how low your pack had sunk." I kept eating, hoping I'd have time to finish the bacon-dressed green beans and mashed potatoes once I'd devoured my steak.

"Would you want to finish school?" Finnick asked, and to my surprise, his voice wasn't sarcastic or cold. He seemed genuinely interested. His dad, on the other hand, was looking appalled.

Ignoring his dad, I swallowed my mouthful. No one had ever asked me if I wanted to finish school, or get my high school equivalency. "Yeah. I love to read. I mean, I don't own any real books, just some paperbacks I found in the trash, but back in school, I loved checking out books. And I kept learning after I quit, so I might be able to place out of some classes. I actually found a bunch of old textbooks in the dumpsters when I was scrounging for food for me and the other unranked kids, and I taught myself algebra."

Ugh. I didn't really care what he thought of me, what the others thought. So why was I trying to convince them I wasn't dumb?

"You like math?" Finnick looked intrigued, his green eyes gleaming. "I just finished my master's in physics. I could tutor you—"

Margarette cut him off. "She would need a Northern tutor, Finn. She's going to be a Northern Enforcer."

259

Finnick looked like he wanted to argue, but he let it go. I wasn't going to, though. "I agreed to be a visitor at Northern, Margarette. I don't know where I'll end up. Your pack might not like me." It seemed probable; I couldn't imagine what an unranked hick like me could offer a pack that renowned.

"They'll love you," Glen announced. "If they know what's good for them."

Brand cleared his throat. "What she needs to learn is how to shift and hunt. For that, you want to come to Mountain." He squeezed my hand. "If Northern doesn't suit you, you're welcome in my home, Flor. We could use an Enforcer with your skills. I want to see what kind of damage you can do with a real staff."

I smiled back. "Thanks, Bearman." I didn't mean I was going to accept his offer, but the other two Heirs acted like I had. Glen, Finnick, and all the other males started shouting suggestions.

"Wait a minute, we have weapons, too."

"She could be an Enforcer in any pack!"

"I've already offered her a place—"

"She's already been adopted by Northern!"

"That can be *changed*."

The racket went on and on, chairs scraping on the floor, hands and arms flying as they argued, none of them paying attention to me. None of them listening to me. I covered my ears, the yelling almost as bad as the swirling emotions that filled the room with harsh, musky scents.

It was the perfect time to sneak away, but I was still exhausted from my fights, from being mostly dead, and from being surrounded by strangers. And for all I knew, I'd cause some inter-pack incident by leaving. So I curled up into a ball on my chair cushion, rocking slightly. No one noticed.

And then I was surrounded by a smell I knew. Rich caramel and fire. A scent that said quiet and calm.

"Luke?" I asked, opening my eyes. Where had he come from?

Before I could ask, he had picked me up and carried me into the hall. The others started to follow, but he shut the door gently in their faces. He took a few more steps and stumbled, his hands tightening on me. I pulled myself free and quickly stood, tucking my arm around his waist to support him.

"Luke! You're still hurt." I peered at his abdomen, the spot I'd stabbed. I could smell fresh blood.

"I'm fine."

I tasted the lie at the back of my throat, like chewing aluminum foil. "I'm so sorry." I never thought I'd apologize to him, or any of the Southern Enforcers. But I had hurt him, and he had still defended me, challenged and defeated the Alpha to save me.

"Never," he said in his soft voice, lifting my chin with his hand so I stared into his icy blue eyes. "Never apologize to me. There's nothing I will ever be able to do to earn your forgiveness, though I'll never stop trying. My heart, I will never deserve a rank equal to yours." He leaned forward and pressed a kiss to my forehead. I leaned into it. "You need sleep."

"Yes." I sure as heck did, if I was dreaming Luke Callaway was calling me his heart.

"Follow me." He led me to a room that had always been locked, then pulled a key out of his pocket. "I'm the only one who has this key. And now it's yours." He pressed it into my hand.

His room? His caramel scent filled the space. It was furnished only with a bed, two chairs, and a desk. Not much more than my own dorm room. The blankets looked warm, though, and smelled fresh like the laundry line, and like him. I turned to thank him, but he was already gone.

I fell onto the bed and was asleep before I could call out my thanks.

30

LUKE'S STORY
GLEN

I lay next to Finnick on the floor of a guest bedroom, listening to my parents arguing. They'd been at it for over an hour. They were quiet, but with shifter hearing and shoddy construction like the Southern Pack House boasted, there was no such thing as quiet enough.

After Luke had collapsed in the hallway in front of his bedroom, where he'd placed a sleeping Flor, Mom had gone into organizer mode. She'd assigned one room for me and Finnick, but we were too wired up to sleep, and a feeling of dread and expectation hovered over the Pack House. Shifting to wolf form had made it impossible to talk, though I was pretty sure neither of us wanted to. But we listened.

Mom's voice rose. "Of course I saw what happened with Brand—we all did. And yes, there's something with Luke and Glen as well. But she might reject them all at this rate, Bradley. She's panicking."

Finnick's dark gray ears perked up, his eyes narrowed. My wolf whined.

"Does she not feel a mate bond with any of them?"

"She's been fighting for her life, literally for years." A pause. "Do you know what she told me, when I was doing her makeup? I asked what she did for fun around here. She said she's never had time for fun, that she's been working for years. Working and hiding. And the other shifters here... Well, have you seen or heard any of them asking about her? Even the unranked ones are only just civil."

"No friends in a pack this size? That seems unlikely."

"When would she have time to make friends? And it wasn't only that she was forced to work. From dusk to midnight, every day for years, as soon as her work was done, she was hunted. Hunted by the young males. Sometimes not only the young ones."

I forced down a snarl.

"Glen said something about a Hunt. What would happen if they caught her?"

"If they caught her, Calvin decreed she would be forcibly mated to them."

My wolf snapped at empty air, looking for a throat to tear out. Finnick growled low.

"Forcibly?" Dad shouted.

"Yes, and that's why we need to wait. She's never thought of mating as anything but a punishment. As sanctioned rape. Of a child. It's what this wretched pack taught her." Something glass shattered, followed by a longer pause. "Brad, you know if any shifter understands the importance of carrying on a line, of a strong female like her accepting a true bond with one of our own, it's me. Darling, I don't think she should be encouraged to choose a mate right now. She says she won't ever, but I think she's terrified of ending up with a shifter like those in her pack."

"If our son pursues her—if any of them do—it's just another Hunt, isn't it?"

"Yes," she said with a sigh. "I'm not sure what's wrong with her mating instinct. What's wrong with our boys as well—it's not normal for them all to be so drawn to her."

"Does she feel any pull at all to them? Maybe a bit more to one of them?"

"I can't tell. At dinner, she seemed to prefer Brand, but it could have been the proximity. We'll need to seat Glen closer to her at meals... They'll make such gorgeous pups."

Finnick snarled softly.

Dad's answer was sobering. "Margarette, they're all displaying the initial signs that they've met their true mate. Whoever it is will be driven to claim her. The pain will be debilitating—"

"I know. But she needs time. Possibly a long time."

"Time is one thing they won't *have*." Dad cursed. "This pack had something to do with a coven. There could be dark magic at work. Is there any chance she's not the true mate of any of them?"

There was a long pause. "For their sake, I almost hope she's not. It could end their friendship when she chooses."

"Mags, if there is some sort of magically perverted mate bond with more than one of them, when she claims her mate..."

I glanced at Finnick. We all knew. Shifters with an incomplete mate bond who were separated went feral.

But Dad finished. "It could *kill* the others."

I swallowed hard. Could that be true?

"Bradley, that's extreme. The bond will settle, I know it. She just needs more time, and healing from her trauma. Why don't we take them with us?"

"All of them? Even Luke?" He sounded shocked.

"No, you're right—they'll need him here as Alpha. The Council voted. When are you going to execute Calvin?"

"I'm going down now."

"Good. Make it quick, even if the bastard deserves to suffer. I can't get out of here fast enough." A door opened, and footsteps went past our room.

Shit. I had to change back to talk to Finn and Brand, and maybe even Luke, although I had a feeling he was going to have his hands too full to chase after my mate. Good. He didn't deserve her. He could have told us, should have let us know years ago what was happening here. What they were doing to Flor.

In minutes, Finnick and I had changed forms, put on clothes, and were at Brand's door. To my surprise, he and Luke both answered our knock. "Flor's still in my room," Luke explained at my look. "It's locked. It didn't seem right to stay in there with her."

At the other end of the Pack House, there was noise. Probably Dad going to the cell with Mom and the other visiting Council members to take care of the loose end Luke had left.

"So," I began, as we all stood in the muggy heat. The only illumination was from porch lights on houses outside the main compound, and a few security lights at the front of the sprawling one-story house. This whole place was a security nightmare. I could see how Flor had managed to hide from the Hunt for so many years. She'd probably been the one to knock the bulbs out of as many porch lights and walkway lamps as necessary.

The thought of the Hunt had me sneering at Luke. "She took that steak knife to bed, didn't she? Mom said Flor still thinks she's being hunted."

"How could you not tell us?" Brand asked the question we all wanted answered.

Luke stiffened. "Callaway gave me an Alpha command,

gave all of us orders, not to speak of anything that was going on here. When I tried to help her, he..." His voice broke, and he swallowed, his face pale. I wasn't sure I wanted to know what the bastard had done when disobeyed. "She needs to leave Southern. It's toxic for her."

"She needs closure," Finnick inserted, his voice smooth and low. "I find the death of one's enemies can provide that."

"Point them out," Brand demanded, his voice so low, it sounded like a rumble of earth. "The ones that hunted her. So I know which ones to kill."

"Yes," Finnick agreed. "Names, Luke."

To my surprise, he nodded. "My first act as Alpha will be to remove the rank of all of the unmated wolves who participated and banish those who deserve that. Although that may leave me with no Enforcers to speak of."

"How many were there?" Something twisted in my gut. "How many males, Luke?"

"Forty males, give or take. A few found their true mates and stopped." He let out a strange noise. "My Alpha commanded me not to interfere. I did anyway, once, and spent two months in the cell he's in now. He starved me for two weeks, then let the Hunt males in, five at a time, to practice their sparring techniques on me, with pipes and chains."

Luke pulled away from me and tore his shirt off, revealing a back that was covered with thin silver scars. "The next time I tried, Callaway whipped me with silver. He said if I helped her again, he'd whip her. If I even looked at her, he'd let his men have her without a Hunt. I was afraid he'd kill us both, if I dared to claim her." I grabbed his shirt and gently draped it back over him.

"Luke, why didn't you tell me?" Finnick pulled Luke

into a hug. It was the only time I'd ever seen Finnick be affectionate with anyone.

Luke held onto him like they were best friends, murmuring something into Finn's ear before pulling away. "I knew," he said to us all, his voice raw. "I knew she was special. I realized she was my true mate when I was ten."

"You couldn't know that. She would have been a baby!"

Luke nodded. "She was two. Trevor's father, Van, was beating her with a belt for some reason, and I felt like it was me under the belt. I was overwhelmed with the urge to protect her. So I threw myself over her and took the whipping for her." He hesitated, remembering. "It hurt less to be under that belt than to watch her suffer."

"What happened to her?" I swallowed hard. "What happened to you?"

"I heard Del took care of her. I almost died. The Alpha healed me—and punished me—by forcing my shift."

"At ten?" Finnick whistled low.

"He started my Enforcer training then. I did what I could, when I could. I snuck rations to Flor's mom, Lily. I got a friend to hire Lily at the QwikMart, hoping she would find a way to escape with Flor. But she wouldn't leave. She couldn't."

"Why couldn't she?" I asked.

"She was insane."

Brand grunted. "What about Flor's father?"

"She said he died," Finnick said, but he sounded uncertain. Luke stayed strangely quiet.

"No," I murmured. "She said it was complicated. That she couldn't talk about it." Maybe she literally couldn't. Callaway had given a lot of Alpha commands to hide his crimes.

"No one ever spoke of him. I assumed Lily was taken

against her will by one of his Enforcers, and that it broke her mind." We all reacted in horror, and when Luke shrugged and said, "It happens at Southern more often than you'd think," I thought I might throw up.

Brand snarled, "We'll kill every last tainted one on our way out." I almost agreed, but the handwritten words on the paper Luke had given me earlier that week suddenly flashed into my mind.

I spoke my thoughts aloud. "Mate bond severance. Twenty years ago, Callaway paid a coven to sever a mate bond. What if it was his own?"

31

SECRETS AND SNEAK ATTACKS

LUKE

E very secret that festered in the heart of my pack was coming to light, and I wondered if the others even understood how close to the truth they were stepping.

I would not be the one to uncover my mate's secret. Not when I knew the truth might pin her to Southern as surely as it had her mother. Trap her here.

Glen had gone strangely pale. Finnick rubbed his brow, like he was trying to solve a complicated problem. Brand's voice trembled with rage when he finally spoke. "Callaway had a true mate? And broke the bond?"

They all turned to me. "Yes," I answered simply.

"When?" The unspoken question hung in the air.

"Over twenty years ago," I said truthfully. It was only a few days over that.

"Before Flor was born?" Brand muttered.

"Yes." Our eyes met, and I saw disappointment in his gaze. Did he know what I was hiding from them?

Did he know why I had to keep it secret?

He opened his mouth to speak, then closed it and looked up, staring into the night sky as if one of the stars there had the answer to his pain.

Glen spoke softly. "The only pack Flor has ever seen up close was deeply abusive. Many of the matings were nonconsensual. The Hunt has made her see all mate claims as cages. Mom was right. Flor needs more time to heal and get to know us, away from Southern."

Finnick nodded. "If you fight among yourselves, it will make her feel hunted again. You need to keep your wolves in line somehow."

Your wolves? I narrowed my eyes, wondering why he was denying what had been so obvious in the battle, and even before. Finnick was every bit as smitten as the others.

Glen nodded. "My parents will take her to Ontario, and we'll all go with her."

I put a hand to my stomach where the wound still ached. "Except me."

Brand settled a heavy hand on my shoulder. "Will you be all right?"

"I have to be," I replied. "I have to try to save the good shifters here at Southern. The unranked, the children and women. And even if I went to Northern with you, I don't deserve her."

"The Moon Goddess may think you do," Brand rumbled.

Finnick sighed. "He can't leave Southern without an Alpha. Sometimes we have to make choices for the greater good." His green eyes glittered with deep pain.

Brand huffed. "This pack doesn't deserve an Alpha."

My laugh was humorless. "I don't deserve to be their Alpha either. Hell, I don't want it—these people, the pack

I'll serve, is the same one that tortured and tormented my mate." I let out a shuddering sigh and stepped away from Brand. "I'll serve the pack, and when it gets to be too much, being away from her... One of you must come down here and help me."

I saw my meaning dawn on them, one by one. I needed one of them to come back and put me down if I went insane.

When I went insane.

"Don't give up hope," Brand said quietly. "My father found a way to stay alive, alone."

"I don't *want* to live without her," I whispered to them all. "Promise that you'll come. Please."

Finnick opened his mouth to answer, when a flurry of shouts and screams from the other end of the compound distracted him.

"It's him," I gasped. I could smell him, a hint of his old man funk riding the breeze to us. Had they taken him out of this cell for the execution? Why hadn't they just killed him down below?

"Is Flor safe?" Brand demanded.

"There's a guard outside her door who has orders not to leave his post," Glen shouted.

Brand shook his head. "One of us should go to her," he insisted.

We all hesitated, but then the decision was taken from us. We heard Margarette screaming, "Bradley!" and the sounds of battle. Samuel roared for his son, and Brand and Glen sprinted away, with Finnick only a breath behind.

None of us had weapons, but the others had all trained for years for situations worse than this. I waited a few seconds, knowing I would have one advantage: my own pack wouldn't understand that I would be fighting against them.

I rounded the corner and paused for a split second, taking in the horrific scene. The space that had been a fighting ring for the Enforcer Games had become a battlefield.

In the center of the dusty ring, Glen's mother stood over her mate's bloody form. Bradley was still alive, but bleeding profusely. She was using one hand to hold a gaping chest wound closed and had shifted her fingernails into claws to keep our Head Enforcer away.

Van was holding a long silver blade in his enormous hand; Margarette was outmatched. Glen was desperately trying to get to his mother's side, but he was almost buried under a wall of Southern's Enforcers.

Brand's father Samuel was fighting off eight Southerners and wasn't doing well. He was armed only with what looked like two hunting knives, and his attackers all had small metal shields and swords. He was bleeding from dozens of slashes, but he ignored the wounds. Behind him, three Southern Enforcers lay on the ground, their necks slit wide. As I ran, more Enforcers poured in from the side yards.

The shifter from the Borderlands was harrying a group of them, making strange movements with his hands, like he was lassoing them, preventing them from entering the courtyard. I couldn't see any rope, but whatever he was doing was working. The nine or so Enforcers he was harassing were tripping over themselves, dropping their weapons.

Weapons. Brand and Finnick had raced to Brand's father and grabbed the swords the dead Enforcers no longer needed. Finnick dashed away to help Glen, who had gone down on one knee, still fighting.

Brand attacked the three shifters who'd managed to circle behind his father. They didn't see Brand coming, and one of them was dead before he could even blink. The other two whirled, teeth bared, and charged the Alpha Heir.

I ran toward the battle just as more Southerners—one of them a massive shifter who had been one of my torturers years ago—snarled and lunged for Brand. I stepped in between Brand and two of the men I'd trained alongside. One of them screamed at me to get out of their way, to help them.

"Weapon," I demanded, holding my hand out for a blade. He handed it to me.

I quickly flipped it around and used it to cut them both down in the space of a few seconds. The knife stuck in the spine of one as I made sure he wouldn't heal to fight again, but I let it go when I heard Margarette's panicked scream.

"*No!*"

I kicked my fallen pack members to one side, trying to reach her. She had been wounded severely, a huge gash running from her hairline to her neck, blood pouring down her shoulder. Van was lifting the sword again for the killing strike.

There were no more weapons to grab, but it didn't matter. I leaped over the bodies in front of me and threw myself between her and Van.

He snarled, licking blood from his lips. "Out of my way, boy. Your daddy ain't here to save you now."

I snarled back, shifting my fingers into sharp claws, feeling my teeth move into position.

"Your funeral," he sneered and pulled one arm back, the sword glinting.

I heard Finnick call my name, and one word—"Catch!" Out of the corner of my eye, I saw something long and brown flying toward me. I caught and lifted it, blocking the blow that Van had leveled at me.

His blade skidded off my weapon as I angled it to diminish the force of the strike. I heard a snap of wood breaking. Finnick had thrown me a staff, a weak one, with a strange metal screw on one end.

I almost smiled when I realized it was a mop. Her mop.

I could work with it. In fact... I snapped the staff at the spot where Van's blow had weakened it. I preferred fighting with two short staffs anyway. I spun them around, licking my lips as Van watched the splintered ends twirling close.

But fighting an expert swordsman with what amounted to two large sticks wasn't sustainable. He had made sure I never got enough training to best him or any of his cronies. Dad had made certain I stayed weak and small from years of being forbidden to shift.

I was fucked.

Van went on the offense, making me hop over the dead bodies of fallen shifters, forcing me away from Margarette. I was fine with that; I wanted him farther away, but then I realized he had taken me closer to another group of fighters. At a short whistle from him, two of them charged me, and Van disengaged, heading back to his primary target.

"Glen!" I yelled, hoping he could get to his mother, though he was facing down a half-dozen Enforcers many yards away.

Unable to get past the two who struck at me with their blades, I half-watched Margarette pull herself up on her bleeding arms. Then Van was there, yanking her long hair up with one hand and pulling back the sword with the other. He was going to cut her head off, on top of her mate's broken body.

"*Mom!*" Glen screamed.

Samuel roared, Brand echoing him, but they were too far to help. Too late.

Then I heard something that made my heart pump faster, made my wolf inside me howl with terror and panic. A high-pitched scream, filled with years of rage.

My mate had arrived.

32

THE OBVIOUS TARGET
FLOR

I knew something was wrong the moment I woke up in Luke's bed. I lay there in the dark, surrounded by his scent, and terrified by the sound of something sliding against the wall outside the room.

A part of me wanted nothing more than to bury my head under the covers and pretend I didn't notice the faint, metallic scent of blood seeping under the doorframe. But I'd been trained by Del to survive, and I owed it to him to get out of this pisshole.

For a moment, I pondered my best route of escape. I had shifted, or at least Margarette had told me I had. So my senses were stronger now, and my healing should be more advanced. I was still weak, though, and I knew better than to try and shift again. For one thing, it would take too long. For another, I had no idea how to fight in that form.

But I could kick ass on two feet any damned day of the year.

Suddenly, I heard a distant chorus of howls and screams from outside, in the direction of the fighting ring. Were the Games still on? But no, I could make out the clang of metal on metal, and far too many screams. It sounded like a war had begun.

Then I heard a soft footstep just outside the door, and knew my own battle needed attention. I slipped out of bed, wishing I had on something easier to fight in than the fancy clothing from the dinner. At least I still had the steak knife in my waistband. I made sure it was easy to reach, then used the pillows to make a shape under the comforter.

I left the shoes where Luke must have placed them, and scanned the room for any other weapons, but Luke's room was almost as sparse as mine had been. Besides the bed, the desk, and two chairs, he had nothing, not even a lamp. I opened the desk drawer slowly and felt inside carefully, finding nothing but a small ring of keys. The keys to this room?

No, he'd handed me a single key. The only one, he'd said, and he hadn't been lying.

But he'd obviously been mistaken, because someone outside had a key as well, or something that worked like one, judging by the unmistakable sound coming from the doorknob.

The doorknob that was already turning.

I slid next to the door, my back flat against the wall, the keyring in my left hand and the two keys already jutting out from between my fingers, my right hand resting on the handle of the knife at my waist.

I held my breath, and held as still as I knew how.

The room was dark, but the light from the hallway illuminated a familiar bulky shape. I didn't move to attack, though, since I knew this one never went anywhere alone.

Sure enough, a whisper from the doorway had me flinching. "Grant! Kill her and get out here! The fight's startin'."

The shifter standing by the side of the bed took a long sniff, then yanked the comforter back, revealing the pillows. "Go on, Lyn. I got this." He turned slowly to face me, his eyes glinting in the hallway light, his mouth twisted in a wicked smile. "Looks like I caught you after all, little prey. I win the Hunt."

I stepped away from the wall, balancing on the balls of my feet, ready to strike. I didn't want him to know I had a knife, so I held my hands up so he could see the keys. "You win nothin', Grant Lee. I'd slit my own throat before I'd let you touch me."

He laughed, stepping closer. "You've shifted now. You can't slit any shifter's throat with those little things, not even your own now. You'd heal too quick. All you'd do is make yourself a little bloody while I deal with you." He let out another chuckle, lifting the comforter. "I don't mind a little blood when I'm fucking my mate. You'll learn to like it, too."

I saw the move coming and ducked low, letting the comforter he tossed at me fall over me. But I was already moving, not toward the door, not away. I crouched low and ran at him, reaching his legs and knocking him over onto the bed.

Del's words echoed in my mind as I made my move while Grant still couldn't see me. *"Smart shifters are hard to beat. But a dumb one will always expect you to go for the obvious target. The throat, the gut. What you want to do is surprise him, and while he's wondering where all the blood is coming from, get away... or go ahead and finish him off, as long as you have a safe way out of the packlands. Once you kill a shifter here, girl, you can never come back."*

It was a good thing I was on my way out. I had the steak

knife in my hand in one second, and had plunged it into his thigh, right where his femoral artery was.

In the next second, before he could grab me through the slippery fabric of the bedding, I'd crawled up his torso, the keys raised just far enough back to get some momentum. I didn't hesitate, didn't gloat. I thrust the keys on either side of his squat nose, into both eyes.

His scream was so loud, I was surprised Lyndal hadn't heard it. But no one came running in. Maybe my luck was finally turning.

Nope. Pain lanced through me, one of my ribs popping as Grant grabbed me with one arm, cursing at the top of his lungs. "You bitch!"

"Not... *your*... bitch... though," I managed to wheeze as I snaked an arm under his grip, saving the rest of my ribs.

He was squeezing me while he tried to pull the keys out of his eyes, keeping me from running away, but I made it as hard as I could. I kicked, I shouted, I punched and scratched, wiggling this way and that, ignoring the pain in my chest.

When he finally pulled the keys out, Grant's face was bleeding something fierce, and I knew he couldn't see me. It would take a day to heal his eyes. "You little bitch, I'm gonna..." He stood, shaking me, but hesitated. "I'm gonna..." His grip slackened, and he staggered.

"You're gonna die like a mangy dog, killed by the prey, you tick-infested shit stain," I snarled as he finally let me go, staring into space. Just like Del said, this fool was dead, and didn't even know it yet.

I heard a scream outside—Margarette—and collected my steak knife off the ground, jumping over the enormous puddle of blood that had almost soaked the carpet and the comforter.

It looked like the Southern Pack House was hosting a blood festival on the front lawn. Enforcers from the other packs were fighting, but each pack had only been allowed to bring a handful of fighters. And for some reason, only a dozen of them, most of them weaponless, were there.

But every male shifter from Southern was there, with enough steel to run a foundry. The ranked males were the largest ones, and they all fought hard. But even the youngest ones, like those little shits Leroy and Bo, were slashing at the empty-handed visitors with long blades.

The odds were ten to one, and Southern was using every dirty trick they knew to make sure they would come out on top.

"Mom!" Glen's voice had me running toward the center of the ring, dodging and weaving around groups of fighting wolves. Some of them were in wolf form, some in human form with knives, but none of them even blinked as I ran past.

I was moving pretty fast. And it was a good thing, because when I saw Van Blackside with his arm lifted high, and a blade coming down toward Margarette's bleeding throat, I knew no one else would be quick enough to save her.

I funneled every ounce of energy I had into my legs as I leaped over a fallen chair, landing on the dirty, blood-spattered ground with a scream, my knife held high.

I was back in the ring, but this time, I wasn't here for any game. I was here for revenge.

"Van Blackside, it's time for you to die."

33

PERFECT WARRIOR
BRAND

I almost couldn't believe my eyes when Flor appeared. She soared into battle, a miniature Valkyrie, already covered with blood and armed with a small blade. Her scream had every other fight pausing to see what had arrived.

Who had come to fight.

My tiny mate flung herself across the melee, her feet landing lightly as she seemed to fly over the blood and bodies toward Margarette. There was no way she would get there in time to save her. Not one of us could, though we were all trying desperately.

Dad chopped down another Southern Enforcer behind me, but two more took his place. The Southern troops had obviously planned this coup well. In retrospect, it was obvious.

Most of our Enforcers had been given housing much farther away. They had explained it was because those were the nicer homes for housing visitors.

Help wasn't coming, not in time. It was only the Alpha Heirs, the members of the Council who had gone with

Bradley for the execution, and that strange dark-eyed shifter, against all of the Southern troops.

Bradley and Margarette would die, I knew it. Glen was close to them, but he'd been swarmed by a group armed with swords. Finnick was even farther away, fighting back-to-back with Glen's brother Patrick, their sword work almost balletic. Beautiful moves weren't going to save us, though. Technique lost to sheer numbers, every time.

I felt a blade slash my leg, turned and twisted to find my way past my opponent's guard, but my attention was on my mate. She was running, skipping, faster than I'd ever seen a shifter move. But Southern shifters had seen her, scented her, and were raising their heads, eyes gleaming.

I had to get to her.

She howled, a high-pitched, ear-splitting sound filled with a rage so powerful, all the shifters near me stopped fighting for just a moment.

It was long enough for me and Dad to run our blades across our opponents' necks, sending them to the ground. "Go," Dad grunted, thrusting a longer sword into my hand. I grabbed it and ran to help Flor.

The world slowed. I watched her leap between Van and Margarette, shouting a cry for justice. Van was holding Margarette's long hair and bringing his blade down with the other, but he hesitated at the shout.

My little mate let out a snarl and brought up her blade.

Her steak knife.

When she'd palmed it at dinner, it had made my gut twist that she still felt unsafe with me there to protect her. What good would a steak knife do against Enforcers?

But now I saw exactly what a steak knife was capable of. She raised it to meet Van's sword near the hilt, moving her thin, muscular arms in a circle to turn the blade away from its trajectory. Van let the circle continue, obviously hoping to bring the knife back around—to cut into Flor or Margarette's neck, I wasn't sure. His other hand was tangled in Margarette's hair, pulling at it so hard, I was surprised the tendons in her neck hadn't torn.

Maybe they had. Her eyes had rolled back, as if she were seconds away from being decapitated manually.

Flor allowed the blade to continue in the arc, the knife flying in a wide circle above her head, useless. Van snarled a laugh and moved his hand to Flor's wrist to grab the handle of her blade, letting his own fall. He was going to force her to slit her own throat.

But with one hand on her wrist, and his other tangled in Margarette's hair, the burly Enforcer didn't have anything left to stop Flor's next dodge, a ducking movement, inside his guard. I assumed she did it to avoid the blade.

I assumed wrong.

Flor had dropped down so that the top of her head was level with Van's waist, only her arm held high. Somehow, she wriggled her arm, moving so fast I wasn't sure what she'd done—maybe used the blood on her wrist to slip free of his grip? All I knew was that his hand now held the steak knife, and she was free. Then she pressed her cheek against his thigh, as if she was submitting.

But she wasn't submitting. Not at all. She struck, like a snake, her mouth wide.

Van's high-pitched shriek sounded clear and loud over the fighting. I let my gaze drop and saw the blood marking the front of Van's thin sweatpants, the dark puddle growing rapidly.

I could tell what she had done from his face. And from

hers, from the stains that covered her mouth and chin, the wicked, victorious gleam in her crazed eyes.

I had never been so proud, so terrified, and simultaneously sickened in my life.

She'd bitten off... well, from the amount of blood, and the way Van dropped like a stone, whatever *could* be bitten off below the waist.

Van's hand was still caught in Margarette's hair. With a flicker of movement, Flor's knife was in her hand again, and she slashed through the mass of tangled hair, cutting off two of Van's fingers as she did so. Then the steak knife rose again, arrowing like a diving, silver hawk, to land in Van's throat.

With a quick thrust, a twist, and two more slashes, Van's throat lay open, fileted as perfectly as any perch on a stream bed, the muscles laying red and bloody, exposed to the air.

Flor met my gaze across the ring and grinned at me, her eyes glassy, her face slick with blood. "Stupid noisy toad-fucker. I've been wanting to do that for a long, long time." She kicked the dead Head Enforcer with a bare foot, then spat to one side. "Wish I could kill him all over again."

Shouts and howls sounded from beyond the ring as I came out of my stupor. The visiting packs' remaining Enforcers had arrived and were overwhelming the rest of Southern shifters now, tearing into them, though seeing their Head Enforcer castrated and killed by a five-foot-tall woman seemed to have taken the fight out of them.

A heavy hand landed on my shoulder. I turned to see my father and scanned him quickly. "Are you all right?" His wounds were extensive, and the bodies of Southern Enforcers lay around him like a bomb had gone off, but I could see he was already healing.

285

"Good exercise." He nodded, looking me over as well. We were the tallest shifters left standing, and we both looked around, making sure no one else was coming, no more surprise troops.

Then we both turned back to my mate. My little Flor, who was diligently, laboriously, using her steak knife to saw through the neck tendons and spine of the Southern pack's ex-Head Enforcer. The end of her pink tongue poked out one side of her bloody mouth as she worked, intent on doing a thorough job.

"Why's she doing that?" Dad asked softly. "Taking a trophy?"

"I think she needs to be sure he's dead. Glen told me this sort of thing is called closure." I smiled when she finally succeeded. "Isn't she perfect?"

Dad hummed, then patted me on the shoulder again. "She's the one, son. Don't let her get away."

"I won't," I promised, feeling my heart rise up as I watched my savage flower wrap the head in a torn shirt. "I'll do whatever I have to."

As I scanned the ring and noted four other shifters—all the Alpha Heirs, and the strange dark-haired Alpha—all staring at her with expressions that matched my feelings, I knew that promise would be a very hard one to keep.

34

AFTER THE BATTLE

FLOR

I thought I'd known what it felt like to be the pack reject. But nothing had prepared me for the aftermath of the battle. In the space of a week, I'd gone from being the girl everyone hunted, to being the one no one would look at.

I sat in the hallway of the Pack House on the gray carpet —the now-clean steak knife in my hand—and learned what it felt to be invisible.

The remaining Council members were holding a meeting in the Alpha's private dining room only a few yards away from where I sat. Brand's father, who'd asked me to call him Alpha Samuel, had invited me in, but I'd left after a few moments. Even though it made me feel exposed, I sat outside Margarette's door. Someone had to keep watch while she was weak.

When I'd left the dining room, Glen's brother had been guarding outside his mother's room. I knew he wouldn't leave her, but he'd looked exhausted. "Go inside with her, Patrick. There's an armchair in there. Sleep for a while; I'll stand guard."

He'd protested. "You need sleep and food, too."

I'd just parroted one of Del's favorite expressions. "I can sleep when I'm dead. If they get past me, Enforcer, you'll be her last line of defense. Stay inside." At that, he'd agreed.

Margarette was his focus, and mine. She was my way out of here, and more than that, she was the only person who had brushed my hair since... I tried to remember. *Ah, yeah.* Since I was six, back when Mama had her worst breakdown, and Del had had to stop her from trying to drown us both in the creek.

I touched the ends of my short strands, remembering the feel of Margarette's hands on my head, my face. I had felt loved, for a moment.

Her promise to take me away from here felt like the only grasp I had on my own sanity right now. No one had spoken to me since Glen's brother. Or looked at me.

The shifters who passed me now—none of them Southern, as none of *them* had been allowed in this wing of the Pack House—averted their eyes, their expressions blank. Ignoring me entirely. But they hadn't been able to hide their feelings after the battle.

Shock, disgust, morbid fascination, anger, and curiosity had painted their faces, even after I'd been gently escorted to an empty shower room by Brand, who'd guarded the door while I washed off blood... and other things. At some point while I washed off the gore, the other shifters must have been commanded to stop staring and whispering.

I wished I could wash my memories away, so I didn't have to think about what I'd done. Well, what they'd *told* me I'd done, since I didn't remember it all. I'd lost time again shortly after I'd stepped into the ring and seen Margarette in trouble. I'd woken up covered in blood, holding Van's severed head in my arms, wrapped in a ruined shirt for some reason.

Alpha Samuel had gently taken the head from me when no one else dared approach. He'd offered to stuff it, as a trophy of battle.

I'd thrown up then.

But a small part of me was upset—not that I'd killed Van, but that I couldn't remember it. Inside, I was glad he was dead, glad I'd been the one to hold the knife to avenge Del. An even smaller part wished I'd told Alpha Samuel to go ahead with the taxidermy.

At least I'd saved Margarette. Alpha Samuel had assured me she would be fine, though Van's blades had been coated with silver, so every one of the dozens of cuts he'd made on her would scar. The wounds he'd inflicted on Alpha Hillier were life-threatening.

The visiting Enforcers had called for Council troops to be stationed at Southern. Mountain troops were already en route. Apparently, Alpha Samuel had predicted the need for more boots on the ground right after he got here.

We were all in lockdown in the main Pack House until they arrived, every able-bodied visiting shifter armed to the teeth and on guard. I realized I'd never seen Trevor during the battle, or after. So he was still a threat, along with any of his friends who'd survived and slunk away like the cowards they were after the fight.

The worst news was that Alpha Callaway had escaped. With Alpha Hillier out of commission, that meant Callaway still technically had control over the Southern shifters. Even if he couldn't return—as he would be killed on sight—his old commands would hold until he was killed and a new Alpha took his place.

Glen's dad was still unconscious, one kidney and both

lungs punctured with silver. An Eastern pack doctor who had come for the mating events was being run ragged, keeping him and a few others alive. While Alpha Hillier was unconscious, Finnick's father was serving as Interim Council Alpha. He had appointed Luke as Acting Alpha of Southern, until Callaway could be found and executed.

Calling Luke Acting Alpha meant nothing. His fight against the other Southern Enforcers had established him firmly on the wrong side, if the hatred and mistrust on the faces of all the Southerners I'd seen after the battle could be believed. He had no power to compel the others to obey him, and I knew better than anyone just how deep the evil ran in Southern. He'd need to watch his back.

From what I'd overheard, most of what the visitors were calling the "Southern traitors" were being kept in housing close to the main compound. The detention cell had been compromised, the silver bars and locks somehow sliced through for the Alpha to escape. In the meeting, Glen had muttered something about witchcraft, but no one had pursued the idea.

I fiddled around with the steak knife, trying not to look as antsy as I felt. It was still against pack rules for me to have a weapon—and there was no denying that was what it was—but I felt safe enough. Safer than I would if the Hunt came in the night and I was caught unarmed, dressed in a t-shirt and boxer shorts. Clean laundry was at a premium after the fight, and I had no idea whose clothes I was wearing.

Safe. I had never known what that word meant, not really. I closed my eyes for a moment, wondering if I would learn what safe felt like at Northern.

"Little flower, I brought you food." I jumped, shocked

that I hadn't heard Brand approach. He was wearing sweat-pants and a black, tight-fitting cotton t-shirt, and no shoes.

"Thanks, Bearman." He settled next to me, placing three foil-wrapped, oblong packages on the floor between us, and a metal bottle of water. "Mm, tacos." I tore off the foil. "My favorite."

"You've had them before?" He picked up one, not opening it. I got the feeling he was going to wait and see if I wanted all of them myself.

"Go ahead and eat," I said, nudging his leg with my bare foot. That strange warm feeling started up again. I stifled my annoyance, and ate for a few minutes before answering his question. I liked that he hadn't asked it again, as if I hadn't heard him or had forgotten. He was patient.

I hadn't met many males who were patient. Especially not big ones like him. Usually, I hated the way I felt when a male loomed over me, but for some reason being next to him, in his shadow, made me feel protected.

Not safe. But maybe something like it.

"I worked in the kitchen, so I had leftovers," I said at last, the last bit of my second taco vanishing as I remembered. "Sometimes, Del and I would put super-hot peppers in the breakfast tacos, so the ranked assholes would stop halfway through." I laughed. "Some of them would pick out the bacon and leave the rest. After I cleared their plates, I'd just roll it all up—egg, cheese, tortilla, salsa—and eat like a queen."

Brand's angry growl was so low, it was more a vibration than a sound, and it shook the wall behind us. "You are a queen," he mumbled around a mouthful of taco.

I fought back my smile. "What do you like to eat?"

"Meat."

I waited, knowing more had to be coming. But he didn't

say anything else. I laughed. "Seriously, that's it? Meat? Not any specific kind? Well done, rare?"

"I hunt," he admitted, the corner of his mouth twitching, like some part of him wanted to laugh along with me. "There's a lake near our Alpha's Den. Not too near, so there's a lot of game." He paused, and I waited him out this time.

"I hunt alone, sometimes. I like the quiet. The water is dark in the mornings, when the deer and elk come down to drink. As the sun rises, the lake takes on the colors of the sky. Pink, orange, and turquoise. Before the sun peeks over the mountains on the far side of the valley, the lake and the sky are mirror images of each other, framed by pines. The only sound is the breeze, like the earth is breathing, the land itself waking up. And birds, calling out softly to each other."

I sighed. His words revealed a part of his own heart I had a feeling not many were allowed to see. "I wish I could see that."

He offered his warm hand to me, and I took it, marveling at the size of his fingers next to my own. For the first time, that strange heat that pulsed between us didn't irritate me. "I would like to show you. I know you're going to the Northern Pack. But after that, would you be my guest in the Mountain Pack? I could show you my lake. We could hunt."

Hunt together? "I've only ever hunted squirrels. Ground game."

"You could come on a pack hunt with us. We go for elk sometimes, deer more often. You can shift now. You would be very welcome."

It was strange to think that I could shift. I didn't feel strong enough, somehow. There was no inner wolf pacing inside me, wanting to get out. Or if there was, I didn't know how to hear her, or find her.

Alpha Samuel had assured me that plenty of shifters had trouble connecting with their beasts outside of the full moon, especially for the first few months. He'd told me not to worry. The mere thought that Alpha Callaway was out there, alive, waiting to take over the pack while I was trapped here made me desperate to shift and run, though.

Brand waited for my answer, giving me all the time I needed to consider what it might be like, the good and bad of traveling so far.

"I'll come," I told him, settling my other hand over our joined ones, like a pact. "After I go to Northern, I'll come to your lake. We'll hunt."

I closed my eyes, feeling a fluttering in my chest, like a swarm of butterflies had just landed on my heart. What *was* this? I'd never felt anything like it before. Brand squeezed my hands gently, then rose, taking the foil and empty water bottle with him.

Inside the room, I heard Margarette let out a moan. Silently, I opened the door. She was moving restlessly. Glen's brother nodded and slipped out, promising to be back in five minutes.

When he'd gone, I perched on the edge of her bed. "Margarette, what do you need?"

"I had... a nightmare."

"What was it about?"

She struggled to speak, so I grabbed her water glass and gave her a sip. "I died. I went to heaven and saw my sister. She knew... about the battle. About my hair." Margarette's eyes glittered with pain and humor. "And I had to spend eternity... letting her say I told you so."

293

We both laughed. "Good thing I was there to give you that haircut."

"No more... laughing. It hurts." She started to cough, and I held the water up to her lips again.

It was a rare thing, to see a shifter of her rank in such a state of weakness. An unheard-of thing, for her to allow me, an unrelated wolf, to come so near. Wasn't her wolf howling for me to get away? Didn't it worry?

I asked her.

"No," she said, closing her eyes again. "You're family."

My heart swelled at her acceptance before I wondered what she meant. Was I family only if I turned out to be Glen's mate? Only if I stayed at Northern?

She'd slipped back into a healing sleep before I could think of a way to ask her what she meant. Honestly, I was a little afraid of what her answer might be.

Fucking hope again. That shit hurts so much more than a hundred beatings.

I couldn't allow myself to imagine Margarette as some sort of storybook mother. When my own mama had been alive, she'd been too broken to show true affection. The day she'd defended me against Trevor had been one of the few times she'd protected me. I didn't blame her. How could a wolf who'd been tormented like her take care of a child?

At least I'd had Del. I let the tears keep coming, silently. For Del. Remembering the best moments of my life, all of which had him in it.

And Alpha Callaway had taken all of that away. My fingers itched to curl around his neck, choke the life out of him. I felt a growl rumble low in my chest.

Glen appeared in front of me, his hands half-extended, like he wanted to hold me, but wasn't certain I'd let him. "Flor? What's wrong? Is Mom okay?"

I scrubbed a hand over my eyes and slid to the floor, sitting cross-legged. "She's fine, Glen. Sorry, I was… thinking about something annoying."

He huffed a laugh. "It sounded like you were thinking about tearing someone's head off." He paused, hands in his pockets. "You probably don't want to remember that."

"No, I'd like to forget it ever happened." I smiled weakly.

I couldn't tell anyone I already had forgotten it. That I'd blanked out when I'd killed Van. Better for them to think I was some sort of psycho, than to reveal that I was more or less feral. I'd be unranked forever if anyone realized I didn't have control of my actions.

A shudder wracked me. Would I be even worse in my wolf form, killing indiscriminately? Maybe I should never let myself shift.

Maybe that was why shifting felt so impossible.

I shook the awful thoughts away, although a small voice inside giggled at the idea of taking a steak knife, or claws and teeth, to a few dozen more of Van's cronies.

"Do you regret it, though? Killing him?" Glen slid down next to me, but lowered himself to his side, propping himself up on one elbow, so that his eyes were lower than mine. That was odd. All the guys had done that, showing submission, but in small, easy-to-miss ways.

Why would they do that? They were Alpha Heirs, literally the closest thing to royalty shifters had. It scared me to think what would happen if they kept doing that sort of thing in front of others. I knew my pack wouldn't let that sort of thing slide. I'd be seen as reaching beyond my nonexistent rank. Even when I left Southern, there was no guarantee the other packs wouldn't see it that same way.

Glen cleared his throat, and I snapped my gaze to his. "Sorry, what did you ask?"

"I asked if you regretted killing Van," he said, examining me. "But you don't, do you?" He smiled, his white teeth shining. "Good. I love you just like this. Fierce. Unapologetic. Powerful."

Of all those words, one made my brain stop. "Um, Glen? L-love?"

His eyes shuttered. "Yeah, it's an expression."

My brain started back up again, and I spoke to fill the suddenly awkward silence. "So, where do we stand?"

"You and me?" His voice was a croak.

"No." I wasn't even sure where to start with that. "I mean, when do the Mountain troops arrive? When will your dad be well enough to travel? Is Luke going to be able to hold things together here once we leave?"

"You know Luke has to stay?"

I nodded. "Yeah, sure. Sucks to be him. But we're still leaving, aren't we?"

His blue eyes were swimming with mixed emotions as he answered slowly. "We? You sure you don't want to stay at Southern, Flor?"

35

NOT MY PACK

FLOR

hat. The Everloving. Fuck.

I pulled my lips back into a snarl. "What the hell, Glen? Stay in this shithole? You've gotta be kidding." His face said very clearly that he wasn't kidding, and I realized what he was doing.

He was trying to get rid of me. To keep me from dirtying up his perfect pack.

Fine. I did not need him, or them. "If your pack doesn't want me, Brand already said I could come to Mountain. So fuck you and your shitty attitude, Glenda—"

"Shit, no, stop!" he blustered, his face frozen in a peculiar expression. "I didn't mean that. Of course you can come. You are always welcome. But..." He blinked furiously before finishing, "You don't want to stay, not even a little?"

"What the hell would I stay for?"

"For Luke. To stay close," he said slowly. "You know, he thinks..."

"Yeah, he thinks I'm his mate." I blew a raspberry, making him laugh. "That's his deal, not mine. Your mom said I didn't have to make a permanent decision, anyway. I could visit y'all."

He relaxed. "Sure. If that's what you want."

"Works for me. And then I'll go to Brand's pack." I felt courage filling me. "He invited me to see his lake."

Glen's eyes got huge. "Wow. That's his secret spot. Of course he invited you." He frowned. "What about Finn?"

"Finn? What about him? If you haven't noticed, he sorta hates me, Glenda."

He thumped me gently on the head. "I hate that name."

"Good," I said with a grin. "I'll keep using it."

He pressed against me, and I felt the magnetic, spiraling sensation I'd had at the stream start back up where our skin touched. I knew I should move away, but I sort of liked it.

"Flor, I wanted to tell you again that I'm sorry."

"For what?" Then I remembered. "Oh, yeah. Well, to be fair, I wasn't in a locked bedroom or anything. I was by a creek. And I ended up getting a free ticket out of Hell from it so..." I thumped his head back, letting my fingers slide through his golden strands the tiniest amount. "Don't creep on me again, and I'll let that one ride. Wipe it from your mind."

He raised one eyebrow, but changed the subject like the gentleman he was not. "To answer your questions, the Mountain troops are only a few hours out, so we'll all be able to sleep once they arrive. My dad is alive. I've never seen a wolf survive that much silver poisoning, but if anyone can, it'll be him. The pack doctor called for a private Council ambulance to drive him back to Ontario."

"Won't that be too hard on him?"

Glen shrugged. "At least there, he'll have all our own Enforcers around."

"They won't challenge him, or some bullshit?"

Glen looked shocked. "You know the only genuine Alpha challenge is one like Luke called. In a fighting ring, or at least a formal fight, in front of Council witnesses. If an Alpha could be deposed just by killing him, we'd go through Alphas like tissues. And we wouldn't need Alpha Heirs."

"How does an Alpha Heir become an Alpha, then?" I was horrified when I realized what this would mean for Glen. "You don't have to fight your own dad someday, do you? Kill him?"

"No! Who the hell would want an Alpha who'd kill his own parent anyway? That's sick."

"Luke was going to kill Callaway," I snapped. "His adopted father. Was that sick?"

"You know that's not what I meant." He ran his hands through his hair. "Callaway brought that on himself."

I fought to keep my expression flat. Glen didn't need to know all my secrets. "Sorry."

"Anyway, when an Alpha wants to step down, he requests a full Council meeting, usually during Conclave, and hands the power over in a ritual."

"I never heard of a ritual."

"Oh, by the way, you missed your first shift ritual. Sorry about that, but my dad had to save your life."

"Glenda, I've never heard of any rituals. There's a ritual for shifting?" Southern had made me stupid in more ways than I'd thought.

Glen let out a series of soft curses. "Yes," he finally said. "There's a ritual to help guide the wolf into this world, so it doesn't hurt. Well, not as much. The first time always pinches a bit." He waggled his eyebrows.

"Still acting like a degenerate." I punched him in the arm, ignoring the magnetic swirling again as he apologized. "I guess Callaway never did the ritual because he liked to cause pain. The unmated females he forced to shift when they were twenty-one—well, let's just say I was looking for a way out of the pack before that day, anyway." I described some of the shifts I'd watched, the blood and the tearing, the way the Alpha had made some of the males and females stop in the middle to talk about the steps of a shift, like he was some sort of redneck university professor.

Glen's face turned greenish. "From what I understand, your Alpha subverted almost all of the main tenets of pack law. The central ones being the pack protects each other, and the Alpha protects the pack."

"Well, the pack protected some of the shifters here— the ranked ones. Before we go, I'd like someone to talk to the Mountain wolves about making sure the unranked wolves here get food, and aren't worse off than before."

"Luke's on it."

"Luke? He was here while it was all going on."

Glen shook his head. "He couldn't tell anyone. He was under dozens of Alpha commands that governed more of his life than anyone could have known, or suspected. For some reason, one of the commands was not to give food or assistance to any unranked shifters."

Ah, hell. Luke *had* tried to feed me and some of the other kids a while back. I guess it made sense that if Callaway had found out about it, he'd have stopped it from happening.

"He'll have his hands full getting anyone to obey, especially if Callaway's commands are still in place," I said, thinking about how pervasive the rot was in our pack. "Wait. Will all those commands Callaway stacked on him still be in effect?"

Glen frowned. "I don't know; I don't think so. He defeated Callaway in a dominance challenge, so his wolf should have the strength..." His voice trailed off before he shrugged. "Anyway, he'll have help from the Mountain shifters once they get here, and they'll make sure the unranked wolves are taken care of. Luke just needs to get well."

I snorted. "He needs to watch his back. If he's not careful, he'll be killed before the end of the week."

For some reason, Glen scowled at me. "He'll be fine if that gut wound heals."

Guilt surged through me again, like a wave of indigestion. "I'm sorry, okay? I shouldn't have stabbed him. Well, not so hard."

The corners of Glen's mouth twitched, and he teased, "I'd let you stab me hard, if you promised to kiss it better." He made kissy lips and smacking noises until I grinned, too.

"I'll kick it better, ya perv!" I pushed him with my foot, loving this feeling. Teasing, being silly. I'd had almost none of this in my life.

I kicked him again, and Glen poked a finger into my ribs, tickling me. Instead of laughing, I let out a cry, pretending it had hurt. "Don't hit me, Glen!" I moaned. "I'm just a weak little—"

Before I could finish the sentence, Glen was flying across the hall, and Luke was attacking, holding him by the throat up against the wall. Glen's feet dangled, but he was either laughing or choking to death.

"Chill," Glen croaked. "I wasn't hitting her."

"Hitting on me, maybe." I smiled, then felt the oppressive energy coming from Luke. The air was almost vibrating with his anger. Shit, he was a half a second from wolfing out and tearing Glen's head off. "Luke?"

"You will respect her," Luke ground out, like the words

were glass. "If she goes with you, you will respect her and protect her. Do you understand?"

Glen gurgled a "Yes," and Luke let him go. I felt ridiculously amused by the display. Luke, standing up for me? Maybe I was dreaming. Maybe I'd been knocked out in the battle, and I was still in a coma, imagining the whole day.

"Wow, the pack protects its own. Calm down, baby Alpha. You and I both know I can take care of myself."

Luke glanced at me, then glared at the floor. "The Mountain wolves have arrived. I need to meet with them, then we're sending the Northerners back home immediately."

"Immediately? Why?"

"I spoke to some unranked servants with good ears. There was a plot to assassinate Bradley tonight, even before the Alpha's escape."

Glen growled. "The coup wasn't because of the Alpha's defeat?"

"No," Luke said bitterly. "It was already in place. They'd stockpiled human guns, but with silver bullets. A cleaner was taking out the trash in the armory area a few hours ago. The black wolf, Joaquin"—he shot a look at Glen, who nodded like they both knew who that was—"led him inside. There were enough guns and silver ammunition to kill every visiting wolf three times over."

"*What?* Did you know of this, Luke?"

Luke's jaw worked, like he was having trouble answering. "No. My fathe—Callaway had been funneling money to Van, who must have made the purchases. I saw money vanishing, but I assumed it was for more of the same crap as usual."

"Who has the guns now?" I asked.

Luke snorted. "Well, that's the interesting thing. Those

particular weapons had all been ruined. Barrels bent, the silver ammunition melted down into a big metal puddle with some sort of fire."

I whispered, "We would have seen a fire that could melt metal, Luke."

"A magical fire," Glen breathed. "You suspect Joaquin?"

My heart raced. I knew how to run from the Hunt, knew how to hide from wolves. But not from magic.

"We can't find him to ask. And we're not sure if we found all the weapons. We can't keep all the Southern ranked shifters locked up forever; they're half the pack."

They were going to let the ranked shifters loose. "I need to go," I gasped. "The Hunt."

Luke grabbed my shoulders, holding me still. "Shh, it's okay. I won't let them hunt you. You have your knife, yes?" I nodded. "I'll get you better weapons. Will that help?"

"You need to sneak weapons to all the unranked females," I demanded. I was getting the hell out of here, but the girls who stayed would need them if they started the Hunt up again after I was gone.

Luke nodded. "I'm Acting Alpha, for now. I can change rules, even if I can't enforce them with an Alpha command. I've already announced that unranked shifters can carry weapons, two apiece. The shifters from Mountain will help keep things under control."

"But if Callaway's commands still hold…"

"Yes. They aren't strong enough to override that command."

"Mops," I said softly. "Mops, and steak knives, and gardening tools. Open the sheds and silverware drawers. And the fucking pantries. They're all so starved, none of them could even…" My voice trailed off. It was not my problem. This wasn't my pack anymore.

So why did it feel like I was abandoning them? Like I should stay?

Luke cleared his throat. "Would you give me a minute of your time, Flor? Alone." Glen had already opened the door to his mom's room and was getting her things packed. He nodded, his brow furrowing as he turned away.

"Sure." I would listen to whatever Luke needed to say; I owed him that much for throwing me the mop. I followed him to the sitting room where we'd had dessert the night before.

Only the night before? It felt like years.

"Are you okay, Luke?" I asked, keeping my voice low. He frowned, confused. I gestured to his shirt.

"Ah. This." He lifted the edge of the fabric, revealing rows of abs marred only by a wicked, long cut, just now scabbing over.

I had to fight not to apologize. "It's gonna scar."

"I hope it will."

"Why?" I reached out, letting my fingertips touch the unmarked skin near his waist, running my hands over those ridged muscles I'd stared at so many times. I'd never gotten to see them this close. He was perfect.

His fingers closed around mine, and I felt it again. A surge of longing, a heat that left me burning inside in places I'd only just begun to feel.

"If it scars, it'll be something I have of you. A memory that you were real. When you're gone…" His voice broke. "When you're gone, I'll touch that scar and remember all that I had and lost, because I was a fool and a coward."

I wanted to protest, tell him he wasn't those things, but a part of me agreed.

Suddenly, an odd feeling filled me. A silent whine. I closed my eyes for a moment, concentrating on what it was.

It was my wolf. I could feel her, faintly. I took a deep breath, listening to her.

She paced inside my thoughts, angry. Unsettled. She didn't like this, didn't want to leave him. Another long, pain-filled whine filled my mind.

I sent her thoughts of calm.

She sent me a snarl.

I opened my eyes, inexplicably angry at what I knew was my own soul. My own stupid inner self. What did she know? She'd only met Luke in the past few days. She'd seen him at his absolute best.

Of course, I was the one still touching his warm skin, tracing his muscles.

"It doesn't seem fair," I muttered, still moving my fingers slowly on my favorite muscle, the line that cut down from his waist toward his groin. His abdomen twitched underneath me like my touch was irritating, but he pressed closer as well.

"What's not fair?" he breathed, shuddering. Maybe he felt the way I did, like he wanted me both nearer and much farther away.

If he was farther away, I could think. If he had been farther away, I wouldn't have said what I did next. I leaned closer, letting my fingers dip below his waistline. "You get a souvenir, and I don't."

He took a shaky breath, and I let my fingers move higher, memorizing the way the hairs, dark and coarse, broke up the softness of his skin. The way his nipples were puckered, like he had been swimming in the creek. Were they hard like mine got when I thought about him? I let my fingers slide higher to find out.

"Flor," he hissed, his hand closing around mine.

"It's not fair," I said, my voice far away. "I dreamed of

you for all those years. When I was being hunted. I would find a place to hide, and I would dream that you would come and save me. And you never did." He let out a sound that was heart-breaking, devoid of hope, but I went on. "But I dreamed you did, and when you saved me, you took me away, and you kissed me." I frowned at his chest. "It's not fair. You get this scar to remember me by, and I get nothin'. Not even a kiss."

I sighed. "And I've never been kissed, not by someone I chose, not when I wanted to be. Not when I wasn't being hunted." I looked up into his impossibly silver-blue eyes. "I want you to be my first real kiss. Before I leave."

When Luke didn't move, or speak, or even blink, I knew I'd made a mistake. But except for the blood rushing to my head, I couldn't move either.

My face felt like it had caught fire. Who even was I, right now?

I knew the answer to that, and it was the reason Luke was stalling. I was the pack reject. The too-skinny, uneducated outcast. I knew that. I knew a reject was all anyone at Southern would see me as.

What was I doing, begging my lifelong crush—the gorgeous Acting Alpha of my almost ex-pack—to kiss me? I'd like to blame my inner wolf, but she had gone quiet now, like she was waiting to see what would happen next.

Finally, Luke stammered, "W-what?"

I scowled as hard as I could, cursed myself out internally, then took another breath. This fucker owed me. "You heard me." I repeated my demand. "I've never been kissed, not for real. So kiss me."

Luke blinked, obviously shocked. "Flor, I don't deserve—"

I'd heard people talk about lady balls, but I never

thought I'd grow a pair of my own. It was getting easier, the longer he hemmed and hawed, to feel justified in my simple damned request. I cut him off with a short laugh. "I know that. But you don't get to say no now."

I paused, stunned as I thought about what I'd just said. It echoed things that had been said to me. The blood drained from my face as quickly as it had risen, and I rushed to explain, "I didn't mean that. I won't make you. I don't ever want to force someone to do something like that, when they don't want, if *you* don't—"

And then I couldn't say anything else, because he had pressed his lips softly to mine.

It was everything I had dreamed about, and yet not enough. Warm, gentle, a soft press of his mouth on mine. He dropped smaller, breathy kisses around my lips, on my jawline, my cheeks. I closed my eyes as he moved slowly, reverently, kissing along my hairline, and then on my eyelids.

Worshiping me. His kisses felt like a prayer. Or an answer to one.

He moved back to my lips then, and the kiss changed. His mouth opened, his tongue touching my lower lip as if he were asking a question. I parted my lips, and suddenly, I wasn't being worshiped anymore.

I was being devoured. His tongue invaded my mouth, plundered me, stripped away all my defenses. Tentatively, I responded, exploring his mouth as his hands gripped my waist, then moved up over my ribcage, spanning my torso, his thumbs brushing the very bottom swell of my breasts.

My nipples tightened, and I gasped as he moved his thumbs back and forth, mimicking the way his tongue moved in my mouth.

What would it feel like to have his mouth there, his

tongue on my breasts? I squeezed my thighs together as a new fire kindled in my center, sending flames to lick at my core. What would it feel like to be kissed... everywhere?

My small whimper was lost in Luke's mouth as he tasted me thoroughly, almost savagely, his hands moving over my arms and shoulders now, and to my neck, pulling my short hair back from my ears, his strong fingers mapping every inch of me that he could reach. As if he was memorizing this moment, rubbing his fire and caramel scent as deeply into me as he could, and taking my own as he went.

The kiss had been a spark that had grown into a bonfire of need, and I fought to keep every inhibition I had from burning away. I longed to have his arms around me, his lips touching me everywhere, his tongue moving over the hidden parts of me that pounded in time to my pulse, that ached with need.

"Luke?" I murmured, taking a quick breath, pulling back. Did he feel this, too?

"Oh, Flor," he moaned against my neck. "I've waited my whole life for this."

His whole life? What did that mean? I tried to break away, but he buried his face in my neck, inhaling my scent.

"Cinnamon and sugar and jasmine... I can't believe I'll never have the chance to..."

To what? My mind was spinning, and some part of me wanted to reassure him that he would get the chance to do whatever. He would; I wouldn't leave.

But the thought of staying here was like an icy bucket of water poured over me.

Shivering, as if I'd only narrowly escaped some unseen danger, I pulled back, extracting my arms from his embrace.

Luke groaned, one hand moving to his abdomen, the other to cover his face.

"Luke?" Had I hurt him again? He opened his eyes, and I saw that he was suffering. But I could tell his frustration wasn't directed at me.

"I didn't deserve that kiss, Flor," he murmured. "I didn't deserve that, or any part of you. I never did. I'm glad... I'm glad you're going." My gut churned like I might be sick, but he went on. "Find someone, some pack, that'll do right by you. That'll protect you, treasure you. That'll make you feel like you don't have to hide who you are, how strong you are. How you're different. I wish I could have been that for you. I hope someday you can forgive me."

How I was *different?* What did he mean? I swallowed to speak, but before I could frame the question, he was walking away.

I wanted to smack him. I wanted to ask what he meant. I wanted to insist that he come back and kiss me again. Instead, for some reason, I yelled. "Well, I don't forgive you! And I didn't even like that kiss. It was gross, and wet, and... disgusting!" The air around me filled with the metallic scent of a lie.

His shoulders shook as he sped up. *That rat's ass.*

"Are you laughing? Luke Callaway, I'll never let your mop water mouth near mine again, do you hear me? Not ever!"

He vanished around a corner.

And from my life.

36

REJECTED AGAIN
FLOR

I stayed mad as long as I could. It helped with the hollow feeling that crept through me as I got ready to leave Southern forever.

"You don't have anything else to pack, little flower?" Brand asked, nodding to the bag I'd found at the end of my bed. It had Luke's scent on it, but inside were all girl things: a pink toothbrush, some small bottles of conditioner and moisturizer, and a comb with rhinestones in it that looked exactly like one I'd had for a few days when I was around ten, which some ranked girls had taken from my school bag.

I shook my head, and Brand took the bag in one hand and my arm with the other. I tsked and switched sides, so my right hand was free.

He glanced at the handle of my steak knife and nodded, understanding immediately.

Finnick said, his tone as full of starch as ever, "You know you won't need that knife at Northern. They have real weapons. Margarette will give you anything you want. Weapons, jewelry, clothing."

I glared at him, trying not to be impressed by how he looked. Like one of the sexy male perfume models in magazines, the ones that came with scratch and sniff panels. He was dressed in an honest-to-God three-piece suit, his red hair slicked back with some sort of hair gel. He arched an eyebrow at me, and I blinked to stop staring.

"I'll earn my weapons and clothing there by working," I snapped, dropping Brand's arm. "And I don't need jewelry." I flicked my metal ear tag with my left hand. "I already have mine."

A flicker of pain or rage flashed in his gaze, and he stepped close, leaning down to my ear. His musk and ginger scent swirled around my face as he whispered, "If you were mine, I would cover you in jewels. I would show you what a woman like you deserves, show the world your beauty." While I was still frozen in shock, he inhaled deeply, like he was trying to fill his lungs with my scent, then stepped back.

I met his sharp green eyes, and before I could stop it, a question tumbled out. "But I'm not yours, am I? I'm not your mate. Your true mate."

His jaw clenched so hard, the muscles of his jaw were outlined for a long moment. "No, Florida Wills. I am not your true mate, and you are not mine." The air thickened with a bitter, acrid scent. He was lying. I knew it.

But he was doing something else, too. I slapped one hand over my heart, as a knife was plunged into my chest.

No. I looked down. There was no knife.

Gasping, I held my hand over the scar that was burning as if it were splitting open. I opened my mouth to beg him to stop, but he bared his teeth, and repeated himself. "I am not your true mate, Florida Wills, and you are not mine."

The pain intensified, though the scent of deception

dissipated as quickly as it had come. Somehow, that was worse. He wasn't lying now, even if he had been before.

I whimpered at the feeling of something deep within me tearing. Finnick opened his mouth and drew a breath to speak again, and somehow, I knew when he did—if he repeated those words—everything would change.

Inside, my wolf howled.

"Finn," I whispered, not sure what to say to keep him from saying those words a third time.

He was trembling, his eyes filled with something like regret. "I couldn't be your mate, Flor. I wouldn't ever make that mistake," he finished at last, his own voice a rasp.

The words hit me, hard, but not like the others. This time, it was the understanding of why he was saying this to me. That I could never measure up. Never be worthy.

I managed to draw a breath to reply out loud. "Fuck you, Finnick. Fuck you all the way back to your fancy pack. I don't care if I ever see you again. I hope I don't!" I tasted my own lie, like aluminum in my mouth. Finnick's nostrils flared as he smelled it. But he didn't call me on it.

Inexplicably, his eyes shone for a moment, as if he were suppressing tears. Then, his jaw tightening even further, he gritted out a goodbye to Brand. Brand only growled back as Finnick turned and stalked away.

"He's l-limping," I stammered, wondering why I was so out of breath. Why it felt the exact same way as being held down and kicked in the gut. Like he'd been trying to break through my ribs with a few stupid words.

"Stupid fucker did it to himself," Brand grumbled, his arm going around my shoulders. I leaned into him, my limbs aching almost as much as my gut did, my head spinning. "Don't worry, little flower. He'll pull his head out."

"What?" Glen asked, coming up on my other side. He

tucked a lock of hair behind my ear, then motioned to the waiting black SUV. Identical vehicles had been arriving all evening, and the Pack House was practically surrounded.

I glanced at Finnick's back, then over at the Pack House, where I suspected Luke was watching from a curtained window. "Are we ready to go? I can't wait to leave this piss-hole forever." I ignored the wary looks from the visiting shifters, and the whispers I heard as I walked to the SUV. I didn't want to know what they were saying about me, and I didn't care.

"We are." Glen opened a door for me. "And you never have to come back, Flor. Not unless you decide you want to."

I raised my voice. "I'd rather eat rats for another nineteen years, Glenda. Get me out of this place."

"As you wish," he replied gently.

Our driver followed behind a shifter ambulance carrying the Northern Alpha pair, and another two SUVs pulled in behind us. Brand was on my left, Glen on my right, and my future lay ahead.

At last, I was going to a place that wanted me. Where I wouldn't be hunted, or scorned, or abused. I knew it wouldn't be perfect, but it had to be better than Southern.

I had no reason to feel anything but joy.

But as the SUV turned the corner to head to the gates, and I craned my neck to see behind me, a vast, hollow space opened up inside me, and my eyes filled with tears.

A lean, dark-haired figure stood on the front porch of the Pack House, alone. And as he raised his hand to wave goodbye, it felt like I was leaving something vital behind.

Memories, perhaps. Or dreams.

Or even a part of my soul.

EPILOGUE
BACK INTO HELL ~ LUKE

I was too weak to let her leave unobserved. Or perhaps my love was too strong.

Either way, I watched through the windows as she spoke to the Alpha Heirs. Watched as the shifters around her dropped their gazes, some nearly bowing to her as she walked past like a queen in disguise, not that she noticed. A few of them swallowed hard, as if they wanted to speak to her, but none of them mustered the will to do so.

Of course, Brand and Glen were sending out waves of Alpha energy, driving the other males away. She probably thought no one wanted to approach her.

I smiled, remembering her oblivious way of moving through the world, simultaneously aware of every small threat that existed, yet unaware of the way she drew others like flies to honey.

She'd been blissfully unaware of the way I'd stared at her for years, and had never understood that the Alpha's threats and commands were the only reasons the other unranked shifters hadn't flocked to her.

Everything about Flor was magnetic, her quiet, subtle

power and strength swirling like an invisible cloak around her. Sure, some of the higher-ranked shifters hated her, but only because their wolves knew instinctively that she was their superior in every way.

She was my mate. I'd known that since we were both children, caught in a trap that bled all the joy and light from the world. But I was almost certain she was the other Alpha Heirs' true mate, too. Even Finnick's, though it had been all I could do not to open the door I'd been hiding behind and give him the beating he deserved for rejecting her.

The words he'd used, and repeated, had come close enough to a formal rejection that I knew they had hurt her. They'd gutted him almost as painfully as I'd wanted to when I'd seen her pain. He'd vomited blood on the side of the Pack House for a while before asking one of the Mountain shifters to drive him to Northern, claiming he'd changed his mind about Flor.

Of course, he'd come up with a rationale, insinuating that she might bear further watching. If I didn't trust Finnick with my life, I might have believed his cleverly phrased falsehood. He'd watch her, all right. Watch her like a wolf watched a rabbit.

Flor was no rabbit, though. Yes, she was small and battered, but the angle of her chin, the hard light in her eyes, her ready stance and wary attention to every detail around her, made it clear that she was the strongest shifter at Southern.

She should be. She was Callaway's daughter, after all.

I watched her slide gracefully into the SUV after Glen, Brand throwing me a glance as I stepped out onto the porch, before he followed her. I nodded my thanks.

His father had given me some advice on how to survive the separation that was coming, which had shocked me. *"I lost myself to my wolf for years after my beloved died. But I do not believe you should let yourself shift. I'm not sure your wolf would allow the separation."*

I'd agreed, knowing my wolf would run straight to her side, which would be the final death knell for the vulnerable Southern pack... and she didn't want me.

Of course she didn't.

Brand had brought her bedding to my room in a sealed plastic bag, warning me to make it last. I'd laughed, but he'd made me promise not to open it for as long as possible. "You said you knew she was your mate. But you were able to be apart from her. I'm afraid this separation will be different."

He was right. This one would be longer. And it would end in my death, if she never returned. I hadn't told him, but I'd already locked my room so no one could change the sheets she'd slept on in my bed. I'd use them to stay sane until the last trace of her jasmine and cinnamon had vanished.

At least she had the others—Glen and Brand, even Finnick—to help her through it. Even if I died, she would survive. As long as she was safe, what happened to me in the long run didn't matter.

"Don't come back," I whispered aloud as the SUV turned the corner. I raised my hand, imagining I could see her doing the same inside, pressing her small fingers to the glass. "Stay away, stay safe, and be happy, Flor. I will always love you."

I loved her, but I couldn't ever save her. I wanted her, but I couldn't keep her safe here.

I prayed that the other Alpha Heirs would be enough. That they would do better.

Then I turned my back on the only Southern shifter I'd

ever cared for, the only scrap of heaven I'd ever found... and walked back into Hell to try and save the ones that were stuck in the abyss with me.

THANK you for reading Pack Reject. Reviews and ratings are the best way to share your feelings about Flor's story. Please take a moment to leave a few words. It makes a huge difference for indie authors like me!

The Splintered Bond series continues in Pack Refuge.

ACKNOWLEDGMENTS

I am deeply grateful to my betas who helped turn this serial into a "real book," even if it took a few actual phone conversations and even some hair-pulling (but not the fun kind) to get it shaped up!

Thank you to Tami, Bekka, Courtney, Megan, Kristin, Deb, Iris, Shannon, and Maria for doing the heavy lifting! Keep sending the names of your exes and enemies, and I'll keep handing them to Grigor or Flor. Thank you as well to Cara Bryant, Elizabeth Dear, Sarah Reynolds, Indie Sparks, Ravin DeMarco, Liza, Renee, Raewyn, Darcy, Jamie, Beatrice, Lorie, and the rest of my Vella crew. Your comments are everything.

My Glitter & Spice and Knotty & Nice subscribers on Ream are a gift from the Moon Mother! Thank you so much to: Veronica, Darsea, Lindsay, Susanne, Mareike, Barbara, Stevie, Jamie, Kathalena, Cici, Danielle, Kimberly, Jacquie, Kat, Kiley, Sarah, Molly, Jen, Kelsey, Elo, Liz, and Taryn.

Also by Merri Bright

The Billionaire's Betasitter Series (MF Omegaverse)

Knotty New Year

Sunshine's Grump

Grumpy's Holiday Sweater

Valentine's Heart

Rainbow's Storm

The Splintered Bond (Paranormal Shifters)

Pack Reject

Pack Refuge

Pack Ruin

Pack Rage

An Ancient Bond, A Pack Reject Story

About the Author

Merri Bright spends her days dreaming up naughty angels, misunderstood demons, sexy shifters, growly Alpha males, and frequently refuses to limit her heroines to just one love interest.

Please join Merri's Mischief Makers on Facebook where you'll discover random giveaways, sneak peeks of new novels, book recommendations, and silly/sexy/funny stuff. You can also email her at merri@merribright.com.